Mordecai's Ashes

Arlana Crane

Edited by Allister Thompson

ISBN 978-1-7772012-1-0

ACKNOWLEDGEMENT

With many thanks to Beth Johnson, Lisa Sawatzky, Vanessa Zahara, Jasmine Hope, Lael Johnson, and especially my husband James for all the help, feedback, criticism, and encouragement that made finishing this story possible.

1

Karl's phone was buzzing somewhere in the bed, shaking him out of a deep sleep. It took eight full rings for him to dig it out from under the comforter, and by that time it had stopped. He cursed under his breath and flopped back on the pillows. The phone in his hand buzzed again and he put it to his ear, eyes still closed.

"Hello?" Karl growled.

"Are you still asleep?" His older sister's shocked voice echoed slightly.

"Not anymore," he retorted.

"Karl, it's after one o'clock there! This is ridiculous. You're not a teenager anymore. I am not letting you stay in my apartment so you can laze around all day like you're on some kind of vacation."

"Tilly, I'm unemployed. I'm divorced. I'm broke. And I'm tired. What exactly do you think I should be doing at the moment?"

"Anything! Looking for a new job, starting a hobby, going to the gym!"

"What time is it there?" Karl interrupted before she could continue. "Isn't it the middle of the night?"

His sister Matilda was halfway through a two-year contract teaching English in Beijing. The tenant leasing her Vancouver apartment in her absence had abruptly decided to return to Ontario, and Karl had been more than happy to move off his brother Jakob's couch and into the comfortable high-rise. He hadn't realized that an increase in sisterly attention was part of the deal.

"It's seven fifteen in the morning. I leave for work in twenty minutes." Matilda's tone suggested this should be obvious, but Karl wasn't totally sure what day of the week it was, let alone the time in a country halfway around the world.

"So you just thought you'd check up on me," he asked irritably, flinging his free arm across his face to block out the sun.

"I am not checking up on you," she protested. "I'm calling to ask you a favour. Well, give you a message. Well, mostly a favour."

He grunted. "Which is it?"

"Look, I'm only the one calling because Mum didn't want to, but since you're not busy anyway, I thought it might be nice if you could help her out."

"What's wrong with Mum? What does she need help with?"

"Nothing's wrong with her. She's fine, but you know Aunty Milly passed away?" Their great Aunt Matilda was Tilly's namesake, and the two women had been more alike than Tilly cared to admit.

"Yeah, the funeral's not until Saturday. It's not Saturday, is it?" Karl sat up in sudden alarm and instantly regretted it.

"No, you idiot, it's Monday." Tilly sounded shocked. "But Aunty Milly named Mum the executrix of her will, which means Mum is responsible for clearing out Aunty Milly's house and taking care of donating her things and everything. The owner wants to renovate it so they can sell. So they're pushing, not very politely, to have it done as soon as possible, and Mum's not pleased about it, and well, I thought, since you aren't busy..."

"Yes, we get it, I'm not busy," her brother growled and rubbed his eyes.

"If you hurry, you could catch the three o'clock ferry. Mum's heading to the Island after she finishes her hair appointment. You could meet her on the ferry, and you could both stay with Liam tonight. I'm sure she'd really like the help."

"Won't Liam help?" Karl didn't mind the job, but he didn't particularly want another sibling commenting on the state of his life.

"Sure, he would, he was going to, but he's on a long haul up Island. One of his drivers called in sick or something, so he's busy until late."

She kindly refrained from adding *unlike you*, but Karl got the message.

"Alright," he said, swinging his feet over the side of the bed and rubbing his forehead with his free hand.

"Really? You'll do it?" Matilda sounded both relieved and pleased.

"Yeah, of course. Do you want to give Mum a call and tell her to look out for me on the ferry? I need a shower before I go."

"Of course, I'll call her right now." All of the criticism had melted out of her voice and she added, "Thank you, Karl, I really appreciate it. If I was there, I'd..."

"I know, you'd do it yourself."

It was true. She was always the one to jump when their mother "didn't really need any help." Moving to Asia meant she didn't have to anymore, but it didn't dispel her guilt. Apparently, it meant that guilt landed on Karl now.

He yawned as he hung up the phone and wondered whether there was any Gravol in the apartment. The way he felt, even a smooth crossing might be unpleasant. With a shake of his head, Karl dropped his phone on the nightstand and padded across the hardwood to the bathroom for a shower.

***

Rapidly accelerating out of the ferry lane, Abigail Larsson said, "So, you actually decided to show up."

"Yeah, well," Karl settled himself more deeply into the soft leather of his seat, "I wasn't busy or anything. There might be some heavy lifting."

Abigail merely sniffed in reply. She drove the little red Porsche aggressively, north along the highway through downtown Nanaimo.

Once they had cleared the city limits and he could relax a little, Karl asked, "What do you have to do as executrix, anyway?"

"Ensure the terms of Aunt Matilda's will are carried out."

"And those terms are…" Karl prompted.

"I don't know. I haven't seen the will yet, have I?"

"You haven't?" Karl was surprised.

"I'm meeting with her lawyer tomorrow morning. He has the will. I assume she'll have left whatever there is to me. She had no children of her own, and I am her only niece." Abigail drummed her fingers thoughtfully on the steering wheel. "Of course, I wouldn't put it past her to have left it to some animal shelter or something, just for spite. She never really liked me much, and I think she would enjoy making me do all the work to clean up after her and then leave me nothing for my trouble."

Karl glanced sideways at the contemptuous tilt of his mother's profile and refrained from commenting.

***

The landlord's daughter met them at the house, keys in hand and a list of furniture that belonged with the house. A jittery woman chain-smoking cheap cigarettes, she didn't wait around to ensure the list was followed, just handed it over with nicotine-stained fingers and jumped back into her aging Cadillac, spraying gravel in the direction of Abigail's Porsche as she pulled away. Abigail compressed her mouth more tightly but said nothing. She stood next to Karl, and they surveyed the house together.

It was tiny, even by the standards of the neighbourhood, with the sort of pebbledash stucco that had been popular in the fifties, now chipped and water-stained. The cheap asphalt shingles on the narrow roof were curling in places, and most of the white paint was peeling off the trim around the door and windows.

Abigail held the keys out to Karl without looking at him. She was still staring at the house. Karl wondered if she had ever been inside such a crummy little place in her life. Her face indicated not. He took the keys and crossed the narrow strip of grass, keeping to the path already worn down to dirt. The three steps up to the front door were sagging wooden boards, unpainted and uneven. He had to put his weight into the front door before it would shift.

Inside, a narrow hall traversed the house from front to back, living room and kitchen on the left, bedroom and bathroom on the right. There was no dining room. Karl had a feeling there wouldn't be much to leave in a will. Looking at the list of furniture, there wouldn't be much to pack, either. His mother followed him up the stairs with tottering steps. Her nostrils flared, and her upper lip curled as she looked around.

"You'll need to get some boxes," she said to Karl. "I saw a liquor store at the end of the street."

She pulled out her phone and began tapping on it, not even pretending to consider fetching the boxes in her spotless car.

***

By 8:00 p.m., Karl had successfully sorted the contents of his great-aunt's house into three short stacks of wine boxes, those for the dump, those for donations, and those with any items of possible value that his mother felt might be worth revisiting. For someone who didn't need any help, she was willing enough to let him carry out the actual work, while she poked around and pointed out which items went where. He was just wondering how they were going to transport the boxes, few though there were, in a car without any trunk space, when his brother Liam's truck pulled up on the street behind the Porsche.

Liam was only four years older than Karl, but his thinning blond hair made him look older than his thirty-one years. He was shorter than his younger brother and possessed both a greater dynamism and a quicker temper. The only member of the family who lived on the Island, he ran a successful trucking company out of Nanaimo. The company logo was emblazoned on the door of his truck, and on the back of his jacket, Karl noticed.

"All set?" Liam asked, taking the steps in one quick bound. "What a dump," he added, looking around the stripped-down house. "Not that I'd expect more from Campbell River." He winked at Karl as if sharing an inside joke. Karl didn't see the humour. The neighbourhood Aunt Matilda had lived in was old and run-down, but he had spotted some attractive homes on the drive through town, including several as nice as the house Liam was so proud of. Campbell River was a pretty little city, strung out along a hilly section of the coast that ensured at least half of the homes had ocean views. Admittedly, not the ones on Matilda's street.

Abigail didn't show any surprise at her middle son's arrival, just pointed to the boxes and said, "They're marked and I'm starving," before going to sit in her car and wait without patience for them to wrap up.

The men picked up boxes and began carrying them out to the truck on the curb.

"So?" Liam asked. "You done sitting around in Van? Ready to get your head back in the game?"

Karl shrugged. He wasn't sure what "the game" was, exactly, and he wasn't about to ask.

"I'm telling you, bro, all you gotta do is get your class one and you can come work for me."

It wasn't the first time the offer had been made, and Karl didn't feel like going over the arguments again. He was pretty sure he'd turn to panhandling before he'd work for Liam, but he wasn't prepared to engage in the confrontation that was bound to arise if he said so out loud.

"I can give you the up-Island route," Liam continued as he dropped a box into the truck bed and turned back to the house. "Nanaimo to Hardy and back four times a week. The money's decent, and if you decide you'd rather be working with your hands, then you can spend some time in the shop and start getting the hours in for your mechanic's ticket. Either way, you won't be killing your body like you were on the rigs, you'll be making decent money, and you can start getting your life back on track."

On track to where? Karl wondered, but he didn't bother asking out loud, just shrugged again and said, "I don't know if trucking's for me," before grabbing the next box.

***

It was a long night, curled up under a too-thin comforter on Liam's lumpy family room couch. The sofa in the main floor living room had looked more comfortable, but he didn't like to move once his sister-in-law had made this one up for him. He was rescued from his attempts to sleep by his sister-in-law's ancient cat landing on his face at 5:00 a.m., and he hurried to let the animal out before it urinated on him. He had met this cat before.

Stumbling up to the kitchen, he found a Keurig machine and a phone charger. He perched on a stool at the counter to sip his coffee and scroll through his tethered phone while he waited for the house to wake up. His nephews pounded down the hall around seven, and he was grateful when their mother trailed in after them, yawning and tying a robe over her Lion King nightgown. He never enjoyed Liam's boys much. They were pushy and rude, too much like their father for his taste, and he preferred them bullying their mother to badgering him at such an early hour.

By the time his mother appeared, coiffed and made up for their meeting with the lawyer, Karl had eaten two plates full of undercooked pancakes slathered in margarine and cheap syrup and drunk enough coffee to mentally keep up with his nephews' bickering.

Abigail took one look at the sticky plate her daughter-in-law held out and said, "Oh, don't trouble yourself; I'll just grab a coffee on the way." Karl was more than ready to leave and followed his mother out the door with an apologetic glance to his sister-in-law. Liam followed, apparently oblivious to their mother's rudeness.

***

Abigail sat across from her aunt's attorney with her sons flanking her. The lawyer, Mr. Amiel, cleared his throat tremulously and adjusted his rimless eyeglasses before beginning to read. He looked about eighty, Karl thought, contemplating the age spots on the bent head under thin strands of grey hair. Clearing his throat once more, he began.

"To my niece, Abigail, and her daughter, Matilda, I leave the contents of my home, including my china, my jewellery and my darling kitty Tibs, to divide between them as they see fit."

"We didn't find any cat when we were cleaning out the house." Karl wondered if they'd missed the animal.

"I believe Mr. Tibs passed away earlier this spring," Mr. Amiel replied, looking up from the document.

"Oh, thank god," exclaimed Abigail, who had never liked cats. "Matilda can have the china; she's always liked things like that. There really wasn't any jewellery worth keeping."

Mr. Amiel waited for her to finish before bending over the document again, searching for his place for several long seconds before continuing. "To my grand-nephews, Jakob and Liam, I leave the contents of my bank account, to be divided equally between them."

"What?" demanded Abigail, leaning forward abruptly. "All of her money? To the boys, and not to me?"

She didn't look at Liam when she spoke, but he flashed a brief smirk in her direction.

"That's right," replied Mr. Amiel, looking up from the will, searching his desk for another document and consulting it cautiously before adding, "I believe the final balance, after the bank fees are deducted, comes to two hundred and seventy-four dollars and change."

Liam's smile faded. Abigail settled back in her chair, arms crossed. Karl shifted his feet under his chair. He hadn't expected to get anything, he didn't mind, but he wondered why his siblings were included and he wasn't.

"And finally," Mr. Amiel continued. "To my youngest grand-nephew, Karl." Karl sat straighter in his chair. "I leave Abrams Investigations, including all of its files, equipment, contacts, and building, intact, as it was left to me by my brother, Mordecai, in the hope that he might desire to carry on the work that my brother enjoyed for so many years."

Karl sat unmoving and uncomprehending. Both Liam and Abigail turned in their chairs to look at him then turned back to stare at Mr. Amiel. Liam's gaze was fixed, but Abigail's eyes grew briefly distant.

"Daddy's agency," she breathed. She appeared at a loss for words, a rare event in Karl's experience.

"Agency, what agency?" asked Liam. "I thought your dad was a cop."

Abigail blinked. "He was, when I was younger. He started the agency after he left the service."

"When was this?"

"Oh, before you were born. Before any of you were born. He and I weren't speaking by then. We haven't spoken in years." Her voice trailed away. She looked up sharply at the lawyer.

"There was a building? What building?"

"It is a small, free-standing commercial building on North Park Street in Victoria." Mr. Amiel turned to address Karl. "I have all the ownership documents, including the lease for the ground-floor tenant and the agency's business license. It is still valid, although it will need to be renewed soon if you decide to carry on operations."

"Tenant?" Karl asked.

"Yes, there is a second-hand bookstore on the ground floor. The agency occupied the second floor, and I believe the third floor is currently vacant, although it has occasionally been rented in the past. The main-floor tenants have leased the space for many years; however, the lease does allow for termination if the building is sold." He paused delicately.

Liam spoke up. "That's a pretty prime location. Just outside of downtown. Very accessible. I bet it will sell for a packet. Jakob will have a better idea of the exact value. You'll list it with him, of course?" He looked across his mother at Karl.

"List it?" Karl still didn't know what to make of all this. It was so unexpected.

"Well, yeah, you aren't going to actually run a detective agency, are you? You wouldn't know anything about it. I suppose you could hold on to the building as an investment, if Jakob says this isn't the right market to sell it in, but you'd want to list those offices for lease, so you'll need him either way."

Their oldest brother, Abigail's second child, was a commercial real estate broker in Vancouver.

"Can I go see it?" Karl asked Mr. Amiel.

"Certainly. I have the keys to the building, along with all of the paperwork for you." Mr. Amiel continued to outline the details in his slow, tremulous way, but Karl was only half listening. A detective agency? His grandfather had been a detective? How had he never known this?

2

"So? You want to go check out this agency? We could drive to Victoria and be back at my place for dinner. It's less than four hours." Liam's eyes were glowing. He bounced lightly on the balls of his feet. They were standing on the sidewalk in front of the lawyer's office. Abigail was fiddling with the clasp on her purse, not looking at her sons, but Karl thought she was listening.

"Nah, I've got things to do in Van. You can drop me at the ferry, if Mom's staying over. I can walk on."

It wasn't true. He had absolutely nothing to do in Vancouver, but he realized he did not want them to come with him. Not for his first visit to his grandfather's detective agency.

Liam looked disappointed, but Abigail settled her purse firmly on her shoulder and said, "Yes, I think I'll stay here one more night, get everything wrapped up before I head home."

She walked briskly across the parking lot, her heels clicking on the cement, and settled behind the wheel. Karl slid in beside her, and they made the drive to the ferry terminal in awkward silence.

***

Standing on the forward observation deck of the ship, the wind whipping his face, the smell of the sea in his nostrils, Karl wondered how he had lived away from the ocean so long. The five years in Edmonton married to Kate, working outdoors in every kind of prairie weather, all felt like a bad dream now. He realized he wouldn't be going back there, even if Calfrac did call him back to work. He inhaled deeply and closed his eyes as the spray off the bow blew back to him.

***

The next morning, Karl walked through his sister's condo, room by room, hunting down his few but very scattered possessions. He was struck by the absence of any real colour in the place. All the wood was a dark chocolate brown that seemed to absorb any light, while the stone, walls, and fabrics were some shade between snow white and pale cream. All of Karl's clothes fit into a hockey bag, and the books, mementos, and gaming system he'd brought back from Edmonton weren't enough to fill an apple box from the grocery store. He managed to lock the condo without dropping either of them and left the key with the concierge before heading down to the parkade to load his truck. The four-wheel drive Tacoma was out of place in this metro Vancouver lot, but it had been the best vehicle he could afford back in Alberta, and it was paid for.

***

It was raining when Karl parked his truck across the street from the address on Mr. Amiel's documents. The building stood on the corner of North Park and Quadra, with the ground-floor bookshop facing Quadra. The entrance leading to the offices above was on the North Park side. It was a three-storey brick and wood building with bay windows on the upper storeys, plate glass on the ground floor, and old-fashioned dentil moulding around the edges of the roof. It was also badly in need of a paint job. The rain streaming steadily down the windshield of Karl's truck didn't improve its appearance. Karl scanned the neighbourhood before getting out in the rain.

The funeral parlour across the street must have been designed in the seventies by someone with a flair for the dramatic, but at least it had a fresh coat of white paint and its shrubs were neatly trimmed, its grass recently cut. The gravel lot adjoining the agency was weedy, with dead brown grass encroaching upon it and a drift of leaves left over from a now denuded tree piling around the row of black rubbish bins at the back wall of the building. The tree might be pretty in summer, but at this time of year it looked woebegone.

Karl decided he should let the owner of the bookshop know he was around before going up to the office. He didn't want to be arrested for entering his own property. Turning up the collar of his jacket against the drizzle, he hurried across the street and around to the front of the building, his footsteps splashing in the rapidly forming puddles. When he pushed open the shop door, a small bell rang above his head. Shaking the damp hair out of his eyes, he looked around at walls covered in books. Full shelves made narrow aisles down the centre of the shop. There was a low counter running along the left side of the room, but even behind that there were more books in a locked glass case. Old books. He couldn't imagine anyone ever reading this many books. He peered into the gloom of the shop. It was darker inside than it should have been because the big front window was half-covered by more books stacked on the windowsill. It smelled of dust, with just a hint of vanilla. At first, Karl didn't think anyone was there.

Then from the back of the shop came an old man. He was tall, with grey hair turning white combed neatly over the top of his head. He was so thin he should have been frail, but Karl didn't think he was. He held himself too straight, and his step was too firm for him to seem weak, despite his age.

"Hello, young man, what can I do for you?" Karl was reminded of an old-school teacher, one who was not afraid to give you what for if you got out of line.

"Hello," Karl said politely. "I'm Karl Larsson. My grandfather owned the agency upstairs. He's left it to me. I just wanted to let you know I'm here. Didn't want to be arrested for trespassing," he tried to joke.

"So." The man stopped and stared at Karl through gold-framed glasses. "You're Mordecai's grandson. The youngest, right? Are you here to tell us to pack?"

"I'm sorry...pack? What do you mean?" Karl could guess what the man meant, but he didn't want to be the one to say it.

"You're a Larsson, aren't you? I assumed any member of that family would have this place sold within an hour of finding out they owned it, and I'd be out on the street and nowhere to put my books. The wife's been wittering about it for years. Whatever would we do, and all that."

"No. I wasn't planning to turn anyone out," Karl said. After an awkward moment he added, "You have a nice shop here."

"Hmph." The man stared at him for another long moment then turned toward the shadowy depths of the store.

"Come on in, let me show you around before you go upstairs," he offered. "I'm Percy Meiklejohn, by the way. Would you like some coffee? It's an ugly day out there." Karl followed him to the back room, tucked behind a curtain of beads straight out of the sixties. It wasn't a very big room, especially with half the space filled by a large table where dozens of books were in the process of being repaired.

They poured coffee into chipped, mismatched mugs, and the old man started his tour of the shop, slowly pacing up and down the narrow aisles, the fingers of his free hand lightly brushing the spines of the books as he passed. "Here we have travel books, and here's history, followed by historical fiction. Down this aisle we have 'classics,' various authors, I tend to group them by their style of writing so that someone who loves Kipling, say, will find other authors they might enjoy on the same shelf. Of course, we have a section of cheap romance novels because they sell, even though I don't like them myself. Then we have your thriller types and your murder mystery, detective stories, etcetera. And over in this corner I keep the children's books."

But Karl had stopped at the detective books. Percy Meiklejohn was still talking. "I stack new books in front of the window until I have time to sort them and get them on the shelves. When it gets too dark to read the covers, then I know I have to get on with it."

Karl jerked himself out of his reverie and smiled dutifully at this stab at humour. Despite the temptation, he thought it was unlikely he would find any useful hints in Agatha Christie or Ruth Galloway and turned away from the shelf without taking a book.

***

Karl jogged round to the side entrance that led to the upper floors, his collar once again turned up against the steady drizzle. Pulling open the wooden door, he stepped into the tiny entrance landing. Shaking the rain out of his hair, he inhaled the scent of the old building, a combination of dust and damp. The linoleum was worn through in the centre of the landing, and the carpet on the steps was threadbare. He climbed the stairs to the second floor and found that one of the keys on the ring Mr. Amiel had provided opened the only door off the landing. He flipped the light switch, and a single bulb in the ceiling fixture flared briefly then blinked out.

"Figures," Karl said.

He could make out a smallish reception area with a desk and chairs showing as bulky outlines in the gloom. The door to the inner office was on his right, and fortunately, it was open, or he would have been in total darkness. He crossed to this door, felt around on the wall, and jiggled a second light switch. The lights didn't work here either, but at least the room was partially lit by the grey daylight coming in through tall, narrow windows. Raindrops were tracking down the panes, making weird patterns on the scarcely distinguishable carpet.

Karl made his way around the square, solid bulk of the desk and sat in the antique leather office chair behind it. He leaned back, looking around the room. The chair creaked audibly.

So. This was his. The air had the cold lifeless feel of unused space. It smelled musty.

He sat for a long time, listening to the sound of the rain blowing against the window panes, letting the damp chill creep up on him.

Eventually, hunger drove Karl out of his lethargy, so he locked the office and went out to eat. After driving around the block a few times, he found a little shawarma place not too far away. Eating lifted his spirits. On the way back to his truck he spotted a London Drugs and turned in. He picked up a large pack of light bulbs, a heater fan, and a step ladder.

Returning to the agency, he began in the inner office, setting up the heater and replacing light bulbs one by one. He made it to the third-floor landing before he ran out of bulbs, but he thought the empty rooms up there could wait. The light brought the layer of dust on the surfaces into sharp relief and showed up the fact that each of the file cabinets against the back wall was a different colour. The wood of the desk looked like it might be teak. It was beautifully carved, but between the coat of dust and the scratches and stains on top, these details were difficult to appreciate. The walls and carpet were faded to an indeterminate beige. Several stains on the floor looked like they might have been coffee.

Karl wandered out to the single washroom opposite the stairwell and found some paper hand towels. Dampening a handful, he returned to the office and wiped down the desk. Sitting down, he powered up the ancient computer, noticing as he did so that all the cords ran across the floor to a series of sockets set in the wall. The sockets looked suspiciously like an afterthought. He wondered if the building's electrical system was up to code.

Karl spent several hours that day going through the documents provided by Mr. Amiel, poking around the file drawers and the computer system. Despite the lack of upkeep to its physical surroundings, the agency's records were detailed and accessible and appeared to be up to date until around six months previously. Karl didn't think his grandfather had been big on appearances, but he had run a decent operation until the end.

Various corporate contacts, the methods used to complete background checks, tips for tracking down fathers who had failed to pay child support, even the best time of day to catch a fake insurance claimant carrying out home repairs, were all outlined in the files. The beige, grey, and black file cabinets contained almost forty years of case files, all carefully set down in spiky black cursive. Computers did not appear to have been popular with Mordecai either, despite the fact that he had condescended to purchase one at some point in his company's history.

After waiting for the painfully slow dial-up connection to access his email, Karl decided to call the Internet provider. It was only then that he realized he was seriously thinking about staying. Why upgrade the Internet on a business he just needed to clear out and sell? Looking around the room again, now warmly lit with the darkening windows reflecting the light back at him, he decided its shabbiness didn't bother him. It needed a good clean, sure, but it was much more comfortable than his sister's shiny, sterile condo.

Besides the reception area, washroom, and the large main office at the front of the building, there was a back room that seemed to be a cross between workspace and kitchenette. A long counter ran the length of the back wall. Plaster covered the brickwork, but there were no windows in that wall. Looking at the heavy canvas hanging over the bay window facing North Park Street, Karl wondered if his grandfather had perhaps used the room as a darkroom at one time. Into the counter was set a large steel sink, while a refrigerator that might qualify as an antique took up one corner of the room. With the shabby but comfortable couch in the office, he could practically live here, Karl thought; then he chuckled to himself at what his family would say to a move like that.

No, he would need somewhere else to live, but the agency didn't seem like the impossible idea it had when Mr. Amiel first read Aunt Matilda's will. There was no mortgage on the building, and the rent from the bookshop covered basic expenses, even when the agency wasn't operating. And the agency had been profitable, on a modest scale. It was an incorporated business, so he could continue to collect unemployment benefits if he didn't pay himself a wage. If he flunked it, he could always sell the building like Liam suggested, but Karl found he rather liked the idea of being a private eye.

***

Karl spent that night in a cheap motel, and the following morning he began apartment-hunting in earnest. He didn't want to spend more than he could help on accommodation. The mortgage payments on the house he had shared with his ex-wife were still fresh in his mind, as was the fact that he had nothing left to show for five years spent working on oil rigs and pulling in six figures a year. He'd had enough of keeping up with the Joneses, he decided, and he approached his hunt accordingly. His only stipulations were no roommates and on-site laundry.

Remembering the painfully slow Internet at the agency, Karl found a Starbucks near the motel and used his phone to look up apartment options. He was surprised to find that rent was higher in Victoria than it had been in Edmonton, but before the end of the day he managed to negotiate the lease of a tiny bachelor suite in the basement of an elderly woman's cottage. She said she liked the idea of a nice young man living on the premises.

Karl was pleased to note that it was close enough to the Esplanade to smell the ocean, but not so close that the seagulls would wake him in the mornings. The suite had one main room for eating, sleeping, and living in, and a closet of a bathroom. Only the laundry room was shared with the landlady. He told himself it was more than enough for him and signed the form without hesitation.

Karl had spotted an "antique" furniture store down the street from the agency. The next day he found himself an easy chair he liked and a table with almost matching chairs. He drew the line at a second-hand mattress and splurged on a new one at a discount warehouse he heard advertised on the radio. He found a frame to fit it at a garage sale on his block, and he was set.

3

Driving up Island Saturday morning with a fresh cup of coffee in hand and the oldies station playing on the radio, Karl grinned to himself. The sun was finally shining, and the brilliant blue sky behind the verdant shades of the evergreens lifted his spirits. Leaving Victoria behind and passing Duncan, Ladysmith, Nanaimo, and Parksville, he noticed when the bare brown limbs of the arbutus trees began to give way to the dark green of fir and hemlock, interspersed with plenty of pale grey alder wherever the pushy little seedlings had been allowed to take root. He didn't want to risk being early for the funeral, so he chose the Old Island Highway rather than the faster inland route and enjoyed the narrow, meandering path along the coast, smiling each time he caught the glint of sun off the waters of the strait.

Even attending a funeral with his family couldn't get him down on a day like this. He pulled up to the little grey Anglican church his mother had selected for his aunt's memorial service two minutes before the hour and slipped into a pew just in time to nod to his mother and brothers without having to speak to them. The stained-glass windows cast a warm glow over their faces. Karl was not surprised to see that neither of his brother's wives had elected to attend.

The service was blessedly short. Karl suspected his mother was responsible for that. Standing around afterward, sipping weak coffee from Styrofoam cups and waiting for their mother to shake hands with the old biddies crowding around her, Karl's brother Jakob broached the topic he'd been expecting.

"So, Liam tells me Great-Aunt Matilda left you Grandfather's old detective agency. I can send Roberts over to value the building next week, but I'll need you to provide me with copies of the lease documents to determine the best price to list it for. I can look up comps for the office spaces on the upper floors." Jakob lacked Liam's forcefulness, but he was knowledgeable in his field, and he did well for himself.

Karl squared his shoulders, taking advantage of the extra inches he had on his brothers, and faced them both.

"I've decided not to sell, actually," he said, pleased at how confident he sounded. "I think I'm going to try running the place."

Jakob looked like he might not have understood, but Liam snorted into his coffee.

"What? You?" he demanded mockingly. "You're going to run around playing detective? I mean, I know you said trucking wasn't for you, but there has to be something more practical you can do."

"Grandfather made a living at it," Karl said. "I've been going over the books, and that place was a going concern six months ago. All the contact information is there, and the old case files. There's a lot more to being a private investigator than I realized. I think it could be interesting."

Jakob's look was appraising now. "Does this have something to do with Kate?" he asked, setting his cup down on a doily-covered side table next to a stack of hymnals. "If you sell the place, are you worried she'll get a portion of the proceeds? Because if you haven't legally separated, she could be entitled to half simply on account of your taking possession."

Karl frowned. "No, it's not about that. My divorce is going through as quickly as legally possible, including the separation period, thanks. I just think I might enjoy the work. I'm sick of killing myself at a job I care nothing about. It'd be nice to build something of my own for a change."

"Look, Karl," Liam chimed in. "You got married too young. A blind man could see that Kate was a cold bitch who would ditch you as soon as something better came along. But you're still young. You're not totally hideous. Don't let them see your profile, and the ladies won't notice the size of that beak you've got until it's too late, and then they'll think it adds character. There's no reason for you not to get out there, meet someone new, pick a new career path, get your life back on track. You just gotta get your head out of your ass and do something real.

"Not play detective," he added, as if it was an afterthought.

Karl rubbed the disparaged appendage. So, he had a big nose. So what? He didn't see how the shape of his nose was going to affect his career as a detective.

"I'm not particularly interested in meeting anyone new just now," he told Liam coolly. "And I don't plan to play at anything. I'm going to give the job an honest shot and see whether I can do it or not. I don't see why I shouldn't be able to make a go of it when Grandfather could."

"Make a go of what?" His mother had walked up behind him. Her face held the coldly polite expression of a person who has been offered too many condolences for something they aren't sad about. She looked from her exasperated elder sons to her irritated youngest.

"Make a go of what?" she repeated.

"Karl thinks it'd be a clever idea to keep Grandfather's agency and run it himself," Liam butted in before Karl could get the words out. "Even though Jakob says the market's the best it's been in years and isn't likely to be this strong six months from now."

Karl scowled at his brother, then turned to look at his mother. A faint line appeared between her perfectly plucked eyebrows. Her hands tightened their grip on her black silk clutch.

"Do you think that is wise?" she asked.

"I don't know," Karl responded. "I guess we'll see."

Turning from Karl to the other two, she asked, "Do you want to get brunch here in Campbell River or wait until we get back to Nanaimo to eat?"

Apparently, Karl and the topic of his career choices were dismissed. Liam insisted that there was nowhere decent to eat in this town, and Karl managed to bow out of the invitation to stop for lunch at Liam's place on the way back down Island. Sliding into his truck a few minutes later, he breathed a sigh of relief and pulled off the tie he had hastily donned on his way into church.

"Could have been worse," he muttered under his breath as he pulled out of the parking lot and onto Dogwood Street. Karl wondered, yet again, why his mother never mentioned her father's passing, especially when it had come so soon before her aunt's, but he pushed the thought away. Considering she'd refused to talk about the man for as long as he could remember, he supposed it wasn't all that surprising.

4

Karl was sitting at the desk in his office, playing a game on his phone and waiting for the Internet supply rep to show up, when the rotary phone on the desk rang. Karl jumped, dropped his phone under the desk, swore under his breath, and picked up the office phone on the second ring.

"Hello, uh, Larsson Investigations," he said, as he bent to fish under his desk for the cell. He had been debating what to call the company now that it belonged to him, and this was the first name that came to mind. He liked how it sounded.

"Hi, did you say Larsson Investigations? I thought I was calling Abrams Investigations," said a bright female voice on the other end of the line. "We've dealt with Mr. Abrams in the past," she added helpfully.

"Yes, that's right," said Karl, straightening in his chair. "We're under new management, but we are offering the same services to our existing customers. What can I do for you?"

Apparently, he sounded convincing, because the woman at the other end didn't quibble. Her name was Janelle, and she was from a local family law office. They needed a father who had failed to make child support payments for the past three months tracked down and a court summons delivered to him.

"His mail is being returned to our office marked 'no longer at this address,' but of course that could just be a ruse," she explained. She provided Karl with the man's name, birthdate, physical description, and last known address. Karl went through all three pens in the desk drawer, trying to find one that he could take notes with and eventually ended up punching the information into the notes section on his cell phone. He also made a mental note to pick up some office supplies.

"Is there anything else you can think of that might help me track him down?" Karl asked, wracking his brain for useful details he might have seen in the case files he'd read so far.

"Do you know where he works or what type of work he typically does? Are there any known friends or family that he could be staying with?"

"Um." Karl could hear papers being shuffled on the other end of the line. "He's worked various positions in three different Nanaimo area bars over the past year. He may try to find cash work in order to avoid paying tax or child support on the earnings, in which case he'll be in trouble with the CRA as well as the family law court. I can give you the names of the former employers, but I don't know if he still works for any of them. Oh, and he does have a sister. She's been uncooperative with our office in the past, but if you can find her home address it would be a place to check."

Karl noted the names of the bars and the sister and promised to keep Janelle in the loop on any progress he made. She, in turn, would courier the documents that needed to be served to his office so he would have them ready to go once Matt Carson was found. Once he had served Carson, she explained, he would need to come into her office to swear an affidavit to that effect. It all sounded very official to Karl, but Janelle seemed to think it perfectly commonplace. Karl thought that if he could pay the bills delivering paperwork, being a detective would be even easier than he had hoped.

***

By the end of the following day, Karl was starting to think it might not be so easy after all. Matt Carson had trashed his last place of residence before skipping out on the rent. The sister, when Karl found her, swore violently and threw her coffee in his face. Fortunately, it was only lukewarm, but Karl didn't enjoy walking around smelling like stale coffee with cream for the rest of the day. None of Carson's former employers had heard from him in months. If he was working, it wasn't for them. All in all, Nanaimo seemed like a total bust.

Sitting in his truck, wondering whether he should head home for the night or try to find somewhere local to stay, Karl had gotten as far as deciding that he definitely wouldn't be calling Liam when it occurred to him that he might try scoping out a few local bars. If he stuck to establishments like the kind Carson had worked at in the past, he might just get lucky, and he could do with a beer. He checked into a cheap motel that advertised free Wi-Fi then drove into the city core, parked at the casino, and started his tour.

Karl called it a night after his fourth beer in as many bars and took a cab from the Queens Hotel, not an actual hotel, back to his motel to crash. He slept late the following morning and ate a Tim Hortons breakfast on a bench by the Harbourfront Walkway, watching the sea planes take off and listening to the screaming of the gulls. Wandering out to the end of the fishing pier to kill some time, Karl watched an overexcited small girl with a high-pitched voice reel in her first fish while her father coached her. He breathed deeply, savouring the salt smell of the sea and the warm sun on his face, and eventually he made his way to the nearest pub to begin his afternoon's work in earnest.

***

Karl stood just inside the door, squinting in the dim light. It was only his second stop of the afternoon, and the sun was still bright outside. Smoking in any public building had been illegal for years, but this place still smelled like stale cigarettes and the more recent skunkiness of low-grade weed. Karl's nose wrinkled involuntarily. He took a step forward and felt the sticky floor pull at his shoes. *What a dive*, he thought, and then he spotted the neck tattoo he'd been looking for and froze. All concerns about cleanliness disappeared from his mind as he stared at that tattoo, momentarily transfixed.

The man with the tattoo was sitting at the bar. The tattoo said *Callie*, and Karl wondered briefly if that was the name of the kid he had failed to pay support for. He was probably the same height as Karl, but at least a foot wider. He leaned thick, heavily tattooed forearms on the bar, nursing a can of Lucky in large, scarred hands. Karl walked up to the bar a little along from him and glanced over casually.

"Matt?" Karl's voice was all cheerful recognition, as if he'd just spotted his long-lost best friend. "Matt Carson, is that you?"

"Yeah, that's me, who are you?" Carson frowned at him, unfriendly but unconcerned.

Karl thrust the lawyer's envelope in his face. Carson's head reared back, and his hand came up to seize it automatically. Karl stepped back, gave Carson a nod, and said, "That, my friend, is a summons to appear in family law court on charges of failure to pay the prescribed support to your ex-wife, Linda Carson. You have been served."

Carson looked at the envelope, looked at Karl, and came up off the stool and around in one smooth, spring-like move. His fist hit the side of Karl's head like a jackhammer, and Karl hit the floor like a felled tree. A very painful tree. That was seeing stars.

The bartender came out of nowhere to catch hold of Carson's arm, spinning him away from where Karl lay, gabbling a mile a minute.

"Whoa, Carson, my man, you really showed him! But you knocked your beer over. Shame. Tell you what, next one's on the house."

He managed to get Carson back on his stool and waved the girl behind the bar to bring a fresh drink over.

"You." The bartender stabbed a stubby finger with a blackened nail at Karl, who was just starting to push himself up from the floor. "Out."

Karl didn't argue. His head was ringing, and he tasted blood. He wove his way between tables and chairs like a drunk and had to lean against the wall outside for a minute to give the spinning a chance to stop. Sucking in a deep breath, he gagged on the smell of stale piss, alcohol, and body odour. Looking over, he saw an old man in ripped jeans, work boots, and a filthy grey sweater sitting on a stack of yesterday's newspapers, his back propped against the wall, a can of ravioli in his left hand, the cupped fingers of his right suspended halfway to his gaping mouth. Red sauce dripped onto the front of his sweater as he stared at Karl.

"You okay, man?" he asked with genuine concern. His pocked cheeks bunched in a sympathetic grimace.

"Yeah," Karl said with a shake of his head. "I'll be fine."

He pushed off the wall and made his way unsteadily to his truck. Inspecting the damage to his ear in the rear-view mirror, he tried to remember the last time he'd let himself get sucker punched like that. It had to be at least junior high. With an older brother like Liam, he'd learned to duck young, and he'd taken up boxing seriously in high school, placing, if not winning, in his weight category at the provincial tournament every year he'd gone. He had maintained his membership in Boxing BC until his third year of college, when he and Kate started to get serious. He hadn't put on a pair of gloves in years, but he still couldn't believe he'd left himself so wide open under those circumstances.

"Stupid," he growled as he started the truck and popped it into gear. He needed to get fit again if he was going to do this thing for real.

Karl stopped at a drugstore for an ice pack and Advil and spent an hour lying on the motel bed, chilling the side of his face, before it occurred to him that the lawyers might like to know where Carson was living these days. With a groan, he heaved himself up, checked out of the motel, and headed back to the bar. He spotted the same homeless guy he had spoken to earlier digging through the dumpster in the alley beside the bar. He parked his truck on the street and walked down the alley to stand by the dumpster, watching the other man's activities until he deigned to look up.

"Can I help you?" He might have been the receptionist in a stuffy office from the tone he used. Karl responded in kind.

"I hope so. I was wondering if you would do me a favour."

"What kind of favour?" The man was suspicious, but curious too.

"I don't want to go back in, but I'd like to know if someone is still in there. If I give you the price of a beer, will you look to see if a guy with a neck tattoo that says *Callie* is still inside?

"He was sitting at the bar earlier," Karl added, helpfully.

"Make it the price of a bottle, and you're on," replied the other man, passing a black plastic garbage bag that clanked to Karl before clambering over the side of the dumpster and landing on the pavement. He dusted himself off then took his bag of cans back so Karl could dig out his wallet. Karl handed him a twenty, and he dropped his bag at Karl's feet, said, "Watch my stuff," and headed around to the front of the bar. Karl looked around the alley and spotted a rickety blue bike with a battered baby carrier hooked behind. He picked up the bag of cans and stowed them in the carrier next to a bundle of fabric that might have been clothes.

The man was gone for less than five minutes, and when he came back, he had good news.

"Yup, still sitting at the bar, nursing his beer and cursing all ex-wives everywhere," he told Karl. "I got a look at his keys, looks to me like he drives a Ford pickup," he added as he pulled his bike away from the alley wall.

"Thanks. Thanks a lot!" Karl replied.

"Hey, any time." The man threw a leg over his bike and wobbled off down the alley, and Karl headed back to his truck to wait Carson out.

He had parked where he could see the front of the bar and the parking lot. There were two Ford pickups that he could see. He wondered if he should worry about a disguise and eventually dug an old pair of aviators out of the glove box and found a ball cap behind the seat. The sunglasses helped counter the glare of the late afternoon sun that shone right in his eyes, and Karl settled in for a long evening.

In the end, it wasn't as long as he'd feared. Carson rolled out the door shortly after seven and beat a more or less straight path across the lot to the bigger of the two Fords Karl had spotted. Karl started his engine and pulled into traffic when the Ford was far enough up the street that he shouldn't be noticed. He kept at least two vehicles between them as he followed the Ford through residential backstreets to a shabby neighbourhood where more than one house had boarded-over windows and a general air of abandonment.

Karl was far enough back to pull into a side street when he saw the Ford stop in front of a house that wasn't in much better shape than its abandoned neighbour. He looped the block and came back around in time to see Carson enter through the front door. He slowed, waiting until Carson was well inside and out of sight before cruising past and snapping a picture of the house with the truck parked out front. He made an audio note in his phone of the house address and the truck's make, model, and license plate number, just in case it would turn out to be useful, then turned his truck in the direction of the highway.

It was dark by the time Karl crossed the Malahat, grateful that the Toyota was built for climbing as he wove his way up the mountainside before descending back to sea level and the city. It was too late to catch the lawyers by the time he reached Victoria, and his ear was still throbbing, so he headed for his basement retreat and called it a night.

5

The next morning, Karl was up with the sun, showered and shaved before eight o'clock. Checking out the bruise on his temple, he reflected that he'd had worse in his boxing days, and he made a mental note to look into getting some boxing gear once he'd been paid by the lawyers. He was at their office when it opened at nine, ready to report the success of his mission. Janelle, the young paralegal who had brought him in on the case, took notes of everything he told her and had him wait while she typed and printed the affidavit, then brought out one of the firm's lawyers to administer the oath. It was all very formal and somewhat intimidating, but also a little bit fun.

"We don't officially pay extra for getting punched," Janelle told him, the dimple in her right cheek showing for a moment. "But if you added an extra consulting fee for the information about the vehicle Carson is driving now and his new home address to the standard document service fee, I don't think there would be any objections. After all, that will be helpful if he doesn't show up for court and we have to get a warrant issued for his arrest."

She promised that if Karl would send her the invoice right away, she could have a cheque for his fee in the mail the following week, and Karl left her office elated. He had done it. He had solved his first case. In the bright light of morning, getting punched seemed like a bit of an adventure and not the end of the world. He just needed to get back into practice, that was all. Why wait for the lawyer's cheque? He tracked down a second-hand sporting goods store and found a battered but usable heavy bag, a slightly newer speed bag, and some decent practice gloves. He still had his old boxing shoes, even though he hadn't worn them in years. He piled the gear into the front seat of his truck and headed over to the agency.

It only took two trips to the hardware store to get the bags hung in a convenient corner of the office, and Karl spent a sweaty half hour doing interval drills. He couldn't believe how quickly he ran out of breath and determined that he would be running on his lunch breaks from now on. He'd need to see about a jump rope and some free weights too, before long.

Collapsing back into the chair behind his desk, Karl still felt the energy of success, despite his temporary breathlessness. He hunted down the mess of spreadsheet-based invoices he had found in one of the few files on the computer when he first reviewed the business books, found an old invoice for the law office Janelle worked at, and used it as a template to make her the requested bill for his recent services. Hitting *send*, he felt a further thrill of satisfaction. He was earning again. He was really doing this.

Karl wished he could tell someone about it. He toyed with the idea of calling Jakob or Liam, but their mockery of the idea of him "playing detective" was fresh in his mind, and besides, he didn't want them too interested in the agency. He wasn't ready to share it yet. He pushed himself out of his chair and paced the length of the office several times before he thought of Percy Meiklejohn. The shop would be open. He thumped down the stairs and hurried around to the front of the building, pleased to see that the lights were on. The little tinkling bell over the door reminded him of his first visit to the agency, and he grinned at the recollection.

"Ah, young Larsson," Percy Meiklejohn greeted him from behind the counter of the shop. "And how are you this fine day?"

He was sorting through a box of books, and he continued to take each book out of the box, inspect it carefully, and then place it in a different stack on the counter as Karl crossed the shop to stand in front of him.

"I solved my first case," he said as nonchalantly as he could manage. He couldn't help grinning, just a little.

"Well, well. My congratulations." Percy smiled at Karl over the top of his glasses.

"It wasn't anything big. Just a father delinquent on his child support." Karl shrugged modestly. "I just had to track him down and serve him with papers, that's all."

"That might be a very big thing to his wife and children," Percy observed. "Why don't I make a fresh pot of coffee, and you can tell me all about it. Including how you got that cauliflower ear," he added as he rounded the counter and headed toward the back room.

Karl was in the middle of his story, just getting to the part where Carson had knocked him down, and Percy was chuckling appreciatively, when Karl swung his arm wide, and his elbow brushed an ornate lidded vase sitting on the windowsill. It tottered for a moment, and he caught hold of it with both hands to stop it falling off the ledge.

"Careful, son, you don't want to go spilling Mordecai's ashes, now," Percy said.

"Mordecai's what?" Karl released the jar quickly.

"Mordecai's ashes," Percy answered with a whimsical smile. "There's over forty years of friendship in that jar."

"But why do you have my grandfather's ashes?" Karl demanded, shocked into near rudeness. "Shouldn't they go to my mother?"

Percy laughed out loud. "Do you think she would want them? I can wrap them up for you to take to her if you like."

Karl's mouth dropped open, then his gaze fell to the scarred surface of the table. "No," he said after a pause. "You're right. They're better here with you."

Percy's continued chuckles irritated Karl. What a ghoul, to keep his best friend's ashes sitting around like that, not even worrying that they might get spilled or lost. Worse, however, was the truth behind his comment on Karl's family. Karl knew perfectly well that his mother had zero interest in those ashes.

This fact was inadvertently verified that very afternoon when Karl's sister called. Seeing her number on his phone, Karl let the call go to voicemail. He knew Matilda well enough to know that she wouldn't be calling unless someone, probably someone other than her, wanted something, and he didn't feel up to any favours at the moment. His head was still throbbing gently. When he saw the message notice flash on his phone, he stared at it for a second, then went to the kitchen and found a fresh cup of coffee to fortify himself before listening to the voicemail.

"Karl, honey," Matilda began. Karl rolled his eyes. When Matilda said *honey*, he knew she was about to condescend, and he did not like being condescended to, even by his favourite sibling.

"Mum told me that you inherited grandfather's old agency from Aunty Milly. How she ended up owning it I can't even imagine, but you should know that Mum is really uncomfortable with the idea of you trying to run that place."

"She didn't want to say anything about it." Karl rolled his eyes again. "But I think you should seriously reconsider this decision. You know how painful that relationship has always been for Mum." *Actually, I have no idea*, Karl thought irritably. "And it really is a waste of your talents." Another eye roll. "Please think it over. I'm sure you'll make the best possible choice."

Karl pushed the button to end the recording at this point. He thought if he rolled his eyes any more, they might come loose in their sockets. He considered ignoring the call, but that would make it much more likely that he would hear from her again. In the end, he settled for a text response.

Thanks for the message, Till. I'll keep it in mind.

He hoped that was vague enough to prevent Jakob showing up to appraise the place but also sufficiently promising to keep Tilly happy for the time being. She was usually prepared to give someone time if she thought they were going to come around to her way of thinking in the end.

Stumping down the steps to his basement at the end of the day, Karl wondered what the matter with his family was. What kind of a daughter didn't care what happened to her dead father's ashes? They had all attended Great-Aunt Matilda's funeral, due to her sense of familial obligation, but she had never even mentioned her father's death, never mind attending a funeral. And why did Karl himself have no memory of the man? Even if his mother didn't speak to her father, he could remember his grandmother visiting. Wouldn't Abigail at least have allowed her children to meet their grandfather? Had she really hated him so much that Karl running his old business would upset her? Why?

6

The call from the family law office had gotten Karl thinking, and the next day he began to work his way methodically through the list of contacts in his grandfather's case records, informing law offices, insurance agencies, and employment bureaus that Larsson Investigations was open for business and happy to provide them with all the services of the former Abrams Investigations. Two weeks later, Karl had run a total of four background checks for cautious employers and landlords, tracked down two more delinquent child supporters, and delivered divorce papers to a very angry woman in a large house, with a small dog who bit him on the ankle while its owner screamed at him. Being a detective wasn't exactly what he had anticipated, but there was an interesting variety, and he thought he might turn out to be good at it.

He was sitting at his desk just about lunchtime, debating walking up Quadra Street for some sushi or down North Park for pizza, when the door to the outer office banged open. It was a finicky door and rarely opened smoothly. Before Karl had time to get up from his chair, a man appeared in the doorway. He looked around the office with casual insolence before turning to Karl and appraising him in his turn.

"Uncle Kris, hi." Karl stood up and came around from behind the desk, holding out his hand. "How are you?"

Kristopher Larsson was a heavier version of Karl's older brothers. His blond hair was thinning on top, and his stockiness was more fat than fit these days, but the family resemblance remained strong. The grip of his handshake was as painful as Karl remembered.

Karl waved his uncle into a chair and offered him coffee, which he declined, then sat behind the desk and waited. Kris wasted no time coming to the point.

"When was the last time you saw your cousin Kelsey?"

Karl had to think about that for a second before he could remember. "Uh, Grandma June's funeral, I think," he replied. "And before that at Jakob's wedding. It's been a while," he added reflectively. He had always liked Kelsey. She was the only one in the family who was younger than him, and that was by at least eight or nine years, he thought. She had been a cute, chubby, annoying little tagalong at family gatherings when he was a teenager, but since his own graduation and move to the prairies, they had completely lost touch. He wondered what she was up to these days.

"She's run away from home," Kris informed him bluntly. "Neither her mother nor I have seen her in weeks."

"Have you called the police?" Karl leaned forward, concerned.

"I called them when her mother wouldn't stop harping at me about it, but they say there's nothing they can do. She's nineteen," he added by way of explanation.

"Wow, nineteen? Already?" It had been a long time.

"Yeah. I'd say let her do what she likes if she wants to be a brat about it, but her mother's convinced she'll be hauled off by white slavers or something, and she wouldn't shut up until I said

I'd do something." Karl frowned at his uncle's language, but Kris didn't appear to notice.

"I ran into Jakob the other day in town, and he mentioned your little endeavour." He gestured around the office with obvious contempt. "I figured hiring an investigator ought to calm Melinda down for a while, and at least a member of the family can see nothing gets in the papers or on social media."

"Is that important?" Karl asked. He had just been thinking that social media would be the best place to start looking.

"*Yes*, it's important," snapped his uncle. "I'm up for reelection to city council, and I don't need my daughter making headlines for something this stupid." Karl remembered Jakob saying that Uncle Kris had a finger in half the shady real estate deals around Surrey. He hadn't realized he was into city politics as well.

"Is there any reason you think she might be on the Island? Or did you want me to look around Vancouver for her?"

"She wanted to come to the Island with some friend of hers, get a job and an apartment, and bum around like some illiterate hippy, apparently, only her mother said no. She should have started university last month at Simon Fraser. We only agreed to a year off after high school if she'd knuckle down and get on with it at the end of that time. I didn't want to agree to that, but her mother thought she'd do better if she took a break. It's already been a year and half, and now this!"

He shook his head and sneered at his ex-wife's foolishness.

"Still, even Melinda realized she had to start acting like an adult some time. When she put her foot down, Kelsey took off. She only had one bag, as far as Melinda knows, and no car, but she could have walked on the ferry, met her friends on this side."

"Do you know the name of her friends, the ones she was hoping to stay with?" Karl asked hopefully.

"Melinda says it's some girl named Alice or Alissa, something like that. If you can get hold of her, she'll probably know where Kelsey is. If she'll tell you."

Karl knew Kelsey's friends weren't likely to talk to her parents about her, but a cousin might be different. Apparently, Kris had the same idea.

"Look, see what you can find out," Kris continued. "And if you can get her to come home, I'll pay a bonus on top of whatever you charge for hunting down missing teenagers."

Karl had been looking over the business books whenever he had nothing better to do. The accounting system was ancient, his grandfather had been addicted to manual entry spreadsheets, and he thought the prices were a little low, so he added twenty percent to the old standard retainer fee, and his uncle wrote him a cheque without batting an eye.

After Kris left, Karl logged in to Facebook and hunted down his cousin's profile. The picture was an abstract painting that resembled no one Karl had ever met, but his ex-aunt was on her friends list, and so was his sister Tilly. It was like Tilly to keep in touch with her, even though they were so far apart in age. He wondered if she would have blocked incoming messages, to avoid her parents. Scrolling through her friends list, he didn't see any

Alice, but there was an Alysa. He thought it wouldn't hurt to try. Thinking carefully and trying hard not to sound like a creepy stalker, he composed his message.

Hi, I'm Kelsey's cousin Karl. I don't think she's getting my messages; do you think you could pass one along for me? I just moved to Victoria, and I heard she might be living on the Island. If she wanted to check out my new detective agency, she can stop by... He typed in the address from memory. If Kelsey was anything like the kid he remembered, a detective agency might bring her out of hiding, even if a long-lost cousin wouldn't.

***

"This place is a dump."

Karl started and looked up from the file he had been reading. A young woman stood in the doorway. She was perhaps 5'5" or 5'6", with a figure that polite people would call curvy, a trucker's cap over messy brown hair, and mud-brown eyes that stared defiantly at Karl. He noticed she had a spot on her chin that looked like it had been picked at.

"Well? You wanted to see me?" She walked into the office and flopped into the client chair across from Karl, hunching her shoulders and glowering at him.

"Kelsey?"

"Obviously."

"You, uh." He caught himself in time to change *you got bigger* to, "You grew up."

"No, I'm still twelve." Her voice held a note of petulance he didn't remember. "Of course, I grew up." After a pause she added, "So what'd you want to see me about? I'm not going home, if that's the idea."

"You figured that one out, eh?" Karl didn't see any point in denying it. He laid aside the file and studied his cousin across the desk.

"Figured my mom would be having kittens by now." She smirked, which was at least an improvement on the glower. "Yeah. But I didn't think she'd sic a detective on me. When'd you start this gig?"

She looked around the room quizzically, apparently less disgusted by its appearance upon second appraisal.

"Recently," Karl replied. "And your mother's genuinely worried about you."

"Ugh, you used to be cool. What happened?" Kelsey demanded. She slumped back in the chair and crossed her arms across her chest.

"I'm still cool," Karl protested, realizing as he said it how uncool it sounded. "So…" He cast around for an argument that didn't sound too uncool. "What's wrong with university? I had fun there."

"Yeah? And how much good has it done you? Haven't you been a rig pig ever since?"

Karl laughed. "Well, yes, but I had some laughs, made some good friends, met my wife…"

"The wife that left you and took you for everything you had?"

Karl didn't have an answer to that.

"University is a stupid waste of time if you aren't training to be something specific." Kelsey's voice was scornful. "Sitting in a classroom, listening to lectures for hours a week, taking all these general requirement courses. It's not an efficient way to learn anything, even if I did have an idea of what I want to become, which I don't."

She added, "I just want to go to work, earn a living, make my own life. And not in Port Moody!"

"What's wrong with Port Moody?" Karl asked, confused.

"It's where my mom lives. With my stepdad. And it's lame. Almost as lame as they are. That's why they wanted me to go to Simon Fraser," she continued, "because I could live at home and take transit to school. Which is not going to happen."

Kris tried to think of something to say to keep her talking, keep her engaged. "Do you have a job?"

"Not yet, but I've been applying." She didn't sound as confident now. "It's so stupid. There are tons of things I can do, but my mom never let me have a job growing up, so I basically have no experience. Just answering phones and filing for my dad last winter. And he won't give me a reference!" The frustration in her voice was palpable, and her eyes suddenly welled with tears. Karl felt a jolt of panic at this ominous symptom.

"You could work here," he blurted.

Kelsey blinked and looked at him in shock. "Seriously? You would give me a job?"

"Sure, why not?" Karl shrugged. "I'm in and out of the office a lot. You could watch the phones, look after the filing, the same sort of thing you did for your dad."

"Do those things still work?" she asked, pointing at the enormous phone on his desk.

"Yeah. Hilarious, aren't they?" He picked the receiver up, gestured vaguely with it, and put it back in its cradle.

"But there's one condition," he added, thinking of his uncle's cheque, still sitting in his wallet, uncashed. "You call your mom and you let her know that you spoke to me, and that I convinced you to call her. And you give her your home address and tell her you have a job.

"You don't have to tell her where you're working," he added hastily.

"Yeah, that might not earn you any points." But Kelsey was really smiling now, sitting straighter in her chair and looking Karl full in the face. She looked a lot more like the cute kid he remembered that way.

"And you have to check in with her at least once a week while you're working here," he added for good measure.

"Check in?" Kelsey raised an eyebrow.

"I don't care how, call, text, whatever you like, just let her know you're alright so she doesn't go bothering Kris about you."

"Heaven forbid Kris be bothered by something to do with me." Kelsey rolled her eyes, but the bitterness in her voice made Karl wince.

"That's not what I meant," he protested.

"Whatever." Kelsey shrugged impatiently. "Shall I start tomorrow then?"

"Sure, tomorrow will be fine." He was grateful she hadn't suggested starting immediately. He wasn't sure what he was going to do with her, and he was already wondering what he'd just gotten himself into.

"Fine," said Kelsey, pushing herself up out of the chair. "See you tomorrow."

"See you," said Karl, then added, before she reached the door, "Hey, Kels. It's good to see you again."

"Yeah." She gave him a half smile and a nod over her shoulder before she left.

"Well," said Karl, looking down at the file he'd been reading without seeing it. "I guess we'll see."

***

Kelsey was sitting on the bottom step, picking at the edge of the hole in the linoleum, waiting for him, when Karl arrived the next morning.

"I'm gonna need a key if you're not going to get here at a decent time," she told him, pushing herself heavily off the step and dusting her broad backside with one hand. "Also, you should really get a lock on that outer door, or you're going to get homeless people camping in here. I'm surprised you don't already."

Karl followed her up the stairs wondering, once again, what he had gotten himself into.

***

"You have got to be kidding me with this computer."

Kelsey's voice reached Karl in the back room as he was making coffee. He came out to find her squinting at the monitor on the reception desk as if it were a bug under a microscope. It was a very old, very bulky monitor, with a very small screen. It belonged to the computer that had occupied Karl's desk when he first took over operations.

"Do you even have a website?" she asked Karl without looking up.

"Not yet," Karl replied. "But," he added with a grin, "that would be a great project for you to get started on."

"On this thing?" she demanded, her eyebrows disappearing into her bangs. Karl didn't think she'd had bangs the day before, but he wasn't entirely certain. He had picked up a refurbished laptop at a place called Gizmo's his first week in Victoria, but there'd been no need for a second machine before now, and Mordecai's old computer was truly ancient.

"Tell you what," Karl said, reaching for his wallet, "why don't you go see what…five hundred will get you at Gizmo's." He pulled out half of the sheaf of cash intended for his landlady and handed it to her. He could get more cash later.

"Probably not much," Kelsey scoffed, pocketing the money nonetheless.

"They specialize in refurbished systems, and I'm guessing it'll be better than this." He waved his hand at the desktop.

"True." She swung her purse over her shoulder and headed out the door without further comment. Karl returned to the workroom for his coffee and a little peace and quiet.

***

Kelsey was gone for most of the morning, and Karl was starting to wonder if she would be coming back at all when the downstairs door banged and he heard her footsteps clomping up the stairs. He saved the case file he'd been typing and wandered out to see what she had found. Apparently, quite a bit. She carried a large nylon shopping bag in each hand, bursting with a surprising assortment of items. There was a desktop computer with a monitor, keyboard, and mouse. Also, paint, brushes, stencils, and cleaning supplies, a drill, a lock, a hole saw, a hammer, and a set of chisels.

"Um, what's all this?" Karl asked.

"I told you," Kelsey replied. "The main door needs a lock. And you're not going to keep calling this place Abrams Investigations, are you?"

"No." Karl had intended to repaint the sign on the street door but hadn't gotten around to it yet. He decided Kelsey was best left to herself and returned to the inner office without asking about change. Listening to her puttering about in the front office, he thought he might get used to having some company around the place.

By the end of the day, she had the new computer up and running, the lock installed, and the doors painted and drying. They would be ready for the new business name to be applied in the morning. Karl felt a bit nervous when he heard a YouTube tutorial on how to install locks playing in the front office, but the key she gave him turned smoothly when he tried it at the end of the night, and it locked the door securely. He wouldn't have thought of painting all the doors black, but he had to admit it looked good. Really sharp against the white trim. He realized he would need to rethink what he should pay her. If she were going to be this useful, minimum wage wouldn't cut it.

By the end of the week, Kelsey had cleaned the carpets, repainted the walls in the reception area, introduced herself to Janelle from the family law office, and gotten the hot water working in the bathroom. She had even put new linoleum down in the entry. She had also informed Karl how much he should be paying her. It sounded reasonable to him.

7

"Where are you going?" Kelsey demanded. She was sitting at the reception desk, painting her fingernails an iridescent shade of purple. She had been with the agency for almost a month now, and her improvement activities had slowed down as she'd run out of urgent projects to tackle. She was starting to get restless.

"Possible insurance fraud," Karl answered, waving the file in his hand at her as he headed for the door.

"Wait! Are you going to be gone all day? What am I supposed to do?"

"What about the website? Aren't you working on that?" he replied.

Kelsey flattened both hands on the desk and stared at him with her eyebrows raised incredulously. "That's done. It's been done for a week. Haven't you even looked at it?"

"I didn't realize." Karl thought she might have mentioned it, and he meant to check it out, but right now he needed to get into position, or he might miss Oglevie leaving. "I'll take a look when I get back."

"I'm coming with you." Kelsey jumped up, screwed the lid on her nail polish, and punched buttons on the new phone system she'd installed.

"Uh, it's not going to be very exciting. I just watch the guy until he does something he shouldn't be able to do and try to get pictures or videos of it. That's basically all there is to it.

"And it can take hours, maybe even days," he added as she shoved sock feet into the combat boots beside the desk.

"Like a stakeout in a cop show?" she asked, shrugging into her biker-style leather jacket and slinging her purse over her shoulder. "Cool."

"Kind of." Karl held the door open for her and suppressed a sigh as she preceded him down the stairs.

***

They sat in a driveway across the road and a block away from Oglevie's place, the truck partially screened by large azalea bushes only starting to bud but already leafy enough that no one was likely to spot the two of them sitting inside. They had watched the owner of the house drive away before selecting this driveway to park in, and Karl counted on being able to stay in the spot most of the day without disturbance. He sipped an extra-large coffee and watched Oglevie walking up and down on his deck, talking on his cell phone. Kelsey had stripped off both boots and socks and was painting her toenails the same purple as her fingers.

After a couple of hours sitting around, a venti macchiato, and three coats of paint on her toenails Kelsey said, "You were right, this is boring."

Oglevie sat sunning himself in a deck chair with his shirt unbuttoned, revealing a large amount of pink stomach and curly chest hair.

"What's supposed to be wrong with him?"

"His back," Karl replied. "He's claiming a severe work-related back injury, and he wants long-term disability. If he's really injured, he's entitled to it. If he's faking, they want to know."

"Do you have a spare tire in the back?"

"Yes." Karl looked at his cousin, wondering what brought that up.

"I have an idea." Kelsey rapidly pulled her socks on, followed by her boots, dug in the glove box until she found a tire gauge, and then jumped out of the truck. Swinging briskly around to the rear driver's side, she crouched down and began fiddling with the tire.

Karl checked that Oglevie was still on the porch and got out of the truck. By the time he reached her, Kelsey had the cap off the valve stem and was letting the air out of the tire with an alarming hiss.

"What are you doing?" Karl demanded.

"Shhh, he'll hear you," said Kelsey, glancing in the direction of Oglevie's house.

"But what are you doing?" Karl repeated in an insistent undertone.

"I'm flattening your tire," explained Kelsey.

"I can see that," said Karl. "Why are you flattening my tire?"

"Well, I can't very well ask him to help me change a perfectly good tire, can I?" Her tone was exasperated, as if he was being particularly dense. Karl reminded himself that she was only nineteen. At the same time, he began to see her point.

"Isn't that entrapment?" he asked doubtfully.

"I'm pretty sure that only counts if the police do it," Kelsey replied. The tire was quite flat now, its sides bulging out until they almost touched the pavement where it sat. Kelsey carefully replaced the valve stem cap then stood back to survey her handiwork. "Besides, we're not taking him to court; we're just finding out if his back really is pooched or not."

She turned to Karl and held out her hand. "Keys?"

"They're in it," said Karl.

She boosted herself up into the driver's seat, started the truck, and looked both ways. She was about to pull out of the driveway when Karl leapt forward and rapped his knuckles on the window. She slammed on the brakes and rolled down the window.

"What?" she demanded.

"Phone."

She rolled her eyes as she handed him his phone from the seat beside her, rolled the window back up, and drove off up the road in the direction of Oglevie's house. Karl crouched behind the azalea bush, phone in hand, and watched. Oglevie was still sunning himself on his porch, playing some game on his phone that beeped and booped. Karl could hear his truck's tire slapping against the pavement and cringed at the thought of the rim. He watched his truck jerk to a stop just past Oglevie's driveway and decided that combat boots really weren't a great choice for driving standard.

Kelsey jumped down from the driver's seat and made a show of walking around the back of the truck, throwing up her arms and kicking the tire. Karl hoped she wasn't overdoing it, but Oglevie did seem to be watching her from his seat on the porch. She stood with her hands on her hips, squinting around her, then, apparently spotting Oglevie for the first time, headed up the driveway in his direction. Karl decided it was almost time to start recording. He dropped to one knee and carefully positioned the phone lens so that he could clearly focus the camera between the leaves without any obstructions, but also without being seen.

Kelsey stood at the foot of the porch stairs, talking and waving her arms, clearly giving a dramatic account of her predicament. Oglevie obviously had no desire to move, but after a minute he sighed visibly and heaved himself to his feet. Karl hit the camera's *record* button. Oglevie walked down the stairs and down the driveway, leading the still gesturing Kelsey, who continued to talk the whole way.

He crouched to look at the tire, which was now as flat as a pancake, then walked around to the back of the truck and bent to check that the spare was in place underneath. He didn't appear to be in any pain, but Karl kept filming, hoping Kelsey could pull off the miracle she was clearly attempting. She appeared to be talking a mile a minute the whole time, and Oglevie seemed to find it very annoying. Karl couldn't blame him.

Oglevie dug the tool bag and jack out from behind the seat and set to work lowering the spare tire. Karl figured he could have done any of this with a bad back, even though it would probably have been more painful than it looked. It was lifting and moving the tires, operating the jack, and getting the wheel nuts off that ought to be difficult. Kelsey was following Oglevie around, peering under the truck and into the cab over his shoulder, talking constantly. Oglevie was starting to hurry.

He reached under the truck one-handed and lifted the tire in a twisting, straightening motion that should have been impossible for a man in his condition. Karl could have cheered, but he stayed silent and continued recording, figuring he might as well get all the evidence he could. The brisk jerk Oglevie used to loosen each of the wheel nuts should have been agony, but Kelsey's continual chatter seemed to be bothering him a lot more than his back. He set and pumped the jack so rapidly, Karl worried that it might not hold and felt a moment of panic at the thought of his liability if the truck landed on Oglevie and actually gave him the sort of injuries he had been faking, but the truck stayed put.

Lifting, twisting and bending, Oglevie had the tires changed in record time, the flat thrown in the back, and the tools and jack returned to their homes behind the seat. Kelsey gave a little cheer when the jack dropped the new wheel to the pavement, and her gushing thanks sent Oglevie scurrying back up his driveway and into his house. Karl ended the video recording as the front door banged shut.

Kelsey drove a loop around the block and picked him up on the side street next to the house with the bushes he had been hiding behind. She slid over to the passenger side, and Karl climbed in behind the wheel, looking at her with genuine amazement.

"How did you pull that off?" he asked.

Kelsey shrugged. "I'm the disappointing daughter of divorced parents. I know how to get what I want."

She buckled her seatbelt. Realizing he was waiting for a fuller explanation, she elaborated. "I whined. The more I whined, the more he just wanted to get rid of me. It was only a matter of time before he started to rush and forgot to act pained."

Karl couldn't help grinning as he popped the truck into gear.

8

Karl finished typing up the report on Oglevie's fraud case and forwarded it, along with the video evidence and his invoice, to the insurance adjuster who had requested the investigation. Kelsey had already left for the day, and he checked his watch, surprised to find it was so late. Since it was a Friday night, he knew the Copper Owl would have live music, and it was a good spot to grab a bite and a beer. The bar had a vintage feel that Karl liked, and its proximity to the agency made it a regular after-work stop.

He was just reaching for his coat when his phone rang. Checking it, he recognized his sister Matilda's number. He'd been wondering how much longer she could keep herself from "reaching out." He rolled his eyes and let it go to voicemail, shrugging into his coat while he waited for the message to come through.

Rather than leave a voicemail, she turned to text, which Karl thought was a mistake. Her deeply concerned tones were so much more effective at inducing guilt.

Karl, did you really hire our cousin Kelsey to work at that agency for you?

I'm surprised you would be so irresponsible. It's one thing to throw away your own potential, but to include Kelsey in this scheme is much more serious.

You know she should be in university. Her parents are very upset about it.

And I'm surprised that you would ignore our mother's wishes the way you have. She's very hurt.

I expected more from you, Karl.

Once again fearing for the state of his eyes if he kept rolling them, and more to stop the flow of messages than for any other reason, Karl fired a text in return.

Sorry, Sis. Can't talk now. Call you later.

The last was a blatant lie, and he didn't expect her to believe it, but he was relieved when his phone stopped pinging. He was used to Matilda being much more persistent, but he supposed being halfway around the world must be putting a damper on her efforts to fix the family.

When he walked in the door of the Copper Owl, Karl spotted Kelsey out on the dance floor with her friend Alysa. He hadn't realized she hung out here, but he supposed it wasn't surprising; there were only so many good bars in the area. They exchanged nods across the room but didn't bother to connect. He took a seat on one of the red vinyl stools at the bar, leaned his elbows on the matching red vinyl padding that ran around it, and ordered a heavy stout.

He was halfway through his first beer and wondering if he shouldn't order something to eat when a commotion on the edge of the dance crowd caught his attention. The entire centre of the venue was packed with dancers, and for a second Karl couldn't see what was going on. Then the crowd parted, and he spotted Kelsey.

Alysa seemed to have disappeared, and Kelsey was grappling with a lanky youth who had clearly had one too many.

For a second Karl wondered if this was a new boyfriend he hadn't heard about, then he realized that Kelsey was trying unsuccessfully to push the young man away, an expression of disgust on her face. The guy leaned in to kiss her, and she twisted away, the flash of fear on her face bringing Karl out of his seat without conscious thought. As he pushed his way across the dance floor, shifting moving bodies firmly aside, Karl could see that the kid seemed to have gotten one hand down the back of Kelsey's dress while his other arm wrapped around her, pinning her in place against the wood panelling that lined the room.

Karl caught hold of the fellow's shoulder and spun him around, causing Kelsey to stumble slightly, and planted a solid uppercut on the point of his jaw. The youth went down and didn't get up. Karl stood staring down at him as he lay there on the carpet for a moment, then looked around and realized that half of the bar's patrons had stopped dancing to stare at him and Kelsey. Two large servers were heading their way, looking grim. He turned to Kelsey and snapped, "Let's get out of here."

She didn't need to be told twice. Scooping her purse up from the floor where she had dropped it, she stepped over the unconscious body at her feet and headed for the nearest exit. She hit the crash bar and practically sprinted up the alley and around the corner. Karl was right behind her. She finally stopped in the shadows on the far side of the parking lot, gasping for breath. Karl stopped beside her.

"Are you alright?" he asked, bent over, hands on knees, and breathing hard, more from residual anger than the brief run. He could feel the blood pumping in the veins in his neck and would have been happy to go back and have a second shot at the fellow inside.

Kelsey nodded; her cheeks were flushed a brilliant scarlet. She straightened her dress. The seam on one shoulder had torn. She looked upset, hugging herself and shivering.

After a minute she muttered, "I'm sorry," staring down at her shoes.

"For what?" Karl asked.

"For that." She gestured back toward the bar.

"How was that your fault?" he demanded, straightening up and looking at her.

"I don't know." She refused to meet his eye.

"Don't be ridiculous," Karl said irritably. "Someone treats you like that, he's the asshole, not you."

"My mom would say my dress is too short," she said, still in the direction of her shoes.

"Your dress is fine," Karl snapped. He paused. "And even if it wasn't, even if you walked in there naked, he still had no right." He couldn't believe they were having this conversation. What year was it anyway?

After a second he grinned and added, "But please don't start going naked. You're my cousin. That'd just be weird."

Kelsey snorted and looked up at last. "My dad would say I was lucky any guy bothered." Her voice was almost matter-of-fact about it. Almost, but not quite.

"That's just…" Karl felt a little sick. He finally shook his head and started walking across the parking lot. "You want a ride?" he asked over his shoulder.

"Yeah."

She followed him back to his truck, and they rode to her place in silence, except when she gave him directions. Before getting out, she turned to say, "Um. Thanks, and all that."

"Sure," he replied, and she nodded briefly, jumped down, and climbed the steps that ran up the side of the garage to what must have been her front door. Karl watched her inside then headed home. Somehow, he didn't feel like eating anymore.

***

Karl heard the rattle of his speed bag when he opened the office door the next morning. Kelsey's coat and purse were piled haphazardly on her desk, so he assumed she was the one in his office and headed to the kitchen for a coffee before coming back to investigate. He found her shaking her right hand and rubbing the wrist ruefully.

"Can you teach me how to hit like you did to that guy last night?" Kelsey asked without bothering to greet him. "I tried punching that thing." She gestured to the heavy bag. "And it felt like my wrist would break. How did you hit his face hard enough to knock him out and not hurt yourself?"

Karl took a fortifying sip of coffee before setting the mug on his desk and coming over to where she was standing.

"Show me how you hit it," he said. Watching her wind up, he reached out and caught her wrist before she could do herself any real damage.

"Not like that. You really could break something with your hand bent at that angle. You have to keep your wrist straight."

He straightened it for her then held his own fist up to demonstrate. "You want a straight line from your elbow to your first two knuckles. And when you hit, you've got to put your shoulder behind it, like this."

His demonstrative jab was hard enough to make the bag jerk and shudder. He'd been working on his technique for a couple of months, and he was starting to get his old form back. Kelsey gave it a try.

"Okay, ow," was her comment, but she looked surprised. "But only my knuckles. I felt that in my wrist, it was like a shock, but it was better than before."

"Yeah, your hands will hurt at first, but they'll toughen up. You'll need to work on it if you want to be any good, but I don't mind you practicing here as long as I'm not trying to work. You should get some practice gloves that fit. They'll keep you from scraping all the skin off your knuckles."

He glanced down at her hands, the dimpled knuckles already reddened by the few attempts she had made so far.

"I can pick you up a pair from the place where I got mine, if you like," he said.

"Awesome, thanks!" Kelsey headed back to her desk with a bounce in her step, and Karl settled into his day's work with a smile tugging at the corners of his mouth.

9

"Hey, I need a copy of your license," Kelsey informed Karl a few days later as he carried a fresh cup of coffee from the kitchen through to his office.

"And who's your supervising Investigator? Did you get one of your grandfather's old friends to take you on or something? And why haven't I met them?"

Karl had stopped in front of her desk, looking at her blankly. What was she talking about now?

"How hard did you find the Private Investigation Licensing Exam? Did you pass it the first time you took it?" she continued, still squinting at her screen, apparently unaware that he wasn't following her at all.

"The what?" Karl asked, a sinking feeling beginning somewhere in the region of his solar plexus and quickly travelling all the way down to the soles of his feet.

"The Private Investigation Licensing Exam," Kelsey repeated.

When Karl just stood there staring, she finally looked up and frowned at the frozen look on his face.

"You did take the exam, right?" she asked, like it was a rhetorical question. And after another pause, "You are properly licensed to be a private investigator in the province of British Columbia, right?"

"Um, the lawyer said that the business is licensed," Karl said as the floor tilted slightly beneath his feet.

"Yeah, it's licensed," said Kelsey, pointing at the wall next to his office door. "The license is right there. But that's the business license, which needs to be updated and renewed." She waved an official-looking form with a thick yellow envelope at him. "But you should be licensed too. It's a requirement for anyone working in the security industry in this province. Didn't you know that?"

"Um, no," said Karl, now definitely worried.

"And it never occurred to you to look it up?" asked Kelsey.

"No," said Karl.

Kelsey stared at him incredulously. "You never took any training at all? You just started running around investigating things any which way you could think of?" When she put it like that, it didn't sound very smart.

Karl shrugged defensively. "I read a lot of the old case files, looked at how my grandfather had done things in the past. I didn't even know there was such a thing as private investigator training."

"Well, there is, and I suggest you sign up to complete it ASAP," Kelsey told him, urgency raising the pitch of her voice. "Although where you are going to find a supervising investigator who will agree to work with you is beyond me."

"A what?" The floor was definitely tilted now, and the walls were beginning to revolve.

"A supervising investigator," Kelsey repeated impatiently. "You need to be supervised by someone with experience for the first year after you finish your training. You know what, forget about that, we'll deal with that when we come to it. The first thing to do is to get you qualified."

"Where can I do that? Is there a private investigator school?" Karl asked, still wondering why none of this had occurred to him when he first took over the agency.

"The classes are available online. I'm going to sign you up for the Basic Security Training course, that's the first requirement."

"Yeah. Okay. Great," said Karl as the walls slowed and the floor began to right itself. An online class? He could handle that.

"I need your credit card to pay the registration fees." Kelsey held out her left hand, pecking at her keyboard with her right.

"How much is the course?" asked Karl, fishing out his wallet and extracting the card.

"Like, three hundred and fifty bucks," Kelsey said, taking the card and turning back to the screen in front of her. "I should probably take it as well, since I work here. You have to take another course after that that's specific to being a private investigator. That's six hundred, but I might not need it. I'll have to look into it further. I'll let you know."

"Okay," said Karl, retreating to his office and leaving her with his credit card. He had real investigations to work on, even if he wasn't qualified to do them. Kelsey would inform him what he needed to study and when.

Sure enough, by the following day Kelsey had not only registered them both for the basic security training course, she had also worked out a plan to keep them in business in the meantime.

"Isn't that forgery?" protested Karl, staring down at a page with a signature at the bottom that looked surprisingly like the samples of his grandfather's writing he had found in old files.

"Of course it is," Kelsey replied. "But it's not like he's going to show up and object, is he?"

"What if they figure out that he's dead?"

"Then we're screwed." The worried look in her eyes belied her matter-of-fact tone and casual shrug. "His investigator's license is good for the moment. They don't seem to be aware that he's dead yet. If we renew the business license under his name and list him as our supervising investigator, then we buy ourselves some time. So long as we pass the exams and get our full licenses without anyone asking questions, we should be fine. We just need to make sure we don't give them any reason to ask questions."

Karl didn't have a better suggestion, so he left her to it, but the anxious knot remained in the pit of his stomach beneath his amusement at how matters relating to the agency had so rapidly morphed into a question of *we*.

***

"Aha!" Kelsey's shout from the front office a few weeks later snapped Karl out of a reverie.

"They're here! Karl, come and look, they're here!"

Karl grinned as he pushed himself out of his desk chair and headed for the outer office. She sounded exactly like she had when she was a kid on Christmas morning, discovering that Santa had come in the night.

"What came?" he asked, pulling open his office door, still smiling.

"Our licenses!" She was still shouting, and she waved two official-looking vanilla envelopes at him.

"Hold on." She threw up her hand dramatically. "Don't move. I almost forgot!"

Leaving the envelopes on her desk, she hurried into the back room, appearing a minute later with a bottle of cheap prosecco and a pair of champagne glasses that had *The Empress Hotel* printed on them in gold lettering.

"Go on then, open them," she ordered, attacking the wire hood around the cork with gusto.

Karl slitted the first envelope open with the scissors on her desk, flinching when the cork popped, breathing again when he saw that the wine had not come foaming out all over the carpet like it did in the movies. Taking first one license and then another out of the envelopes, he laid them on the desk and stood looking down at them, in awe of what they represented.

"Don't touch these yet," said Kelsey, pouring the golden liquid into the glasses.

"The new business license came in the mail last week, but I was waiting for these."

Carefully setting the full glasses down on the desk next to the bottle, she pulled out a drawer and lifted out another envelope and four black picture frames with white matting.

"Here." She thrust the final envelope at Karl and began prying the back off one of the frames. It only took three tries to get all four documents — the business license and the investigator's licenses of Mordecai Abrams, Karl Larsson, and Kelsey Larsson — lined up on the wall straight enough to satisfy her critical eye, then she perched on the edge of her desk and picked up the wine glasses, passing one to Karl. He joined her, sitting beside her on the desk, his long, lean frame taking up far less surface space than her short, wide one.

"Cheers," said Karl, holding up his glass.

"Cheers," Kelsey replied, clinking glasses with him.

They sat in silence, sipping the bubbly and admiring the fruits of their labours. Of course, it was primarily the fruits of Kelsey's labours, so Karl had no objection to her holding the same qualifications he had, but at the moment it was Mordecai's qualifications he was thinking of. Not just a piece of paper to hang on the wall, but almost forty years of practice with police training to back it up. The phrase *dead men's shoes* ran through Karl's mind, and he lifted his glass to his grandfather's license, silently toasting the stranger he owed so much.

10

It was a broiling Thursday afternoon in late spring when John Fullerton arrived at the agency. Karl had the office windows open, but the warm, wet air still made the building feel like a pressure cooker, and Kelsey had begged the afternoon off to go to the lake. Karl couldn't blame her, but he also couldn't neglect the stack of background checks piling up on his desk any longer either. He could feel the back of his shirt sticking to his chair as he ran various Internet searches. The street door slammed, and he heard brisk steps climb the stairs, then a voice called from the reception area, "Mordecai, old man, you've cleaned the place up! Lookin' good."

The speaker walked through the door of Karl's office with the confidence of long familiarity then caught himself midstride.

"Who are you? Where's Mordecai?"

He was well past middle-aged, with the deeply lined face and grizzled hair of a life lived outdoors. The plaid shirt, jeans, and leather hiking boots would have backed this appearance up if they hadn't been so clean, crisp, and pressed-looking. The professional leather satchel in his left hand added further contrast. Karl smiled his professional business owner's smile. He'd been practicing it for a while, and he felt like it gave the right impression of confident competence needed to win over old clients.

"Hi." He stood, stepping around the desk, and holding out his hand. "I'm Karl Larsson, I'm running the agency these days, but I take it you knew my grandfather?"

"Grandfather?" The man looked confused, but he had a firm handshake, nonetheless. "I didn't know Mordecai… Wait, knew? What do you mean? Mordecai's dead?"

"I'm afraid so," Karl replied, returning to his chair. "I'm sorry. Did you know him well?"

"Well enough. Well, damn." His guest threw himself into the visitor's chair with the same familiarity he had shown before, dropping his satchel casually on the floor. He rubbed a hand over his face distractedly then seemed to feel he needed to give an explanation.

"I've been stationed overseas for the past eight months," he explained. "But I would have thought Percy would let me know."

"Percy Meiklejohn?" Karl asked with interest. "You know him too?"

"Of course. You can't know Mordecai long without getting to know Percy. If you can't, well, I guess I should say couldn't, find Mordecai up here, you could usually catch him downstairs, drinking Percy's superior coffee and BS'ing. Crazy to think the old fart's gone. When did he pass?"

Karl shifted uncomfortably in his chair as the old guilt knotted his stomach. "A while ago," he replied as casually as he could. "I've been operating the business for the past few months.

"I inherited it," he added by way of explanation, but even that statement felt like it should be explained. Why had the agency been left to him, after all?

"Wow. Well, welcome aboard. I'm sorry I wasn't here to pay my respects."

Yeah, me too, thought Karl, but he just nodded sympathetically.

"I guess I should probably introduce myself, hey?" asked his visitor with a quick smile, and he leaned forward to extend his hand across the top of the desk. "I'm John Fullerton."

"Karl, Karl Larsson," replied Karl, as they shook for the second time.

"Larsson…kinda rings a bell," said Fullerton, leaning back again. "Mordecai probably mentioned you at some point. My memory must be going, that's all."

He shrugged expansively, and Karl tried to smile in response.

"Our family's not especially close," he offered, then changed the topic. "So, what do you do? Were you just a friend of my grandfather's, or did you work with him too?"

"Oh, work first. We got to be friends after he'd helped me out on a couple stories. I'm a reporter," he added in response to Karl's expression. "With the *National Post.* I've done a fair bit of work on the international scene, but whenever I needed a local man on the ground for good first-hand information about the situation on the Island, I'd come to Mordecai."

"Well, I'd be happy to fill the same role, if you think there's something I can do for you." Karl tried not to sound too eager, but helping a news reporter investigate stories sounded a lot more fun than the security checks he currently had going.

"Sure, why not. In fact, you being a younger man might make it easier on this one. Hard to believe an eighty-year-old would be interested in designer drugs for any reason other than investigation, when you think about it. You might get farther."

Fullerton eyed Karl speculatively. Karl was intrigued. "Drugs?"

"That's right. You remember how big fentanyl was in the news a couple of years ago?"

Karl nodded briefly.

"And then carfentanil was a big problem, but it got less coverage, right?"

Another nod.

"There's only so much news value you can get out of a stronger version of the prescription, when the prescription itself is so potentially lethal. People get desensitized; it just doesn't sell any more as news." Fullerton's voice was cynical and faintly bitter.

"Are you saying there's a new drug that you think needs to be reported?" Karl probed, trying to figure out where this was going.

"Oh, sure, but there's always some new drug, that's what I'm telling you. This story is bigger than that, because it's not just about what's coming in; it's about how it's coming." Fullerton was leaning forward now, his elbows on his knees, his gaze intense. Karl wondered if his grandfather would have grasped the significance of all this more quickly than he was. He still couldn't see what the man was driving at.

"Look," Fullerton continued. "Any major incoming shipment of drugs has typically been brought into Vancouver by one of two routes, overland from the States, which is getting more and more difficult, or else by sea. But any of the ports around Vancouver and for hundreds of kilometres up the coast are watched as carefully as the international border, since Vancouver is literally the western end of the Canada-US border."

Karl nodded. This was common knowledge; he didn't see where the exciting news story came in.

"The ports are watched, like I said, but the drugs still come in. The police make busts all the time, and the coast guard work their asses off in coordination with the RCMP, but it's still the easiest way to get large shipments into the lower mainland, and from there to the rest of western Canada."

"Except lately it hasn't been working that way. Or I should say, the latest designer drug of choice hasn't been coming in that way. I don't know if you've heard of Odin's Tears?"

Karl thought it rang a bell, there had been a headline or two about deaths at university parties, but Fullerton was right, he hadn't paid much attention. There was always some new drug like that popping up. He made a vague gesture, and Fullerton continued.

"Someone has come up with a new form of poison, highly addictive, highly lethal, and they've found some way to come at the import process sideways. The city police, the RCMP, the coast guard, no one's picked up a single incoming shipment. But they're coming in. By the ton. And they're killing kids. Young kids. Most of them younger than you."

Fullerton's voice shook slightly with this last statement. Karl found himself leaning forward, listening intently, but now he adjusted himself in his chair, watching the man across from him closely. There was something about him and his story that bothered Karl. He was too intense, too emotional about it all, despite his careful self-control. This wasn't just a reporter on the trail of a good story. This was something more.

"So do you think you know how they're doing it then? Bringing the drugs in?" Then, as a thought struck him, he added, "Couldn't they just be producing the stuff locally? Right in Vancouver, or one of the suburb cities?"

"That was the first possibility the police looked into when the problem started getting out of hand, but they're pretty certain now that that's not the case. The drug might be reprocessed, made up for distribution here, but the original source is Latin America. The basic ingredients are just so much more accessible, not to mention cheaper, down there. It's not just affecting Canada, either. Drugs are a hell of a lot easier to move south into the US than north from Mexico. Once it's in Canada, it can be moved down into the States, too."

"Okay, so how are they bringing the drugs in? What have you figured out that the police haven't?"

As soon as the words were out of his mouth, Karl realized how skeptical they sounded, but Fullerton just smiled grimly.

"I think they're coming in via the Island," he replied simply, then he leaned back in his turn to watch for Karl's reaction.

Karl thought about it. The Island was over four hundred and fifty kilometres long, with thirty-four hundred kilometres of coastline and less than a million people living on it. It had dozens of tiny port towns up and down the coast and professional fishing boats that sometimes went almost as far as Hawaii, following the schools of fish. Getting shipments onto the Island might be easier than into Vancouver, but they would still be on the Island. Then what?

"I admit that the Island might be an easier drop point, but they still have to move anything they're bringing in to the mainland, and that's got to be just as much of a problem as landing it in a Vancouver harbour," Karl argued.

"You really think so?" asked Fullerton. "When was the last time you were asked about what you were carrying when you took the ferry to the mainland? Ever see any dogs sniffing around or been asked to submit to a random security screening? They have the right, technically; it's in the BC Ferries policy, but they only exercise that right if they have a tip-off or some reason to be suspicious. Trucks full of fish and crab come over every day of the week, when the season's right, and no dog's gonna smell pills through that stink, even if they did have them out, and no ferry worker's gonna ask them to open up. Never happen."

Fullerton was clearly confident of his claim, and Karl had to admit, he'd never had to show so much as a driver's license to drive onto the ferry, never mind seeing dogs or security checks. The Island might be a great place to grow pot, but any hard drugs came in from the mainland, not the other way around. At least that's what he'd always assumed.

"Do you have any evidence that this is the route it's coming in by?" he finally asked. "Or is that just a theory?"

"At this point it's a theory with a few rumours and hints from off-the-record sources that seem to back it up. I need to determine if it's true, and then I need some pretty substantial evidence to back it up before I can take it to print. That's where you come in," Fullerton added.

"What exactly do you want me to do?" Karl asked, intrigued but apprehensive.

"Find out if I'm right," Fullerton replied. "Find out if the shipments are coming in, and if they are, then where and how. Who's involved? What type of boats are they using, and what sort of vehicles to transfer it all to the mainland? Is it coming in packaged for distribution, or are they using some place here on the Island for processing? Find me all the details and collect all the proof you can. That's about it," he concluded calmly.

"Oh, and the paper will pay the usual retainer, working expenses and bonus if we get the story, of course."

"The usual retainer?"

Karl tried not to show his excitement at the number Fullerton mentioned.

"I can't withhold information about criminal activity from the police," Karl pointed out.

"Of course not. I wouldn't expect you to." Fullerton's reply was quick. "I just want you to coordinate informing them so that I get the scoop on the story. That's all."

Would his grandfather have considered this proposal as coolly as Fullerton seemed to do? Karl had no way of knowing, but no matter how impossible the whole thing sounded, he still wanted to take it on. More than he liked to admit—even to himself. This was proper detective work. This was the sort of case he'd been hoping for from the beginning.

"So, are you in?" Fullerton asked.

"Oh, I'm in," Karl replied.

***

Locking the street door later that evening, Karl wondered if Percy could give him any background on Fullerton that might help explain his vehemence. He wanted to understand his new employer's motives better before he went too far. He pushed the shop door open and walked in to the sound of roaring laughter coming from the back room.

"And you didn't tell him?" Fullerton's voice sounded choked with amusement.

"Not my place, now is it?" Percy responded, not quite as deadpan as usual.

"And you've just been keeping tabs and reporting back this whole time?"

"As instructed."

Both men laughed again. Karl decided he didn't feel like interrupting a reunion and let himself back out quietly. At the very least, it sounded as though Percy did know and like Fullerton, which was probably a mark in his favour.

11

Karl thought long and hard that night. How in the world was he supposed to break into the local drug scene? He'd only ever smoked pot twice in high school. It had never been his thing, for the same reason cigarettes hadn't: sports. To be any good as a boxer, he needed clear lungs. And he'd never been ambitious enough to think PEDs were worth the risk. Was it possible to just go out and buy the stuff on a street corner? Well, he decided, trying to pick some up would be an interesting place to start, so late Friday afternoon he pulled on his scruffiest old clothes, combed his hair differently than usual, and headed out to shop for some drugs.

Cruising through downtown Victoria, Karl realized that he didn't even know where to begin. Victoria didn't have many areas that could reasonably be called a "bad" neighbourhood. Newer areas were sparkling clean, old neighbourhoods were gentrified. At most, there were a few streets where the houses looked tired, but even there the owners were clearly trying to keep up appearances.

Karl wasn't sure what he had expected. Something out of the movies, maybe? A rundown neighbourhood somewhere with burnt-out cars and broken windows in half the houses? A couple of obvious thugs swapping cash for packets of white powder on an aging basketball court? Hookers strolling along in pairs, calling lewd offers to passing drivers? He gave his head a shake. What year was this anyway? Real crime, the organized, lucrative kind, had to be online, or at least by phone these days. Why stand on a street corner when you can have a website?

No, he didn't think it could be that easy, but people did still buy drugs in bars sometimes. He'd heard friends, or friends of friends, talk about doing it. He'd even seen a few exchanges down dark side streets that couldn't have been anything else. He just needed to think of a ruse to convince someone as cagey as a drug dealer that he was an easy mark. Someone they should target. Not a threat. Basically, he needed to convince them he was stupid.

Well, Karl had seen enough stupid people in bars that he thought he could play the part, at least for a little while. As he drove, he rolled different cover stories around in his mind. He knew he didn't want to try this thing anywhere he would usually hang out. Not the sort of scenario he would like to be recognized in. And he would need to make a stop at the bank. Drug dealers probably didn't accept credit cards. Not that he'd want those expenses showing up on his account if they did.

Eventually, Karl tracked down a place called Big Bad John's, hoping that the bar might live up to its name. From the outside it didn't look like much, just a plain black storefront on the main floor of the old Strathcona Hotel. The hotel itself was sufficiently antique to qualify as a heritage building, with its six storeys of white brick facade decorated with corbels and dentil molding. The black door to the right of the hotel entrance was only identifiable by a small wooden sign hanging over it. Parallel-parking farther up the street, Karl crossed nervously to the door and pushed it open to find himself standing in a small tiled vestibule, facing a set of fake barn doors with a variety of signs posted on them sporting sayings like "Hangovers Installed and Serviced." Above the door ran a shelf holding wooden barrels, old whiskey jugs, and even an antique shotgun.

Taking a hesitant step through this second entrance, Karl was surprised by a crunch under his shoe. Looking down, he saw that the floor was covered in peanut shells, bowls of which sat on every table. The cheesy Western theme had been carried through the place alongside a combination of grunge and clutter that made the half full room feel oppressively crowded. Someone had turned the concept of a dive bar into something kitschy, and Karl already knew he wasn't a fan. Taking his second crunchy step toward the bar at the back, he thought at least this wasn't somewhere he would want to hang out later.

Karl had to sidestep more than once on his way down the room to avoid bumping into one of the many bras hanging from wagon wheel chandeliers and ropes strung up around the narrow room. The graffiti and memorabilia that covered every available surface were messy, but at least it was less awkward than a face full of strangers' musty undergarments. Following a sign, he found the tiny bar in a back corner with only a couple of stools squashed together in front of it. He had hoped for a little more space and a bigger audience at the bar, but he squeezed onto a stool at the end and called for a beer in a voice full of false bravado.

He had decided on his cover story; he just needed to get the attention of the right person and give himself an excuse to strike up a conversation. The first step was establishing his financial standing. With a flourish, Karl pulled a wad of twenties out of his pocket and peeled one off for the bartender. Nothing said money to burn like a fist full of cash. Both the bartender and the guy sitting next to him gave the cash a sideways glance, and Karl looked around expansively, making sure he had an audience.

"Pretty sweet, hey?" He said it loudly, as if he thought the bartender was hard of hearing. "You don't get this every day."

He waved the cash in the bartender's face before stuffing it back in his pocket.

"Finally got paid out for my wrongful dismissal. Bastards should have known better than to try to screw me like that."

Karl's abrasive tone grated his own nerves, but he was getting the attention he wanted. The bartender dutifully said, "Congrats, man," and swept the excess foam off the beer he was pouring with his finger, flicking it onto the floor before placing the glass in front of Karl. Karl picked it up and made a toasting motion before bringing it to his lips, although he cringed inside at the flecks he could see floating in the golden liquid. The sour taste confirmed his suspicions: the lines hadn't been cleaned in a long time. At least it was cold and not too flat.

The guy at the other end of the bar was clearly ignoring Karl, unimpressed by his rudeness, but the bartender and the guy next to him showed vague signs of curiosity, and Karl thought he had caught the attention of the players sitting at the pair of VLTs that stood against the adjacent wall, even though their eyes remained glued to their screens.

He worked his way through half the mug, commenting rudely on the decor of the place between sips. The player at the nearest VLT snorted at a particularly pointed reference to the bras, confirming Karl's hopes that he was listening. Karl asked the bartender how long he had worked here and what he thought of the general setup, but the guy had hardly opened his mouth when Karl banged his glass down dramatically and pulled his phone out of his pocket to study an apparently absorbing text message. He grinned and nodded to himself, tapped a rapid response, and then stared at the screen some more, transfixed until a reply popped up.

He had actually messaged Kelsey *Send me a text*, but the *Huh* that she wrote back provided the cover Karl needed. He laughed under his breath, sent back *Nothing, just testing something*, and put the phone face down on the bar before picking up his beer and swigging it again while he glanced around, ensuring his audience was still there.

"Looks like it's my lucky day," Karl announced to no one in particular, swilling more beer, intent now on getting through it as quickly as possible.

"More good news?" The bartender must have had his tip in mind, because he managed to sound curious rather than irritated, and Karl grinned at him appreciatively.

"Yeah," he replied. He picked up his phone and waved it in the same manner that he had the cash. "I got this super hot chick texting me. Sort of a friend of a friend. She just broke up with her boyfriend, and I think she's feeling lonely, if you know what I mean."

Karl winked broadly at the bartender, and the man managed to maintain his *impressed by the idiot* expression. Karl drained the last of his beer and wiped his mouth with the back of his hand.

"Gimme another," he said loudly. "And how about a round for the bar?" He gestured to include the VLT players. "Gotta share my good luck. Karma," he added vaguely, as if that explained his impulse to generosity, and he pulled out his wad of cash again as the bartender passed out drinks. Sharing his good luck suddenly made Karl much more interesting, and more than one of his fellow drinkers raised their glasses and said, "Cheers, man." He caught the player at the closer of the two machines eyeing the cash as Karl stuffed it back into his jeans before jerking his attention back to the screen in front of him.

Karl smiled to himself as he took another gulp of beer, then picked up his phone and squinted at it, once again oblivious to his surroundings. He let his left foot bounce a nervous rhythm as he peered at a nonexistent message. He grinned and nodded again. The mythical "hot chick" was clearly giving him reason to hope. He messaged *Send me another text* to Kelsey, drank some more beer, then started asking the bartender about himself again as if the conversation had never been interrupted. This time he waited until the other man was talking, then sucked his breath in sharply through his teeth when Kelsey's reply popped up, indicating an unexpected twist in his pursuit of love. The bartender stopped talking and managed not to roll his eyes.

"Damn," Karl commented, sotto voce, but still audible to anyone nearby. His reaction had nothing to do with Kelsey's *You're kinda weird sometimes, you know that?* He looked up at the bartender, glanced at the drinker sitting next to him, and leaned forward to include them both in his next communication.

"She says I can come over if I can pick her up some..." Karl double-checked the phone before continuing with a clearly audible false undertone. "Odin's Tears? Do you know where I could get some of that?"

He looked from one to another with eager naïveté, mentally crossing his fingers that they would accept his obvious inexperience based on the excuse that it was "for a girl." The bartender paused for a fraction of a second before continuing to wipe the counter and said, "None of that stuff around here." Karl didn't think he sounded very convincing. The guy next to Karl shook his head and mumbled something that sounded like *Idunno*, while the man at the end of the counter just shrugged, finished his drink, and headed for the men's room.

Karl looked vaguely around, doing his best to channel the right mixture of hope and desperation. His neighbour seemed to find it unnerving and, with a nod of recognition for the shared drink, he too moved off through the bar, finding a dart game to watch as his excuse. Karl slumped over his phone, disconsolately poking at the screen, radiating disappointment. He thought the bartender might be his man. That the others might have left to give him a clear field. But the bartender had started wiping out glasses from the washer and seemed to have lost interest in both Karl and his money.

It was beginning to look like he was out of luck, and Karl felt himself slump with real disappointment as this reality sank in. All that effort and money, wasted. And he would have to finish this drink before he could move on to a new bar to try again. Just then the phone in Karl's hand rang, startling him so that he almost dropped it as he fumbled to answer. He abandoned the rest of his drink and turned to go. The intense stare of the VLT player he had noticed before surprised him, but he was already jamming the phone to his ear and heading for the entrance.

"Hello," he snapped into his phone.

"The private dick actually answers his phone." Liam's emphasis on *dick* was not subtle.

"What do you want?" Karl asked as he exited the bar and stood on the sidewalk, waiting for a break in traffic that would allow him to jaywalk back to his truck. Liam laughed, and Karl was about to give up and walk to the nearest crosswalk when the man who had been so attached to his VLT machine came out the door in a rush, stopped abruptly, and then pulled out a pack of cigarettes. Karl turned his steps toward the crosswalk into a brisk pacing up and down the sidewalk, and the other man leaned against the building and smoked with serious concentration and no apparent interest in Karl.

Liam was speaking. "Since you're wasting your time dicking around anyway, I thought you might as well do me a favour while you're at it."

"Like what," Karl snapped, continuing to pace and ignore the smoking player, who was ignoring him with equal diligence.

"One of my drivers has been charged with drunk driving. I can't afford to do without him at the moment, so I thought you could look into getting him off. Don't expect me to pay what you charged Kris for tracking Kelsey down, though. I can't believe you had the gall to cash his cheque and then hire the brat with the money he paid to get her back." Liam almost sounded impressed with that last bit, but it didn't interest Karl.

"Not my line of work," Karl informed him. "If you want to help him, get the guy a lawyer."

Liam snorted. "A lawyer's not going to do him much good with the BAC he blew. There's gotta be some way to get around those tests. Get it thrown out or something. Come on, the guy's not just an employee, he's a friend of mine."

"Sorry, can't help you," Karl replied and hung up before Liam could answer. He wouldn't usually be so rude to his brother; he preferred to keep things civil, at least on the surface, but the man with the cigarette had just thrown it to the ground and was grinding it into the pavement with his shoe, and Karl did not want to lose him. Shoving the phone back into his pocket, he turned to walk past the guy and, just as Karl had hoped, the man caught his eye and jerked his head in invitation. Karl took a step closer, and the man glanced around furtively.

"You know that stuff you mentioned inside?" he muttered under his breath.

"Yeah," Karl responded eagerly and not nearly as quietly. "Odin's Tears. It's supposed to be little black pills, shape of a teardrop. Why? You know where I could get some?"

"I might have a couple, if you've got the cash." The guy was almost vibrating with urgency, and Karl reached deliberately for his money, peeling off bills and accepting the small bag of pills that was stuffed into his hands in return.

The seller turned to head back inside, and Karl stopped him. "Where do you usually get this stuff?" he asked. "Is there someone I could talk to, another time, if I needed more?"

"Can't talk now," the man replied. "Someone might get on my machine. I ask the bartender to watch it for me, but…"

He didn't bother to finish the sentence as he hurried away, and Karl shrugged then looked down at the tiny Ziploc bag he'd been given. His blood was pumping, and he felt a little lightheaded. He wasn't sure if it was excitement or just nerves, but he had pulled it off, and he could feel his confidence rising as he jaywalked across Douglas to get to his truck.

<h1 style="text-align:center">12</h1>

Karl was pleased with the success of his first attempt but didn't want to get complacent. He figured he'd been lucky to hit on someone that desperate for cash. The man's smoking while he waited to talk to Karl had given him an idea, and he stopped at the next gas station he passed. He thought about just getting a pack of regular cigarettes, but he wasn't sure he could manage to smoke one without choking. He had smoked the occasional cigar that wasn't so bad, but he couldn't remember which ones. A little hunting on his phone on line, and he came up with a brand that sounded familiar. He hit the next bar with a pack of Captain Black sweets in his pocket. If anyone asked, he was trying to quit cigarettes.

As the evening wore on, he got into a groove with his routine and could almost believe that he was the abrasive, desperate loser he projected. He managed to avoid buying too many rounds; the project was expensive enough as it was. But Fullerton's money transfer had been his biggest retainer to date, and there was an unexpected thrill to the whole adventure that could get addictive. Two out of three times, he got the same answer. "You don't want to mess with that stuff, man, it'll get you killed." Some even tried to warn him against buying it for someone else. "What if she dies on you, then what are you gonna do?"

But the third attempt usually got him a phone number or a place to try or some nameless individual pointed out who could hook him up. And it wasn't always the grungiest-looking places where he had the best luck. Some offered him alternatives to the particular poison that Fullerton was after, but he stuck to his purchasing goals, glad that Fullerton had told him how to identify the stuff. No point wasting his money on the wrong product; it wasn't as if he would ever use the stuff. He was just glad that it didn't come in a plain white pill, because he didn't think some of the individuals he encountered would have hesitated to lie and sell him something else with the same name.

After his second purchase in Victoria, Karl got more nervous about being recognized and decided to shift his shopping area. He stuffed the baggies he already had into the glove box of his truck and headed over the Malahat to try up Island. He made it to Nanaimo in time to catch a couple of nightclubs open late and had better luck there than in Victoria, although one incident scared him.

He was talking to a guy who looked like the right type, but when Karl went into his now familiar spiel, he was seized roughly by the arm and shoved back into a corner.

"Are you crazy?" The stranger hissed whisky fumes angrily in his face. "Are you trying to get us both arrested?"

"What?" Karl demanded in his normal voice, shocked for a moment out of his self-imposed persona.

"That guy who was just standing next to me." The other guy gestured with a jerk of his head. "He's a cop."

"Shit." Karl's heart was abruptly beating in his throat, and he felt acutely aware of the two little packages currently residing in his jeans pocket, besides the ones in his truck.

"Come on, outside." The stranger again jerked his arm, and Karl found himself being marched out a side door and into the alley. He was so shaken that he didn't think twice about the price that was asked, and it wasn't until he was back in his truck and driving down the highway that it occurred to him the whole thing might have been a ruse to accomplish just that.

In any case, he'd had enough of the criminal life for one night, and he pulled into a small motel on the outskirts of Parksville in the wee hours to sleep it off before continuing his quest. He debated bringing the packets of pills into his hotel room and stashing them in the toilet tank so he could at least try to deny they were his if the cops broke his door down in the night, but in the end he couldn't bring himself to do anything so melodramatic and left them in his glove box.

Karl spent the latter half of Sunday and the holiday Monday town hopping around the perimeter of the Island, hitting a lot of places with Port or Harbour or Bay in their names. He was beginning to see what Fullerton meant about the many potential landing points on the Island. By the time he crossed the Malahat on his way back south late Monday night, he had a tidy haul from his shopping endeavour and an idea for how to begin looking for clues to a smuggling organization, if one did exist on the Island.

***

Karl sat in his swivel chair, staring at the pile of pills in tiny Ziploc baggies lying on top of his desk, when he heard the street door bang on Tuesday morning. He swept the mound off the desk into a drawer and slammed it hastily as Kelsey came into view.

"Hey, sorry I'm late. What the heck were your texts about this weekend? Were you drunk or just having signal issues?" Kelsey saw his face and stopped, her eyes narrowing. "What's up with you?" she demanded suspiciously. "Why do you look like a kid caught with his hand in the candy jar?"

"Nothing. Sort of. We have a new case," Karl snapped. It occurred to him belatedly that Kelsey might have had some insight on how to approach drug deals more smoothly than his initial attempts. Then again, did he really want to be responsible for corrupting his young cousin like that? Probably better not.

"Okay. And you feel guilty about this because..." she prompted suggestively.

"It has to do with drug smuggling on the Island. This reporter thinks that a new street drug is being smuggled into the lower mainland via the Island, and he asked me to look into it. He used to know my grandfather," he added by way of explanation. "They've worked together before."

"Okay, cool. Drugs. Reporter. Grandfather. And you're guilty because?"

Kelsey stopped abruptly, giving him an incredulous stare.

"You didn't use any drugs, did you?" she demanded.

Relieved that this was her response to the idea, Karl shook his head hastily. "No, no I didn't take any. But I did buy a few," he added in a rapid undertone.

"You're kidding me." Kelsey's look was beyond incredulous now. "You went drug shopping over the weekend? Seriously?"

"Yeah, basically."

Feeling sheepish, Karl pulled his collection of baggies out of the desk drawer and dropped them on the desk for her to see. Kelsey dropped her bag on the floor, not bothering to make the trip to her desk to put it away, and walked dazedly up to his desk, staring down at the little pile. Her knees gave way abruptly, and she sat down hard in the guest chair. The chair groaned in protest. Her jacket slid off one rounded shoulder and puddled around her in the chair as she half slumped forward to peer closer at his haul. She shook her head and leaned back in the chair to stare at him. Karl shifted uncomfortably in his seat.

"You know you could totally lose your license for having these, right?" Kelsey commented casually. "Not to mention going to prison. I bet they would call holding this many intent to distribute. Why on earth did you get so much?"

"I was investigating," Karl retorted, the heat rising in his face.

"Investigating. Right. So, what are you going to do with them?" she asked, again staring down at the pile.

"Flush them, I guess," said Karl. "Keeping them probably isn't the best idea."

"Yeah, stashing drugs around the office might not be the best way to stay in business," Kelsey repeated helpfully.

"I guess not," said Karl. "I just wanted to see how hard it was to get hold of them."

He looked up at her, his face troubled. "It is way too easy."

"Well, if you're just going to chuck them anyway, I'll take a few," said Kelsey, scooping all but one bag up off the desk and turning to leave the office.

"You aren't going to take those." Karl pushed out of his chair and was halfway around the desk before Kelsey had time to respond. She laughed right in his face.

"Do I look stupid to you?" she demanded. "I don't particularly want to die, thanks. And I definitely don't want to live my life fighting some horrible addiction."

When he continued to eye her suspiciously, she continued, "I saw this thing online about different experiments you can do to see what's in a pill you've been given, to break down its chemical components. If you're going to flush these anyway, I might as well analyze them first, right?"

The gleam in her eye was positively gleeful, and Karl wondered, not for the first time, why someone who could get so excited about scientific investigation hated the notion of higher education.

"Okay," he agreed reluctantly. "But be careful."

"Oh, I will," she replied over her shoulder, already heading toward the kitchen dark room at the back of the building. "And you can include the results in your case file. You could probably keep that package," she gestured back toward his office as she opened the door opposite, "and attach it as exhibit A or something. I don't think you could get into too much trouble for that, and it would fill the file out nicely. One should be enough for evidence, though, don't you think?"

Lifting her eyebrows cheekily at him, she shut herself up in the kitchen and Karl returned to his desk.

13

It took a week for the stubble on his face to grow long enough for Kelsey to comment.

"You're not trying to grow some hipster beard, are you?" she asked him one morning as she picked up a stack of files off his desk and began slotting them into a cabinet. "Because you look more like a homeless person who hasn't had a chance to shave recently."

"Perfect." Karl grinned at her skeptical glance. "I'm going to try going undercover as one of those transient dock workers you see around. Try a few different places up and down the Island, see if I can pick up anything about these drug shipments for Fullerton that way."

She looked him over critically, one hand on her hip, her eyes narrowed. "Yeah, that might work," she finally admitted before turning back to the filing.

Kelsey had to order several items online before she got anywhere with her experiments on the pills, but once she had the right reagents, she was able to confirm both the dangerous nature of the pills' contents and the illegality of their components. Karl had thought hard about the best way to look into how they were arriving on the Island, and the transient worker scheme was the best idea he had come up with. It seemed the simplest way to get close to an operation run via water without drawing attention to his inquiries. When he called Fullerton to explain his plan, it was received with enthusiasm.

"That's a brilliant idea." Karl couldn't help feeling pleased at the older man's approval. "It's exactly like I said, you being young makes the whole thing so much simpler. Mordecai never failed me on an investigation, not since the first time I hired him — which was probably before you were born — but this one, this one will be good for you to cut your teeth on. You'll get a taste of real detective work, and I bet you never look back."

Karl grinned at this. He had the same feeling. This *was* real detective work. Not like delivering paperwork or watching cheating spouses and insurance frauds from behind some bushes. He was looking forward to it. When Fullerton told him the retainer and weekly expense account he had gotten the paper to approve, Karl was even more galvanized by the possibilities this new contact might afford. Fullerton also said there would be a bonus if the story went to print and that its size would depend on the level of detail Karl could provide him with. Karl thought that if he could work a few news stories a year and let Kelsey take care of the little jobs, he might actually make a decent living off the old place yet.

It was two weeks after Fullerton's initial visit when Karl packed up his truck, left Kelsey in charge of the agency, and headed north again. The weather had gotten warmer and slightly drier in the interim, and he was grateful that this job, at least, wouldn't involve any midwinter work outdoors. He just hoped he would find something before the summer fishing season was out. It seemed like the kind of case that could take time to break, and despite her efficiency, he didn't like leaving Kelsey alone to run things for too long.

He planned to start as close to the north end of the Island as he could get, then zig-zag his way back south until he found something useful or suspicious to look into further. It was just getting dark when he turned off the highway into Port Hardy, cruising along Hardy Bay Road past the seaplane base and the marina. He had been on the road for nearly six hours and hadn't had cell service in over two. The prospect of spending his days entirely out of touch via phone or Internet was disconcerting. The possibility hadn't occurred to him, but it appeared that north of Campbell River coverage was only available in the immediate vicinity of the few scattered townships. Karl made a mental note to buy a good map in the morning.

Although initially tempted by the solid, modern grey building that housed the Quarterdeck Inn, Karl decided he needed something cheaper if he was going to be convincing in his current role and ended up settling for a backpacker's hostel. The idea of sharing a dorm room felt too much like being a kid at summer camp, so Karl sprang for a semiprivate room and was grateful to find the second bed empty.

After depositing his meagre luggage, he went looking for a pub where he might pick up information on cash work opportunities. Sure enough, the barkeep at Sporty Bar and Grill was able to point out the foreman in charge of hiring extra help for unloading the night's catch, and after hastily swilling the last of his beer, Karl approached the man nervously.

He intentionally made his voice low and gravelly when he asked, "Hey, you looking for any extra help unloading tonight?"

The foreman looked him up and down. Karl wore his oldest and most threadbare jeans and t-shirt, and he had intentionally worn them for the previous two days as well, without washing in between. He hoped, combined with the slowly thickening beard, they would give the right air of desperate circumstances. The foreman must have decided that the knotted muscles in his arms balanced out his naturally lean frame, because he nodded judiciously and told Karl to be on the dock at 9:00 p.m.

When Karl walked down the gangway to water level, the first boat was just pulling into its slip, a crew member jumping over the edge and landing firmly on the wooden planks before lashing the rope he held around a mooring. There were a couple of other men standing to the side, waiting for the first tub of fish to be passed to them. They were the exact sort of men that Karl had set out to emulate, and he was pleased to note that he had gotten the general air of hard luck and hard living right, although his clothes were still in better shape than most of theirs. He hoped the foreman would assume that he simply hadn't yet slipped quite as far down the path to destitution. Then the first tub was slung over the side of the boat, and there was no more time for looking around or thinking as they paired up, two by two, heavy tubs swinging between them up the walkways.

The sky overhead was clouded, a dark smear without city lights reflecting off it. The brilliant halogens on the tall poles around the marina shone on the greasy water of the bay, creating shifting shadows anywhere outside their immediate sphere. The lap of the water, the grunts of men lifting bins of fish, and the thump of work boots on worn planks or corrugated steel were the only sounds in the night air. There was no time to talk. There was barely time to breathe. Up and down. Back and forth. As the hours crept by and boat after boat came in, the hike up to the trucks got harder and harder, and Karl finally realized that the incline of the gangways had increased significantly. The tide was going out. The dock was sitting several feet lower than when the night began.

Finally, the last of the boats had been emptied and the sweating workers gathered around the foreman, who began doling out cash. Some of the men grumbled or tried to negotiate their wage, but Karl just silently took the money he was handed and staggered back to where he had parked his truck at the far end of the lot. It was all he could do to make it back to his room and kick off his boots before collapsing across the bed.

Karl put in several days at Port Hardy and Port McNeil then jogged across the Island to Coal Harbour, Winter Harbour, and Port Alice. His initial unease over travelling without a GPS map to guide him had subsided once he realized how few main roads there were this far north and how difficult it would be to get really lost on them, but he had bought himself a Backroad Mapbook just in case. This wasn't exactly reassuring when he looked through it. Highway options might be limited, but the web of logging roads criss-crossing every page was daunting. He made up his mind to avoid straying from the main roads and to be sure he had a full tank of gas before heading out of any town. He had no desire to find himself stranded.

Karl slept in the cheapest local motels and a couple times stretched out in a sleeping bag in the back of his truck rather than pay the exorbitant prices the tourist traps charged. Even though Fullerton had approved a decent retainer and operating fund, Karl tried living off the cash he earned on the docks, getting into the headspace of the character he had outlined for himself before leaving Victoria. He was careful not to stay too long in any one town, worried that his truck might be spotted as too good for the work he was taking or that he might miss the clue he was looking for just down the road.

14

After several nights spent shivering in the periodic chilly drizzle, Karl stopped at a Work Wearhouse and picked up a couple of the thin grey wool sweaters the older workers seemed to favour. The scratchy fabric drove him crazy for the first hour or two, but he had to admit it kept him warm and breathed well, and by the end of the night he thought he might eventually learn to wear it next to his skin the way the old-timers did. There were some real characters among those old-timers, and Karl made a point of drinking with them at the local bars any chance he got. He figured the more contacts he made, the better his chances were of getting the information he needed.

Karl found that most of his conversations followed the same pattern. Sitting at the bar of Salmon River Inn in the Village of Kelsey Bay one night, one of the men he had worked with that evening climbed onto the stool next to his and called for the bartender to bring him a beer. Karl had been struck by the way this man kept up with younger, stronger-looking workers, despite one shortened leg that gave him a rolling walk. He was a tough, garrulous old geezer, and Karl thought probably a good resource to cultivate, so he flashed the man a friendly smile.

"Jim," the man said, holding out a hand ropy with veins, knuckles the size of golf balls.

"Karl," Karl replied with a wider smile and shook the old man's hand. Jim grinned at him, displaying an uneven row of teeth pocked with rot, and turned to repeat his order more loudly in the direction of the bartender who was busy serving a couple at the other end.

"You're new to this scene, aren't you?" he asked, returning his attention to Karl.

"Yeah," Karl admitted. "It's my first season working the docks." Then, even though he was pretty sure of the answer he added, "You been doing it long?"

"Twenty years this summer." Jim was clearly proud of this accomplishment. "It's good for someone in my shoes, 'cause I can collect my pension and still make some cash on the side. Keeps me in drinking money, at least. And I can't afford to live anywhere better."

Jim accepted his beer with a nod of thanks to the bartender when he brought it and took a swig before turning back to Karl.

"But what makes a healthy young buck like you turn to this kind of life? There must be better options for you."

Karl wondered if the old man saw him as a threat to his territory, despite his friendly demeanour. There wasn't much he could do about it if that was the case.

"I figured it was better than nothing while I'm laid off. Like you say, I can still collect EI and make a little cash on the side," he said, shrugging, keeping things casual. "As soon as I get the call, I'm back to the rigs."

This was not exactly a lie, but it wasn't entirely accurate either. While he was still collecting EI rather than paying himself a wage out of the agency's limited resources, Karl had no intention of returning to his old job on the rigs if the opportunity did arise. As far as he was concerned, all of that was behind him, and he could only hope that he didn't get the call until he was in a position not to need EI to keep himself. But Jim didn't need to know that.

The old man grinned again, totally unconcerned with the spectacle that his teeth presented, and clinked his beer bottle against Karl's.

"I hear you, son," he said. "I hear you."

Jim took a long pull at his beer, gave Karl a sideways look, and commented, "I never worked the rigs, but I did use to work the rails."

"Really?" Karl asked in surprise. The idea of working on a train, or even travelling on one, had always intrigued him.

"Sure." Jim bobbed his head up and down. "'Course, it was just the Englewood, but it was still a pretty good job in its day."

"The Englewood?" Karl recognized his cue and was happy to oblige.

"Yup," said Jim. "The old train from Woss to Beaver Cove. Last working logging railroad in the country. Probably the whole continent."

"Wow," Karl replied, suitably impressed.

"Yup. I could tell you some stories," Jim continued, clearly getting into his stride. Karl sipped his beer and settled in to listen.

***

Making friends wasn't difficult in this crowd. Or at least, finding drinking mates who were happy to buy you a round if they were sure you would return the favour. The inanity of these barstool conversations wouldn't have bothered Karl if they produced anything useful, but it wasn't until the third week in June that he finally caught a break.

He was in a little place called Tahsis, drinking at a bar called the Grillhouse that actually floated on the surface of the inlet. The local population was only about three hundred, and even though Karl had to admit it was a picturesque hamlet, snuggled between low coastal mountains with its white, steepled church on the hill and its freshly painted marina buildings, he wasn't sure how much he was likely to find in a place this small. His drinking partner for the night was called Shawn. Karl might have heard his last name, but he couldn't remember it. He was young, wiry, and already too drunk for his own good when he struck up a conversation with Karl, and his rambling account of the various hardships that had led to his working the docks got boring fast.

"But all that, all that is gonna change," he insisted, leaning across the glass-topped patio table toward Karl and blasting him with a face full of halitosis. "'Cause I'm on to a good thing. A real good thing. Gonna turn it all around. They won't be laughing at ole Shawny Shawn after this!"

For the first time that evening, Karl gave him his full attention. "What kind of a good thing?"

"Wouldn't you like to know?" Shawn sneered back at him.

"Yeah, I would," said Karl. Shawn looked at him in surprise at such forthrightness, swaying slightly in his chair as he contemplated this turn of events.

"Okay, okay." He finally began to nod. "You seem like a good guy. I guess I can let you in on it. No point in keeping secrets when there's plenty to go around, eh?'

He laughed, blowing the smell of unbrushed teeth, stale cigarettes, and beer in Karl's face again.

"Meet me up there." He gestured to the marina parking lot. "Tomorrow at five, and I'll take you to meet my source."

He attempted to tap the side of his nose in a gesture of secrecy, but he missed and ended up waving his finger in front of his face instead.

"Sounds good, thanks." Karl found himself momentarily mesmerized by that shaking finger and began to wonder if he wasn't a little drunk himself. He couldn't be sure the exhilaration he felt was the result of having a possible lead at last, or just a beer buzz.

Karl finally made his escape when Shawn spotted someone he was sure was his old buddy Mikey across the dock patio and stumbled off to find out why Mikey was ignoring him. Karl hoped that he would remember their meeting the next day but thought he could likely track Shawn to one of the few places that served alcohol in town if he failed to show up.

To Karl's surprise, Shawn was waiting for him when he reached the marina's parking lot the next day, having spent the night at the more modest Tahsis Motel rather than the Westview Marina Lodging. Besides the price, Karl wasn't sure how well he would sleep in a floating motel. Shawn still stank of beer, and even though it might have been left over from the night before, Karl was happy to drive to their destination, following Shawn's directions.

They drove right to the edge of town, where a semiprivate dock jutted out into the inlet just before S Maquinna Drive disappeared into the back road to Westbay Park. Shawn bounced out of the truck the moment Karl pulled up and waved his arm in excited invitation for Karl to follow him down the walkway, onto the wooden dock, where a single fisherman stood waiting beside a boat piled high with crab traps, several bins set out around him.

"Ta da," Shawn intoned dramatically, waving to the contents of a bin as Karl walked up behind him.

"Crabs." Karl stared down into the bin. A jumbled mass of the crustaceans were clambering over and around each other, attempting to escape, without success. He looked up at Shawn, uncomprehending. He almost asked, *Are the drugs hidden under the crabs*, but caught himself in time. It was just beginning to dawn on him that this had nothing to do with drugs. Nothing at all.

"Undersized crabs," Shawn clarified, clearly still waiting for Karl to display the appropriate enthusiasm.

"These are the ones they can't sell legally, so we can pick them up for a killer deal." He grinned away at Karl, bobbing his head as if encouraging his new friend to get in on the excitement already. "And the average person on the street has no idea they aren't legal size, so you can sell them to family and friends for half what the stores charge and still make a killing."

Karl saw the point. He was sure Liam and maybe even Jakob would be happy to pick up some fresh seafood at a fraction of the retail price, without inquiring too closely into the legality of its origins. However, this was not what he needed at the moment. A truck load of live crabs, undersized or otherwise, were not going to help him confirm the existence of a drug-running operation in the area. Thinking fast, he put on his best skeptical face.

"I don't know, they look pretty small," he said, eyeing up the crabs again. "I mean, undersized is alright if it isn't too obvious, but if I get caught with these there'll be no question…"

"Who's gonna catch you?" Shawn interjected, bouncing on the balls of his feet now. "It's not like you're going to set up a stall and try to sell them on the sidewalk, is it? Just family and friends, I'm telling you, you can make plenty that way."

"Maybe." Karl made his reluctance clear.

"Look, man." The gum-booted, rain-suited fisherman spoke up, "I'll give you a half dozen on the house. Try it out, ask around, see if it'll be worth your while."

He was clearly less eager than Shawn to force this sale through, and Karl wondered what kind of a commission Shawn had been hoping to make off the introduction.

"Yeah, okay," he agreed, still not sure what he was going to do with half a dozen live crabs. Shawn stopped bouncing and looked disgusted, but Karl wasn't about to let that influence him. He was here for drugs, not contraband seafood. He just wanted to get out of the situation as gracefully as possible.

A spare five-gallon bucket was found, six of the largest crabs were placed in it, and Karl was waved off with apparent goodwill by the fisherman, if not by Shawn. Putting the bucket on the floor of the passenger side of his truck, Karl drove off up Tree to See Drive, headed for Highway 28. The constant thumping and scrabbling of the crabs trying to escape the bucket was getting on his nerves by the time he reached a turnoff marked Moutcha Bay Resort, and on a whim he turned in, bumping over the rough road until it widened into a parking lot in front of a building that looked like some kind of eco tourism lodge, sporting shingle siding and solar panels on the roof.

Climbing out of the truck and walking around to the passenger door, Karl noticed what appeared to be round cabins with domed roofs farther along the waterfront. Definitely a hippy hangout. But not, Karl thought, a cheap one. Pulling out the bucket and carrying it by the handle, he walked down the concrete boat launch to the water's edge and tipped the crabs into the sea. With a violent thrashing of their back legs, they made off with all possible haste, and Karl watched them, amused, for a minute before heading back to his truck. The bucket he left next to a rack full of brightly coloured kayaks for the resort staff to find and dispose of.

Lying on a lumpy motel mattress later that night, Karl couldn't help wondering if this was all a wild goose chase. Was Fullerton's theory a dud? Was he wasting his time chasing shadows that didn't exist? He hoped not, but the letdown of Shawn's "big break" took the edge off his initial excitement.

***

At first, Karl didn't want to mention the incident with Shawn and the crabs either to Kelsey or Fullerton; he felt too stupid about it, but in the end he couldn't help telling Kelsey. Her hilariously amused reaction at his discomfort was hardly encouraging, but when he finally forced himself to call Fullerton and update him with the only progress he had made so far, Fullerton's response surprised him.

"This is good." Fullerton's voice crackled through the poor connection. "Seriously, Karl, this proves that the other dock workers are beginning to accept you as one of their own. Of course, a minor criminal with very little to lose is going to trust more quickly than someone involved in a racket like drugs. But it shows you're playing your part well. That you're believable, and that you're seen as trustworthy. Keep at it, and I think you'll get there."

Despite Fullerton's assurances, the monotony of the work and the life dragged at Karl's motivation as the weeks passed. He checked in with Kelsey less frequently, the everyday work of the agency feeling too far away to matter. It all reminded him of his days on the rigs. The mindless repetition combined with physical discomfort and risk of injury dulled his mind and numbed his senses. He didn't know how anyone made this a permanent lifestyle. If he hadn't known, in the back of his mind, that it wasn't forever, that he did have a purpose beyond surviving for just one more day, he thought he would likely drink himself to death pretty quick, rather than face it. As it was, he was so numb to reality in his attempt to blend in that he almost missed the clue he was looking for.

15

It was late, and Karl was climbing slowly into his truck after a long night, the chill night mist collecting on his hair and occasionally accumulating enough to send a cold trickle down the back of his neck. He wasn't looking forward to a night in another empty motel room, and he sat for a few minutes staring down at the dock he'd just left. In a daze, he realized that several of the other men hadn't followed him up the walkway to the parking lot. Instead, they sat around on the gunwales of moored boats or leaned against pylons, settling in, clearly intending to wait. For what, he wondered.

Straightening his aching back and leaning forward in the driver's seat, he shook the damp hair back off his forehead and squinted down at the dock he had just left. They were waiting for something. This wasn't just a pause to have a last smoke and shoot the breeze; these men were gearing up, not down, for the night. Just as he reached this conclusion, however, he noticed the foreman standing with feet planted and hands on hips staring up in the direction of his truck. He realized that he was leaning close enough to the windshield for his face to be visible as a pale blur to the man below, and he hastened to start the engine and pull away as if everything was normal. But he was no longer mentally numb. Something was going down on this dock tonight that the foreman didn't want anyone watching.

Should he double back and try to see what it was? Karl decided it wasn't a good idea, not when the foreman had seen him watching already. He wasn't prepared, and he didn't have a plan. But as he stood under the steaming shower back in the grungy motel, he thought the direct approach just might be the best. After all, if the foreman thought his interest was purely monetary, it could seem less suspicious.

He intended to broach the subject the next night. The only problem was everyone, including the foreman in charge of the marina, packed up and headed out as soon as the last tub of fish was loaded onto the truck and the night's cash payments were handed out. Karl noticed, however, that this was not the same man he had seen watching him the night before. He could have kicked himself over how unobservant he had let himself become.

Looking back, he realized that there were individuals who regularly managed specific marinas, or, in smaller, more remote areas, the single dock or jetty serving the local fishing community. But there were also at least one or two he had definitely seen in more than one location. He knew that a lot of the guys moved around, like him, wherever they heard the best work would be next. But these were the foremen he was thinking of. They shouldn't be transient; they were the ones in charge. And now he thought about it, did the same set of extra guys tend to go with the same mobile foreman from place to place? He wasn't sure.

Karl had been planning to head north again in another day or two, to a little place called Winter Harbour. He decided he'd go in the morning, since whatever had brought the travelling foreman to Fair Harbour had apparently taken him off again, and Karl didn't know how to trace him other than to continue as he was and hope their paths would cross again. It was another week before Karl, working his way around Quatsino Sound, recognized some of the crew he was working with in Coal Harbour. He was almost certain two of them, at least, had been in the group that he had seen that night, staying later than the rest.

Sure enough, a different foreman walked out of the marina office than had been supervising the night before. Karl recognized him from other nights on other docks. He was called Roy, but that was all Karl knew. He locked up behind himself before leading them down onto the docks and directing them to the different slips where the first boats were starting to pull up. Karl wondered if the rest of the regular guys failed to notice this anomaly in the foremen, or if they just knew better than to comment.

As they settled into the rhythm of the night's work, Karl paid attention properly for the first time in weeks. It seemed as if the guys he thought were likely staying for the "late shift," as he'd begun to think of it, hauled up maybe one tub of fish for every two or three that the rest of them carried. Clearly, they were conserving their energy, ready for the long hours still to come. Since he didn't know if he would have the option to stay, he couldn't very well emulate their example, and he kept pace with the rest of the regulars until the last fishing vessel had been emptied and the trucks were pulling away.

He intentionally positioned himself at the back of the pay line, an easy task since most of the guys were more than willing to push their way forward in hopes of making it to the nearest pub or liquor store before it closed for the night. When he took his cash from the foreman, he stood looking down at it for a minute, shifting his weight from foot to foot until Roy snapped, "What's the matter? It's all there."

"Yeah, yeah," Karl mumbled, cringing a little at his harsh tone, rolling the bills into a tight tube in his hands. "I was just wondering…"

He glanced over to where a small knot of men stood waiting.

"…if you could use any more help tonight."

His voice tailed off at the end, but he glanced up, hopefully, from under the hair that hung in his eyes these days.

"No, I don't need any more help tonight. If I did, I wouldn't have just paid you, now would I?"

It was a risk, but Karl pushed his luck. "Look man, I could really use the money. Obviously, you've got something more coming in, or they wouldn't all be hanging around." He gestured to the huddle at the end of the dock, where one or two men were now shooting him dark looks over their shoulders. "What could they be bringing in that's so secret? I mean, I don't care about undersized crab or prawns or whatever. I can keep my mouth shut. I just need the work."

"Shove off. The boss doesn't like people who ask questions, and people who say they can keep their mouths shut usually can't. Get out of here before I have to get you out, or you won't work on these docks again, ever."

Karl cringed away from him, hunching his shoulders and dragging himself up the walkway to the parking lot, glancing back resentfully more than once. He'd parked farther away than usual, hoping his arrival on foot would reinforce the image of financial desperation he was aiming for. He maintained his cringing demeanour until he was sure he was out of sight of the men on the dock, then straightened his shoulders and lengthened his stride as he headed for the alley where he had left his truck.

If they wouldn't let him join them, he had already decided, he'd just have to watch them. It had been a while since he'd staked anyone out, but how hard could it be, late at night and in the dark? Moving stealthily in the still darkness, he unlocked his truck with the key rather than the fob and fumbled in the glove box for the camera he had gotten Kelsey to order online and ship up to him on the Island courier bus. Grabbing the ski mask he had thought to pick up at the last minute, he closed the door, careful not to let it slam behind him, and headed back toward the docks.

Instead of taking the street, where he might meet one or more of the other non-initiates heading for the local pub, Karl snuck through the parking lots of the businesses along the waterfront until he reached the overgrown tangle of trees and shrubs that flanked the little marina. Dropping to his belly on the blanket of rotting leaves and needles, Karl dragged himself forward with his elbows through the bush until he had a clear view over the dock below. This manoeuvre, unfortunately, had caused his sweatshirt to ride up, and an unpleasant amount of damp and pungent mulch was now attempting to work its way into the waistband of his jeans. It took several minutes of wriggling and scooping to remove it all and get his clothing straight enough for comfort, and by that point he was beginning to feel the damp.

Sighing at the inevitable discomfort, Karl carefully unscrewed the lens cap from the camera, tucked it in his pocket, and checked that the settings were right for the highly contrasting nighttime lighting he was dealing with. He had been very specific with Kelsey about what he needed when she was ordering the equipment for him, and she had spent over an hour on the phone with him after it had arrived, walking him through the careful notes, with pictures, that she had sent along with the camera. Initially, he thought this was a bit of overkill on her part, but he was thankful now to be able to push the exact right button to avoid creating a flash that would give him away instantly.

Once he was sure he had the settings right, he trained his lens on the dock below and settled in to watch. He was surprised by how clearly he could see every detail, right down to the hangnail on the forefinger of a man lighting a cigarette. He wasn't looking forward to seeing his credit card bill, but he had told Kelsey the limit Fullerton had approved for expenses on the job. He just hoped she'd paid as much attention to those instructions as she had to his explanation of the camera's functional requirements. It was nice that the marina was kept lit up all night, he thought. It'd be a lot harder to capture what he needed, even with this camera, if his quarry had been working in the dark.

The group on the dock seemed unconcerned about carrying out their activities on what was essentially a lit stage. The time stretched on as nothing happened and the damp, rich-smelling earth slowly soaked his clothing. The shrubbery above him dripped occasionally, and several times a chilly drop went down the back of his neck, making him jump and shudder. He turned up his collar with one hand, careful not to let the camera touch the ground. He wondered how long they were planning to wait and if it was always this late.

It was after three o'clock in the morning when he finally heard the low rumble of an outboard as it idled, as quietly as possible, into the cove. He could hardly make out the boat, since it ran completely dark, and he wondered why they bothered when the dock was so well lit, but just as the thought crossed his mind, the half a dozen lamps in the area went out, and the boat pulled up to a suddenly shadowed mooring, cutting the engine as its fenders bumped the wooden dockside.

Karl cursed under his breath as he hurried to adjust the settings on his camera. He had known this sort of thing might be a problem when he'd ordered the equipment, and he thought he should still be able to get enough clarity for what he needed, but he hadn't been ready for the abrupt change. Already, the men were beginning to offload bundles, working quickly and efficiently in absolute silence, not bothering to haul their load straight up to the waiting truck as they did with the fish. Of course, if this was the stuff Fullerton had sent him to look for, freshness wouldn't be the issue.

Double-checking that the flash was still off, Karl propped himself on his elbows, trained his camera on the boat, and started snapping as quickly as he could without sacrificing the limited image quality of his shots. Fullerton had been specific: "Get faces if you can, but it's especially important to find the name and identification number of the boat. That'll let us track its port of origin, even if it's an international vessel. The number should be on the stern, and it's unlikely they'll have covered it, because that would be a dead giveaway if they did cross the Coast Guard's path."

The vessel was pointed toward Karl's hiding place, and he could see lettering along either side of the bow, so he trained his lens on this first, cranking the resolution as high as it could go to try to pick out details in the near darkness. The faces of the men on the boat looked like vague blurs to Karl, but the camera picked up details he never could have seen on his own, and he continued to shoot, trying for at least one decent shot of each. The men on the dock he could catch as they carried their load up to the truck; he was much less worried about them. The fact that the men on the boat were so careful to remain hidden made them more interesting anyway.

Unloading the boat took less than half an hour, and from where Karl lay in the underbrush overlooking the marina, there was next to nothing to hear in the night air. The occasional soft thump of a bundle hitting the dock, but no voices, nothing to attract attention. The hoot of an owl in the woods sounded louder than anything that came off the dock. And then they were done. The bowline was thrown back onto the boat, and the engine roared briefly to life then dropped to an idle as it reversed and turned. The lights on the dock came up just as the boat was pulling away, the faces of the men driving it already out of sight when Karl caught the shot he had been hoping for all night. Clear and crisp, the stern showed up for that one moment before disappearing into the darkness beyond the circle of light, but Karl had it. The name and identification number Fullerton needed. He exhaled a long breath he hadn't realized he was holding and shifted his shoulders to ease the tension.

Continuing to snap the faces of the remaining men and the pile of bundles now being carried up the long walkway to the waiting truck was easy by comparison, although it required another adjustment of settings to avoid washing them out with the increased light. The only difficulty, Karl realized, was the angle of rock jutting out between his hiding place and the parking lot hid the truck itself from view, and he definitely wanted that license plate. Pushing himself up to a crouching position, careful not to shake the shrubs he hid behind as he backed between tree trunks, he scrambled up the rocky outcrop until he could lie flat, looking over the top and seeing the vehicle in question.

It was a half-ton with a flat deck, and the bundles or bales or whatever were being loaded onto it were covered by a plastic tarp and held in place with ratchet straps as if they were so much lumber or farm equipment. The false foreman banged on the side of the truck when the last of the straps were secure, then loaded the men he had been supervising into a beat-up old van. Taking them where? Karl wondered. Did they typically travel together? Did he do it to keep them under observation? And how did a person get himself accepted into that inner circle?

His truck was too far away to get back in time to follow them, and he didn't want his request to stay late being linked to any headlights the driver might see on the highway. No, he would need to bide his time before trying to follow them to wherever they took their illicit cargo. A different vehicle might not be a bad idea, either, he thought, and he wondered if Kelsey would swap vehicles with him for a bit.

Back at the hotel in the early hours of the morning, Karl pulled the map he had bought when he first moved to the Island out of the glove box and took it in with him, spreading it out across the cheap bedspread. Taking a Sharpie, he began to make careful marks on the shiny laminated surface, noting to the best of his recollection those places where "late shifts," as he called them mentally, had been worked, and the corresponding dates. He had to wrack his memory for details he hadn't been paying attention to at the time, and in some cases it was only a guess, but he was sure there had to be a pattern, and he needed to find it, fast. The fishing season was more than half over for the year, and although that might not stop the smuggling operation, it would make his cover a lot harder to maintain.

Ideally, Karl wanted to get to the next drop point before they did. He didn't want the fake foreman to think he was following them. Then he realized the man wasn't likely to know who had arrived first anyway. He gave his head a shake. This was not a profitable line of thought. After staring at the marked-up map until his vision began to blur with fatigue, he finally snapped a picture with his phone and forwarded it to Kelsey, hoping that she could make more sense out of it than he could. Pushing the mess off to one side of the bed, he crawled under the covers and was asleep as soon as his head hit the pillow.

16

Karl woke to the buzzing of his phone the next day around noon. The sun was shining much too brightly through insufficient hotel curtains. He squinted at the screen before answering and growled hello to Kelsey without bothering to sit up.

"Okay." Her voice was too loud for his ears to handle, and he held the phone away from his head. "I think I've got it figured, but you must have two of your dates backwards."

"It's possible," he rasped back. He hadn't included any instructions with the picture he had sent the night before, but apparently that hadn't slowed her down.

"You must have," she said confidently. "There's a pattern to these dates; there must be a couple that you didn't include on the map you sent me, maybe that you just missed, and like I said, you must have two of the dates backwards, but I think I know the next place they'll be."

This woke Karl up better than a shot of espresso. "You do?"

"I *think* so," she stressed. "I'm working with some assumptions, obviously. They seem to prefer towns that don't have a local RCMP detachment, that are only patrolled periodically by a larger town's detachment. And I've taken into account the proximity of the dock or marina to homes, because that would affect how likely they were to be overheard or observed carrying on illicit activities. I assume places that typically have a lot of tourists this time of year will make them feel safer, because tourists won't pay as much attention as homeowners."

Karl rubbed his eyes, trying to follow it all. "How do you even know this stuff about places you've never been to?"

"Karl. You've been gone for weeks!" Kelsey sounded accusatory. "There have only been a couple of background checks, and I served papers on this one lady, but that was it. Summer is slow here. I had to do something! So I learned everything I could about the towns you've been to, in case it might come in handy. And I bet I know more about the fishing industry you're working for than you do right now."

"I'm sure you do. So where do I go next? And when do you think they'll be bringing in the next shipment?"

"If I'm right, we're looking at two shipments a week, one to a smaller, more remote community on either Monday or Tuesday and one at a more touristy spot on the Thursday or Friday. I don't know if they alternate the two weekdays regularly, but they don't seem to use the same town twice in a row, and I think they likely have them on a regular rotation, so no one place is used too frequently. So I *think* they should be in Telegraph Cove on Friday. Can you get there by then?"

"Yeah, that's only an hour away." Karl squinted around the bright room. "Is today Tuesday or Wednesday?"

"Wednesday," she replied. "So I think you should probably head there today or tomorrow, be seen there, work a shift or two, so they don't think you're following them."

"Yeah, I'd thought of that." He leveraged himself up off the pillows and swung his feet over the side of the bed, looking around for the clothes he'd discarded the night before. Wearing clean things every day was a luxury he had never appreciated before, and he was looking forward to that as much as anything once this case was finished.

"I'll head there today," he continued. "I should be able to work there the rest of the week. I can camp out in the back of my truck. The local accommodations are geared more toward rich sports fishers than the likes of me, but the campgrounds have showers."

He was pulling on jeans one-handed as he spoke. He had his shirt halfway over his head when he heard Kelsey say, "Great, just be careful and don't get spotted snooping."

"Aw, you worried about me, Kels?" he mocked, putting the phone back to his ear and reaching for a boot.

"Not especially," she said with sniffy disdain. "But I don't particularly feel like looking for a new job right now."

"Okay, for the sake of your employment security I'll try not to get myself killed." Karl laughed.

"Good. Let me know how it goes." And with that, she was gone. Karl grinned at the thought of her worrying about him. It felt odd to have someone do that, but he kind of liked it. And, he decided, he really would be careful. After all, more than just his future was riding on the success of this case. Letting the laces on his boots hang loose, he grabbed the map and the rest of his gear and headed out to the truck. He could get lunch on the way out of town.

***

Glancing around at the crew gathered on the Telegraph Cove commercial dock Thursday night, Karl felt a frisson of excitement chase down his spine. There were several faces he recognized from the "late crew" here. Apparently, he wasn't the only one who came to town early to avoid drawing attention to the drop nights. Then he wondered if Kelsey's math was off somehow and if tonight was the night. That shouldn't technically be a problem; he had all his camera gear in the truck, but he didn't like the idea that she could have been wrong. He'd been depending on her calculations, which might be a risky thing to do, now that he thought about it.

The night's work was shorter than it had been at the height of the season. Already the boats were bringing in smaller loads, and soon they would start heading out for the winter, except for the few that converted over for the short rock cod season. Everyone seemed to hold the same pace tonight; there was no holding back by the "late shift" men that Karl could see. He found the work easier now, too. He wasn't exhausted by the end of a shift the way he had been when he started. His mind was still sharp, he could focus on the problem at hand, and his muscles had hardened with the work.

Karl took the cash allotted to him at the end of the night and headed up to the parking lot without hesitation. The man doling out cash wasn't the foreman he wanted, and he noted, out of the corner of his eye, that the late-shifters were in the group headed to the town's less touristy bar, so he fell in with the group and joined the scrum pushing their way into the narrow, dark doorway under the neon sign.

It was a dingy little place, and it smelled of thirty-year-old cigarette smoke. Karl thought they might keep the lights this low to hide the stains in the carpet and the cracks in the vinyl seats of the booths. He took a stool at the bar next to one of the late-shifters and ordered a stout.

The other man glanced over at him, uninterested, and Karl acknowledged him with a nod. He had drunk other beers, in other bars, with this man before, but they had rarely spoken. The work usually left them too tired for more than a drink to wind down before heading to their rooms and to bed, but tonight Karl felt keyed up and alert, ready for anything. He was careful to keep this feeling out of his face, however, as he drooped over his beer, projecting depression for all he was worth.

"You've been around a lot this year," the man commented offhandedly. "I don't remember seeing you before this season."

It wasn't really a question, but Karl replied anyway.

"I only came back from Edmonton late last year. I grew up around here, though."

He felt like leaving it vague was the right approach. His family had lived in Vancouver all through his childhood, and he had only visited the Island a handful of times before moving to Victoria, but he wanted to give the impression that he was local. A local boy returning from the big bad oil field, burned out and desperate. Something along those lines.

"Alberta, eh?" The man was laconic, but Karl was prepared to take advantage of any opening.

"Yeah, I went out there after I finished school. I was getting married and wanted to make enough to get our life started off right. Got a job on the rigs, made some good money, until the price of oil tanked. Got laid off, wife left, same story as a hundred other guys, you know?" Karl took a swig of his beer, trying to convince himself that the bravado was all part of his character, that the conversation didn't bother him.

"I hear that." The man tilted the neck of his own beer toward Karl's, and they clinked bottles, drinking in a silence that was as companionable as any Karl remembered since coming north on this case. Glancing sideways, Karl studied his companion without appearing to. He was small, slightly built, but wiry and tough. His thin, weasely face should have been sharp, but it was relaxed now into a surprisingly pleasant expression. Karl wondered if he might be able to worm an introduction into the late crew for himself if he could cultivate this unexpected friendliness, but he decided it wouldn't do to push his luck too soon. So, after finishing his drink in silence he dropped cash on the bar, said, "See you round," to the other man and headed for the door. The man only grunted in reply, but Karl felt like it was a friendly grunt and thought that he had been right not to force more conversation on him.

17

Karl slept late the following morning, ate a hearty breakfast at the local greasy spoon around lunchtime, and spent the afternoon strolling around the little tourist town, learning its ins and outs, its back alleys and its dead ends. He also found what he thought was the best lookout spot to watch the docks without being seen. There were too many docks to pick just one to keep an eye on. He couldn't decide which was more likely for his quarry's purposes, the commercial docks he generally worked on or one of the private docks that would be busier, later, where any of the yachts might have people sleeping on board. Commercial seemed most probable, but he wasn't prepared to bet on it, and he chose his lookout accordingly.

He ate dinner earlier than he would have preferred and kept it light. He had learned the hard way that fighting through the fog of a food coma was not a fun way to spend an evening on the docks, and before the last of the late summer dusk had darkened into night, he joined the same group of men he had worked with the night before to bring in the day's catch. Up and down, back and forth, the familiar rhythm of the work, the sloshing of the fish shifting in the crates in time with men's boot steps, the salty smell of fish and sea water that seemed almost permanently embedded in his skin. Karl felt it all and wondered how it would feel when it ended.

That night ended earlier, even, than the night before, and Karl took his money and left as calmly as he had before, but this time his friend from the previous night stayed behind, and Karl smiled to himself at the thought that he had doubted Kelsey's calculations. Cutting through an alley that climbed steeply up from the waterfront to the street above, Karl made it to his truck without drawing any undue attention and slid in behind the wheel. He put on a well-worn ball cap and added a pair of eyeglasses he had found on a drug store rack. He brushed up the beard into a bushier mass than usual, hoping that the combination would be enough to disguise the outlines of his face in the dark if anyone did see him. There wasn't much he could do about the truck. At least it was a common model. He hoped it wouldn't be too noticeable.

Carefully screwing the correct lens for this distance onto the camera, Karl settled in to wait, anticipating a long night. The fishing boats had been unloaded on the government dock, and the men who stayed behind were still congregated there, so apparently they didn't mind carrying out their activities on government property. Karl shook his head at their audacity, but he supposed audacity must be a requirement of the industry. Along with a lack of any moral compass and a whole lot of greed.

It wasn't quite as late this time when the distant throb of a boat motor reached Karl. Up the hill from the docks and overlooking the cove, he probably wouldn't have heard it at all if he hadn't rolled the truck window down so he could listen. The minutes ticked by, and Karl only gave the men on the dock half his attention, since he expected the lights to go out before anything happened.

As a result, he was surprised when a particularly classy-looking private fishing vessel pulled up to the dock and the men sprang into action. This was not the same boat as before, and the crew hadn't bothered to kill the lights before it arrived. Why was this time different? Karl had no way of knowing, but he wanted to capture everything he could all the same. Seizing the camera from where it sat on the dash, he trained the lens on this new vessel. Different men on the boat, although the dock crew were recognizable. Apparently, there were multiple carriers bringing in shipments. This was interesting. Karl wondered if the different runners knew about each other, if there was competition involved, and how it was all coordinated.

Could the more casual approach to security have something to do with the fact that Telegraph Cove was more of a tourist spot than Coal Harbour? The matching red and green paint jobs on the various buildings around the cove, the expensive private vessels pulled up alongside charter boats around the docks, all seemed to indicate that this was the case. What had Kelsey said about tourist towns being less conspicuous, because tourists wouldn't be watching out for the things homeowners would? Apparently, she knew what she was talking about.

The haul they unloaded was larger than the previous one, but not enough to make the process much longer. The men worked calmly, steadily, and apparently without any concern for the security of their venture, even without the cover of darkness this time. Karl wondered if that had been for the sake of the other boat's crew, or if it would simply have been too noticeable to kill the lights in this bigger, busier town. As the boat pulled away, Karl did his best, with his lens magnification maxed out, to get a readable shot of its back end. The downward angle made it distorted at best, but he thought Kelsey might be able to do something with it if he sent the digital image to her. She had been talking about learning to manipulate digital images when he had asked her to order the camera, and he thought if anyone could figure it out, she would.

Karl had chosen his lookout well. He could follow the vehicles carrying both drugs and men whichever route they chose to take out of town, and he could do so from a parallel street, higher up the slope of the town, so they wouldn't even see anyone behind them until they reached the highway. So long as he gave them enough space, he thought he would be able to see which way they turned without them noticing him at all.

It all went so perfectly to plan that the very smoothness made Karl nervous. He could see the taillights of the van rounding a corner up ahead as he pulled onto Beaver Cove Road, and since it had been right behind the flat deck until just before he lost sight of them, he was pretty sure they were still together. Now it was just a matter of keeping close enough to see which way they went when they reached the highway. Far easier than following someone in the city.

There was only one major highway this far north on the island, and sure enough, they turned south when they reached it, heading into the Island's interior. He had driven this way many times over the course of the summer, and he'd never felt nervous on these roads before. He could have followed these same vehicles a dozen times without realizing it and without their noticing him. There was no reason why they should become suspicious this time. None of which prevented Karl's heart pounding or his hands sweating on the steering wheel.

He needn't have worried; after forty-five minutes on the highway, he could see both sets of tail lights turn off, heading into the bush. Karl slowed very slightly as he passed, looking for landmarks that would help him recognize the place again, but it was the same as any of a hundred gravel roads off this highway. Some were old logging roads, and some might even lead to homes, but there was nothing to differentiate this one.

He pulled over as soon as he rounded the next corner and thought hard. He needed to identify this particular turnoff on the map, and there was no room for error if he hoped to find it again. But how? Karl dug the MapBook out of his glove box. He hadn't looked at it in weeks, he was so familiar with the main routes from town to town by now. He knew which highway he was on, and he had a general idea of how far he had come from Telegraph Cove, which narrowed things down, but the number of dark, narrow lines branching off the bold red of the highway was still daunting.

He decided he needed to focus on the main roads, the ones with names, speed limits, and traffic signs. The turnoff to Woss seemed to be his best bet. He had never bothered to visit the tiny village due to its distance from the coast, but he had passed the turnoff more than once and knew it was well signed. It would have to do as a landmark for his calculations. Karl put his truck in reverse and backed along the gravel edge of the highway until he was once again opposite the turn where his quarry had disappeared. Putting the truck in park, he made a careful note of the exact mileage on his odometer, took a deep breath, put the truck in drive, and crawled off down the highway doing less than half the actual speed limit. He kept his eyes wide open, constantly scanning for side roads and making a note of each one, left or right, as he passed them. The drive to the Woss turnoff took a lot longer than usual this way, and his eyes were feeling the strain of staring into the darkness, but he knew how many kilometres the turnoff was from Woss and the exact number of turns he would need to count between it and Woss in order to find it again. It was the best he could do.

It was late, and he was tired. Karl thought about simply sleeping at a rest stop like the one at Hoomak Lake but decided he didn't want to be woken by morning traffic while sleeping rough, and there was always the risk of rain. Pulling a three-point turn, he headed back the way he had come, driving at the proper speed, but still counting turnoffs just to see if he could. Yes, the turnoff and the mileage matched. He could find his road again. Grinning, he continued toward Port McNeil, where he should still be able to get a room at one of the local motels. As far as he was concerned, the night's work had been a success.

18

Getting out of the shower an hour later, Karl wondered if it was too late to call Kelsey, but he suddenly felt he would burst if he didn't talk to someone. This whole working solo gig was getting to him. He dialled her number, expecting to have to wait, but she picked up on the first ring.

"So, was I right? Were they there? Was this the night?" Karl couldn't help grinning at the eagerness in her voice. If he'd known she was waiting up, he would have called before he showered. Then he wondered how long she would have waited if he hadn't called.

"Kels, you're a genius. Seriously, remind me that I owe you a bonus at the end of the year if the agency actually makes any money."

She snorted at that, but he thought she would try to make sure there was a profit when it came time to do the year-end books, all the same.

"You were right on every count, and I followed them until they turned off the Island Highway, so that definitely narrows matters down. There are only so many places they can have gone from there. Next time I'll follow them all the way, and…"

"*No!*" Kelsey's interruption was emphatic. "You can't just drive in; do you know how many of the roads up there end in dead ends? It's going to be a bit difficult to pretend you aren't following them if you get stuck with no way out of wherever they stop!"

"Yeah, I realize it's a risk," Karl responded. "But how else am I supposed to figure out where they're going and what they're doing? Technically, I still haven't seen anything illegal."

"I've been working on that. There are certain criteria that I think they would need for their base of operations. Especially if they're doing any kind of processing to their product locally."

"Product? That's what we're calling it now?" Karl was amused.

"Don't interrupt," Kelsey admonished. "I'm explaining my genius here. I've been working really hard on this!"

She paused to collect her thoughts on the other end of the phone, and Karl snickered to himself, but quietly enough that she wouldn't hear him.

"So, they need a certain amount of space, if they are doing any processing. And they need a lot of privacy. So the building or whatever they've got has to be in an out-of-the-way location, but still large enough for their activities, and not too damp or leaky or whatever, because they wouldn't want their *product*," she stressed the word, "getting wet and spoiled."

Karl could tell by the way she was repeating herself that he had thrown her off her stride, and it amused him, but he forced himself to pay attention. It sounded logical, and if she had a theory, he was prepared to hear it.

"I've been searching for vacant commercial locations in remote areas, especially on the North Island, and I've narrowed it down to about a dozen possibilities. I mean, obviously, if it's not listed anywhere online then I might just miss it entirely, but I did manage to dig up a couple that were listed for sale a year or two back and aren't now, but that still don't have any businesses operating out of them either. I figure if someone sold, rented, or leased their property to dope dealers, they wouldn't want it advertised."

"Probably not," Karl agreed.

"So, now that I have a list of possibilities, I need you to send me the exact location where you saw them turn off the highway. Then, when you follow them next time, you confirm if they go to the same place, or where they do go, and I triangulate the information, see if it lines up with my theory.

"Oh, and I think it might be a good idea for you to find a different vehicle to follow them in," she added. "You don't want them connecting it to you, and you're going to Zeballos next. That place is tiny. Do you think the agency could afford for you to pick up a beater for the job? You could sell it again when the job's finished.'"

"I thought of that," Karl replied. "I mean swapping vehicles, not buying one. I was wondering if you'd just switch with me for a week or two? It'd be a lot easier than finding a car that looks crappy enough for the job but was still reliable and affordable."

"You'd let me drive your truck?" Kelsey sounded much too thrilled with this idea for Karl's liking, but it only lasted until the next thought hit her.

"Wait. Are you calling my car crappy?"

"You have to admit, it's not exactly beautiful," Karl said.

"It's a classic," Kelsey snapped back.

Kelsey's car was an ancient orange Toyota Tercel, clearly well loved and cared for by some previous owner, but more recently showing the effects of the Island's salty air in the rust around the wheel wells and on the corners of its doors. She'd showed up with it a month after coming to work for him, proud as punch of her first car purchase, and they had the same conversation then that they were having now. But Karl knew she'd been taking good care of it since, and it had never failed to start so far. In the warm, early fall weather they were having, he thought it could be trusted to get him where he needed to go, even if he didn't relish the idea of having to camp in it, if that became necessary.

"Well, can I borrow the classic?" he asked with mock solemnity. "Will you swap vehicles with me for a week or two, while we sort this whole location question out?"

"Oh yeah, for sure." She was back to being excited about the idea. "I'll drive up to Campbell River tomorrow, and we can swap there. It's too big a place for them to use, I think, so we shouldn't have to worry about being spotted by anyone connected to the case. Then you can get back north before anyone realizes you've left."

Karl still thought she sounded a little too eager about the plan. It was affecting his confidence level, even though it had been his idea in the first place.

***

Karl was afraid that Kelsey might arrive in a trench coat, fedora, and aviators, but she bounced out of the little orange hatchback wearing a tank top, cutoffs, and flip-flops. Looking down at her footwear choice, he asked, "You do know how to drive stick, right?"

"Yeah, I've driven your truck before, remember? On the Oglevie case?" Kelsey was impatient with his fussing.

"That was a block and a half," said Karl. "With a flat tire. In the suburbs. Not on the highway."

"Look," Kelsey reassured him, holding out her car keys and eyeing his truck. "I'll take the old Island Highway back to Victoria. It'll be slower and take me longer, but I can easily pull over if I need to take a call or anything like that."

Karl knew she was leaving out the fact that it would be much more scenic and relaxing driving along the coast than running down the Inland Highway, but he didn't argue, just handed over his keys and pulled his various bags out of the truck, transferring them to the little hatchback without voicing any more misgivings.

"Now, remember," Kelsey instructed, "I need you to be absolutely exact about where they leave the highway so I can triangulate it against my map and see which location is most probable for the hideout. The mileage from the nearest major junction worked, so get me that again and we'll be set."

Karl glanced nervously around the mall parking lot, but the closest person was a young mother several cars away attempting to wrestle a screaming toddler into its car seat and clearly not listening to a word they were saying.

"And be careful," she added fiercely. "Don't get spotted, and don't let anything happen to my baby."

Then she turned rapidly away, pulled herself up into the driver's seat of his truck and, with a quick wave, drove out of the parking lot without stalling or grinding the gears. Karl hoped this was a good sign.

Driving across the Campbell River bridge on his way out of town, Karl discovered the reason for Kelsey's footwear choice. The Tercel did not have air conditioning, and his feet, in work boots, were already beginning to sweat.

19

Not wanting the change of vehicle to be noticed prematurely, Karl left the car parked in the lot behind his motel and walked down to the fuel dock on Monday night. If any of the late shift crew were working in town tonight, he planned to stop in whichever of the local watering holes they headed for after work and see if he could pick up any hints about the following night's drop. Assuming Kelsey was right, and the drop would be happening in this town and on the following night, he should then be well positioned to follow them a second time and confirm their destination.

Before he went back to John Fullerton to report his findings, Karl wanted to get eyes on the actual distribution centre for this operation and be certain that he wasn't making a complete ass of himself chasing a bunch of undersized shrimp or something equally uninteresting to the newsman.

The shortening daylight in the evening reflected the shorter shift on the dock, and it was only ten when Karl pocketed his earnings and followed the others up the plank walkway to the shore and toward the seedier of the dockside pubs. He supposed a nicer place might not have been so happy to see a troupe of customers come in reeking of fish and sweat and all demanding cheap beer or even cheaper spirits. He ordered his usual and took a seat at the bar. His friend from a few nights previously was standing next to a booth full of regulars, chatting with them, but he too came up to the bar to order and, after a sideways glance at Karl, took the stool next to him.

Karl gave him a nod, but remembering his previous taciturnity, did not speak first. But apparently the man was in a more talkative mood today.

"I don't think I ever caught your name," the smaller man commented once he had a drink in hand.

"Karl, Karl Larsson." Karl had intentionally gotten Kelsey to keep his first name and any images of himself off the company website so that he didn't have to worry about aliases when he was working.

"I'm Gabe Ross," replied his companion, and they shook hands in the awkward, sideways manner of men sitting at bars everywhere.

"What are your plans once the fishing season's over?" Gabe asked, clearly making conversation with an effort.

"I don't know yet." Karl was honest. "My brother wants me to get my class one and go work for him driving truck, but," he let his voice tail away, indicating his reluctance at this idea.

"Huh. Working for family? Not my idea of a good time," said Gabe.

"Me neither," Karl agreed. "But I'm not sure what else to do. It doesn't look like there's any chance I'll be called back to work this year, and I've gotta eat, you know? I mean, EI helps, but it's not enough to really live, not when half of it goes to alimony, anyway."

He added the last bit in a fit of inspiration. He wasn't paying any alimony; he'd been lucky there, but it made his desperation sound more legitimate, and he thought it was the sort of thing a man like Gabe would sympathize with.

"Any kids?" Gabe asked.

"No, thank goodness," Karl replied sincerely this time. Swigging his beer, he glanced sideways at the other man.

"What about you? How'd you end up living this life?" he asked, genuinely curious but keeping his voice casual.

"Same general idea," Gabe hunched over his bottle. "Had a good job working for one of the smaller logging operations until it went under. Divorced, only in my case there are three kids, so it's child support as well as alimony, and even if I don't see them as often as I'd like, I want the best for my kids, you know? Braces and summer camp and dance lessons. Playing sports. All the stuff I didn't have. College too, when they're older," he added. Karl was impressed by the man's determination. He could understand how turning a blind eye to whatever they were unloading from the boats could feel worth it, under the circumstances.

"'Course, the ex is always bitching that I just want to be the 'fun dad' while she does all the work, but you don't see her out hauling fish every night to make ends meet, and she seems to have plenty of fun with her new boyfriend, according to my kids." His voice had taken a bitter turn, but Karl could understand this too. It was a common enough reality, but not a pleasant one. He grimaced sympathetically and continued to drink in companionable silence.

By the time they had finished their beers and nodded goodnight to each other, Karl felt like he had made an ally of sorts, maybe even an ally who could get him in with the drug runners. The next night the work was the same, but when Karl turned to leave, the group Gabe belonged to remained behind. Karl gave Kelsey mental props once again for her calculation skills.

Flat gravel lots surrounded the access to both docks, making any close observation from convenient shrubbery out of the question. Rather than run around in the dark trying to find somewhere to watch from, Karl simply collected his car from the parking area and drove back to where the two access roads converged from the docks before heading back through town, parked in a convenient picnic area, and killed the engine. For added effect, he slammed the car door to make it sound as if someone had gotten out, since he still had a partial view of the docks, then he slouched low in his seat and prepared to wait.

Despite the poor angle his location gave him, Karl set up the camera and laid it on the dash, ready to use if needed. It was more comfortable staking out the dock from the car than some bushes, but he missed the vantage his truck gave him. He couldn't remember when he had last felt this short sitting in the driver's seat.

By the time the boat had turned and purred its way out of the cove, clearly more concerned about attracting attention than the previous delivery crew had been, Karl was fairly certain that this was the same boat he had seen on his first stakeout and likely the same crew. There was nothing to prove what the bundles being unloaded contained, but they weren't fish, he was willing to bet on that. Once the truck was loaded and the crew in the van headed out after it, Karl started the Tercel and followed them out of town from a safe distance. It was laughably easy until the truck turned off the Zeballos Main Road well before it reached the highway in an entirely different area than Karl had tracked them to previously.

This worried him. He had expected them to go to the same location as before and hoped for a clearly indicated hideout or storage facility. Something that he could trace them back to. If they didn't have a special destination of some sort, why hadn't the truck simply headed for the ferry? Why go off the paved roads in the middle of the North Island forest? With no way of answering any of these questions, Karl had no choice but to note the mileage and start counting gravel turnoffs between this location and the highway. He just hoped Kelsey could make more of it than he could.

When he reached the highway, Karl once again turned toward Port McNeil as the nearest real town and had trouble preventing himself from dangerously exceeding the speed limit all the way there. He bounded up the steps on the outside of his motel and was dialling Kelsey's number as he locked the room's door behind him.

"Hey." Again she answered on the first ring, and Karl knew she had been waiting for his call.

"Hey, Kels, I'm sending you the location info now. They took a completely different route than last time. It's not even on the highway, so I don't think their final destination can be the same, but take a look and let me know what you think."

Karl sat on the edge of the bed, loosening the laces on his work boots, his phone jammed between his ear and his shoulder as he listened to her tapping keys and muttering to herself. He realized she must still be at the agency, and he wondered if he would be paying overtime for this. If so, he wasn't about to argue. He needed her, and he knew it.

"No, no, this is good." Kelsey's voice crackled slightly due to the poor cell service this far north, even in town, but her confidence came through clearly.

"This narrows down the options, because there is really only one place on my list of possibilities that they could have been going to from these two turnoffs. I can find routes through the logging roads from either spot to this old sawmill I have on my list. It's been abandoned for about a decade, and the property was up for sale for ages, but about a year ago it was taken off the market.

"No sale that I could find any record of, but it's not listed anymore. And there's no company showing that place as their business location, so I don't think it's been officially leased to anyone legit. It's the only building on my list of possibilities that fits both turnoffs. Well, the track you've marked tonight isn't even on any map, but it must connect to the logging road that's less than a quarter kilometre from the highway there, and the logging road would get you to the sawmill in not too long. Quicker than going around to the other turnoff. Yeah, yeah, I think this is the place. It has to be."

Her assurance and excitement were infectious.

"So, can you send me a map? Can you give me clear directions to the mill from that turnoff?" asked Karl.

"I could," said Kelsey. "But I don't think you should go that way. For one thing, I don't want you beating my car over a bunch of gravel roads, when there are paved options that are just a little farther. For another, they're less likely to be watching for you coming from a direction they don't use themselves."

"Okay, but how do I do that? You said there were only two ways in, and that it would be a dead-end road when I got there," Karl asked, confused.

"I said it *might* be up a dead-end road, and you didn't want to take that risk," Kelsey rejoined. "Now that we have a pretty good idea where they are going, I can get you to within a kilometre or two of that location on a different set of logging roads than they seem to be using. That way you can park my car far enough away that they won't see or hear it, hike through the bush, and sneak up on them, check things out, and find out what's actually going on."

"You want me to just head off into the bush from some random back road in the middle of nowhere." Karl was less than comfortable with this idea. He had always been a city kid. Yeah, he had worked in some out-of-the-way places on the rigs, but he had been ferried in and out of those sites by the company he worked for. He was used to having buildings and bridges and other landmarks of that sort, not just a whole lot of trees. With only one major highway serving the North Island, it was easy enough to avoid getting lost as long as you stayed on the main roads, but the miles upon miles of forestry lands, with their labyrinth of old logging roads, some in good repair and some definitely not, was a whole different matter.

"You'll be fine," Kelsey insisted. "I'm sending you a detailed map with landmarks that you can't possibly miss on it. Stick to that and you can't go wrong."

"You know I won't have cell service out there? I could seriously end up lost wandering around in the bush until I starve to death."

"If I don't hear anything from you for forty-eight hours, I'll send out search and rescue."

"Great. Thanks."

"No problem." Kelsey laughed. "Look, if you do get properly lost, you should always head downhill, find a creek, and follow it downstream. That's what my old girl guide leader said." Karl didn't find her cheerful unconcern particularly reassuring.

"So I'll end up in the ocean. Then what?" he demanded.

"Uh." Kelsey pondered that. "I don't remember."

"Great."

"You're not going to get lost; you'll be totally fine. You'll have my map, and if you're really so worried, go buy a compass and just make sure you know what direction you took when you leave the car. Then you can always find your way back to it."

This sounded straightforward, but Karl still didn't love the idea. On the other hand, what choice did he have? He needed to find out what was actually going on here, and he needed to find out soon. So, after a quick hunt online the next morning, he headed for the Timberland Sports Centre, which offered everything from fishing bait to lottery tickets, and a whole lot of outdoor gear. Explaining to the helpful teenager behind the counter that he wanted to try wilderness camping for the first time, Karl found himself bombarded with both survival tips and equipment options, and an hour later he left with a lot more gear than he had planned to buy but also an increased confidence in his chances of surviving a night in the forest, if it came to that.

20

After considering the matter, Karl decided the best time to confirm the hideout's location would be when the crew was actually there. He got Kelsey to calculate the next drop night for him and maintained his current routine in the meantime. Not relishing the idea of doing anything in the forest after dark if he could help it, he waited until dawn the following morning before taking the route laid out on Kelsey's impressively detailed map. She had been right about paved roads. Although the logging road indicated was rough, with cracked asphalt and without any painted lines or traffic signs, it was paved. It also had a large sign with *Restricted Access* printed in red standing at the point where the road left the highway, which Karl pointedly ignored.

Karl didn't know if there were any logging activities currently ongoing in the area, but he didn't relish the idea of coming around a corner too quickly and driving the little orange car into one of the massive logging trucks he had seen hauling delimbed trees up and down the highway, so he kept his speed to a cautious sixty and an eye on the road ahead, only occasionally glancing at the map to check on his whereabouts. It took over an hour to make his way around to the spot where Kelsey had indicated he should leave the car and take to the woods.

Even though the turns, forks, and back-road junctions had been exactly where her instructions said they would be, he still felt nervous as he pulled over onto the soft shoulder and double-checked his odometer against her map. This had to be the spot. Pulling out the magnetic compass recommended by the teen at the sporting goods shop, he carefully compared this against the map as well. Everything lined up. It was now or never.

Secure in the knowledge that he had light, heat, fire, signalling devices, food, water, and bear spray, Karl shouldered his pack, locked the car and, taking the direction his map indicated, stepped off the road. There was plenty of undergrowth, and he picked his way cautiously through it, trying to put his feet down between the short, thick shrubs with the shiny dark green leaves, and skirting massive ferns, some of them over three feet in diameter.

This section of the forest felt old, although the occasional rotting stump told him that it wasn't true old growth. Still, the last time this area had been logged was probably before his lifetime, and the tall, sturdy trees with their broad canopy high above kept the excessive weediness of a younger forest at bay. He had to walk carefully, but he could make his way through this without having to hack away at any salmonberry bushes and without encountering the tall, thorny stalks they had called "devil's club" as children. He was pleased not to find any of them, at least. They hurt.

Continually checking his compass against the instructions on Kelsey's map meant slow going through the trees, but if he hadn't been so distracted, Karl had to admit it would have been a beautiful hike. Most of the way was a gentle downhill slope, which made sense when he thought about it. The logging road he had left Kelsey's Tercel on was farther inland than the road Kelsey said led to the sawmill. Most of the Island sloped down from the central ridge of mountains to the coast on each side. This area was no different.

Gaining confidence as he went and realizing that all he would have to do was head uphill and eventually he would find the road the car was on, Karl's stride lengthened and his spirits lifted. He was feeling so good about the progress he was making that he almost walked straight into the sawmill yard without recognizing it. The dark green paint on the corrugated steel frame blended so well with the forest around him that Karl didn't realize what he was looking at until it was less than a hundred metres ahead of him.

Then he heard a door slam. Karl froze, one leg raised in midstride, then crouched quickly behind the nearest tree trunk. A car started, and he peered around the tree, getting his bearings. Now that he realized what he was looking at, he could see the outline of the building through the tree trunks. It was bigger than he had anticipated, although he had no reason to expect something small. He didn't know how big a typical sawmill was. Keeping low to the ground, he crept forward until he could see the structure and its yard more clearly.

It was a low, square, flat-topped building, without any windows, although the better part of one wall appeared to be made up of tall sliding doors so that two thirds or more at a time could be pushed aside to leave the interior open to the elements. These doors faced onto the massive gravel lot that spread in front of the building, where half a dozen cars were parked, without using even a fraction of the available space. It all looked so open and exposed that Karl found himself doubting anything underhanded could be going on here. Which didn't mean he wasn't going to try to find out what was happening, if he could.

Keeping a sharp lookout and moving as quietly as he could, Karl crept from tree to tree, moving toward the main structure, staying under cover as much as possible. He could see figures moving around the lot below. One individual was carrying bags of some kind to a vehicle and apparently loading them into it, but Karl didn't have a clear view of either the vehicle or the bags. He needed to get closer if he wanted specifics for Fullerton. Moving cautiously to the right, he managed to catch a couple plate numbers from the vehicles parked in the lot with the camera lens zoomed in for clarity. This was a start, but he needed more.

A moss-covered log lay across his path, and Karl stepped up onto it. The instant the log felt his full weight, it gave out under him, the wood rotted to the core. Karl fell headlong onto an old branch jutting out from the log, and it snapped with a pop like a firecracker before Karl landed with a terrific crash on the bush beyond. His right leg was trapped in the pulpy core of the log, elevated at an awkward angle behind him, making any movement impossible without even more noise.

He heard several shouts from the area of the sawmill, but he could see nothing from where he lay because the bush obscured his view. It was also stabbing him under the right eye with a small branch that seemed determined to dig his eyeball out of the socket if he failed to hold his neck at an extremely awkward angle. He tried desperately to listen for approaching footsteps, but the pulse pounding in his ears made hearing difficult.

"Who's there?" came a loud, angry voice, followed by the echoing bang of a gunshot and the thump of a bullet hitting a tree to his left. Karl's nerves screamed at him to jump and run for it, but his position made this impossible. Besides, the other half of his mind insisted he remain completely still and silent. Every muscle in his body was bunched for movement and frozen into immobility at the same time. He could feel the blood pumping in his throat, and he wondered if the combination of stress, tension, and position would be enough to make him pass out.

There was a slam in the lot below him and a new voice shouted, "What the hell are you doing?"

"I heard someone in the bush," the first voice called back. Karl was relieved to note that they still seemed to be in the gravel lot and not searching for him in the woods. This relief was tempered by the starbursts exploding behind his eyelids every time he blinked. It felt rather like a stupid game his brothers used to play, where they would deprive him of oxygen by the simple expedient of placing pressure on either side of his windpipe until he caved and begged for mercy. Thinking of Liam's face leering down on him, waiting for him to break, stiffened the muscles in Karl's back, helping him to hold his head farther away from the eyeball-skewering bush and maintain the necessary stillness.

"Someone?" the second voice called back. "Or something?"

There was no answer to this, and after a few seconds it asked again, "Did you actually see anyone? Or did you just scare the crap out of some squirrel and risk drawing attention to our location with unnecessary gunfire?"

The speaker was clearly annoyed and apparently had some authority over the shooter, because they responded defensively, "That was definitely bigger than a squirrel!"

A couple of other voices joined in half-hearted agreement, but it didn't appear to impress the angry voice.

"Keep your eyes open, don't shoot at what you can't see, and get a move on," the voice snapped.

After a moment, the sounds of packing up and leaving resumed, and Karl did his best to control his breathing and calm his heart rate by sheer willpower.

***

Karl wasn't sure how long he lay on the forest floor, breathing in the smell of fallen needles and rich earth, his heart still throbbing in his ears. It was enough time for the long scrape across his ribs from the branch he had landed on to begin to burn and the muscles in his arched back to seize. Eventually, the distant sounds of car doors slamming and vehicles driving out of the yard below died away, and he was left with the empty silence of the forest all around him, but he still couldn't bring himself to move. A squirrel chattering in the tree directly above him finally snapped Karl out of his frozen state, and he managed to get his hands planted on either side of his shoulders and tried pushing himself clear of the bush.

It felt like doing a declining pushup after planking for about a decade. The muscles in his arms shook and his back spasmed as he raised himself just far enough to avoid eye damage before collapsing to one side, his leg twisting free of the log as he flopped onto his back, breathing hard. Karl realized that he could not feel his right foot. For one panicked second he imagined it might somehow have been torn off, but raising himself on his elbows, he confirmed that it was definitely still attached, just entirely without feeling.

Lying back, he pulled his knee up to his chest, his foot flopping loosely at the ankle, and tried rubbing it gingerly. It felt extremely odd to hold his own foot, feel the flesh and bone with his hands, and yet receive no sensation from the foot itself. It didn't seem to be broken, just...dead. He rolled up into a sitting position, and the scrape across his ribs burned harder. Setting his numb foot carefully on the ground, he lifted his t-shirt and inspected the red stripe across his ribcage where the branch had gouged his skin. It wasn't deep enough to bleed, but it still hurt like the dickens.

Peering between branches and tree trunks, Karl was fairly certain there was no one left at the site, but it still took several minutes before he could pull himself to his feet, and even then, his foot remained too numb to walk properly. He began to pick his way back the way he had come, taking short, cautious steps to keep balanced on his wobbly foot. A stab of pain shot abruptly through his right foot and up his leg, making him stumble. He hadn't stepped on a spike, although it felt as if he had. The numb foot was merely reacting to finally receiving oxygen again. He took another step, and this time there were several stabs.

"Just pins and needles," he muttered to himself, trying to believe that the screaming nerve endings would be fine in a minute. It was longer than a minute. The climb had turned from awkward to excruciating. Eventually, he remembered his compass and pulled it out to try and get his bearings. In his current mental state, Karl wasn't one hundred percent certain which direction he actually needed to go in, but he was headed away from the mill, and it was uphill, after all. He continued to stumble along, trying unsuccessfully to ignore the stabbing pains that shot through his right foot at every step.

He came up over a hill of earth and hit the gravel road unexpectedly, briefly panicked when he didn't see the car, then spotted it a hundred metres up the road. Considering the state he was in, he was surprised that he had come back so close to the route he had gone out on. He limped up the road to where the little orange beater waited, unlocked the door with unsteady hands, and slid carefully into the driver's seat, even though he felt more like collapsing. He struggled out of his backpack and placed it on the seat beside him, then took several slow, deep breaths before starting the engine.

21

Karl drove until after 3:00 a.m. When he found himself drifting onto the shoulder, nodding, he pulled over at a rest stop, leaned the little car's driver seat as far back as it would go, and passed out right there. It couldn't have been more than a couple of hours later when the early sun woke him, and he hit a drive-through for coffee and a breakfast sandwich before finishing his trip south.

His truck was parked badly on the street beside the agency. Karl frowned to himself and executed a carefully precise parallel park in front of it, planning to comment when he saw Kelsey. He did a quick circuit of the truck to make sure there were no new dents or scratches, but it seemed to be fine, just poorly parked. Karl took a deep breath and headed indoors.

He walked into the front office to find a pile of black garbage bags and clothes on wire hangers heaped over Kelsey's desk. He raised his eyebrows and went to check out the kitchen. Other than a couple of boxes sitting on the counter, there was no sign of Kelsey there either. Shrugging, he made himself a cup of coffee and walked over to his office, flipping on the light as he entered.

Kelsey groaned, rolled over on his couch, and pulled a comforter over her head. Ah, there she was. Karl considered going away and letting her sleep, but he had work to do. Ignoring the lump on the couch, he sat down at his desk and warmed up his computer.

He was uploading the pictures from his camera when the comforter was abruptly thrown back and Kelsey sat up with a galvanic heave. She wore baggy sweats and fuzzy wool socks. There was an elastic holding the tangled mess of hair more or less on top of her head. She slouched against the cushions and glared at him through flattened bangs.

"Morning," remarked Karl laconically.

"Is that coffee?" asked Kelsey.

Karl held out the mug that was only just cool enough to drink.

Kelsey took a long draught and shuddered. "I don't know how you can drink this stuff black," she remarked before taking another sip.

"Big night?" asked Karl.

"Alysa and I are officially friends off," she announced, grimacing but continuing to drink the dark brew.

"Oh yeah? Why's that?" Karl turned back to the computer and began attaching photos to the email he was writing to Fullerton.

"Because she's making an idiot of herself chasing a man who doesn't care about her and is just using her," spat Kelsey.

"Did you tell her that?" asked Karl, glancing up from the screen.

"Maybe," said Kelsey, glaring more fiercely than ever.

"Possibly not the best approach," Karl suggested mildly.

"Real friends tell each other the truth," she protested. "Even when it hurts! Furthermore," she continued, gesturing dangerously with Karl's mug. "Real friends do not dump friends for men." She spat the last word out vehemently.

"Right," said Karl, carefully rereading his email before hitting *send*.

"What are you doing back at the office?" Kelsey asked. "Did you find anything? Or just give up?"

Karl ignored her tone and answered calmly. "I think I did, you know. I followed your map, and I found the sawmill building. Weird sort of a layout for a drugs operation, but it sure is secluded enough. And someone's doing something there. Something they don't want anyone looking into. Enough to shoot possible trespassers, anyway."

When she didn't respond, he glanced up to find her listening with wide-eyed interest, which she quickly covered with a renewal of her formal scowl. Apparently, the progress he had made on the case wasn't enough to let him off for the crime of being a man. At least not yet. The corner of Karl's mouth quirked up, but he returned his attention to his screen and offered no further details.

After a minute or two of silence, Kelsey hmphed and heaved herself up off the sofa, wandering out of the office, still carrying Karl's coffee cup and trailing her comforter. When Karl saw her padding toward the door to the stairs, he called, "Are you planning to go out like that?" in a carefully neutral voice.

Casting a withering look over her shoulder, Kelsey said, "No. I'm just checking on something." He heard her thumping, not down, but up the stairs, and returned to the report he was typing with a shrug. Five minutes later, she was back.

"Did you know that the shower upstairs works?" Kelsey demanded, rooting through a gym bag on the floor, pulling out various toiletries as she squatted beside her desk.

"Really?" Karl looked up, surprised. "That could come in handy."

"No kidding," she replied. "That space would actually make a decent little apartment, with the right furniture."

Karl hoped she wouldn't get any ideas as Kelsey headed back out the door, her arms full of brushes, shampoo, and a hairdryer. Karl remembered noticing that the bathroom had a shower when he first looked around the space, but he seemed to remember that there was a large birdcage stuffed in it, which led him to assume it wasn't functional. Trust Kelsey not to assume anything.

Karl's phone rang, and he checked it automatically, then let it go to voicemail when he saw his sister's number. Her texts followed almost immediately.

Karl, did you seriously make Kelsey work on Canada Day?

Karl frowned at this message. He had been up Island on Canada Day. It hadn't occurred to him to mention the holiday to Kelsey, but he was sure she would have taken the day off if she'd wanted to.

Even if you don't care about spending time with your family any more, it's very selfish of you to keep her from visiting.

Light slowly dawned for Karl. The annual family barbeque had been a Canada Day tradition for as long as he could remember. He had managed to avoid going for the last few years of his marriage by booking holidays that just happened to overlap the date, and he had completely forgotten about it this year. Apparently, Kelsey hadn't forgotten but also hadn't wanted to go any more than he did. He couldn't really blame her for using work as an excuse, but he wished she had given him a heads-up about it.

Karl thought for a moment then sent his reply. *Sorry, not trying to be selfish, just trying to run a business.*

He knew that Matilda would forgive her brothers anything if they told her they were sorry, and she was very responsible when it came to business matters, so he wasn't too worried. His mother might be another matter, but there wasn't much he could do about her. She wasn't likely to approve whatever he did.

An hour later, the normal, put-together Kelsey walked through the office door and plunked down at her desk. Other than venting the occasional deep sigh, she made no further reference to her housing situation and even went so far as to bring Karl a replacement cup of coffee, depositing it on his desk and departing without comment. Karl thought about mentioning her choice of excuses to get out of family gatherings, but Fullerton called just as Karl opened his mouth. Karl could tell he was excited just by the way he said hello, but he was considerate enough to feign some concern for Karl's safety, at least.

"They actually shot at you?" was his first question, and then, "Are you sure you're alright? I've been shot at before. It's not a fun experience, and I definitely didn't intend to put you in that kind of situation."

"Yeah, I was far enough away and hiding behind a tree. I don't think I was in real danger," Karl responded. "I could hear them shouting at each other. I think they concluded that they had just heard an animal, which is good news for us. Anyway, I'm fine, but they definitely don't want anyone coming to visit, and I think that you're on to something."

"Fantastic," Fullerton replied. "I want to get over there as soon as possible, see it all for myself, check your findings, but you've done an amazing job so far. I'm particularly impressed with your system for determining their next drop point. That should endear us to the police when we hand it over to them."

"That was all Kelsey," Karl insisted. "She's been invaluable in this case. I'm definitely farther ahead than I would have been without her backing me up here at the office."

"Is that the lovely young lady I spoke to on the phone a few days ago?" asked Fullerton. "Kelsey Larsson, she said her name is, right? Your wife?"

Karl almost choked on his coffee at this question, and it took him a second to get out, "No, my cousin, actually."

"Really?" Fullerton was briefly curious. "Quite the family affair you've turned that agency into."

Karl thought that was a bit of an overstatement for hiring one cousin, but he didn't bother to dispute it. "So, what did you think of the pictures? Anything useful there, do you think?"

"That's a seine," said Fullerton, and Karl assumed he must be looking at the picture that showed the silhouette of a boat outlined against the reflected light on the surface of the water. "A lot of them are out of work right now because of the new catch limits imposed by Environment Canada and some have had to sell their boats for whatever they could get for them. It might not even be the registered owner running it, but it's a place for us to start. That's the kind of research I can get my office working on. They're used to it.

"In the meantime, I want to watch a drop for myself, get a feel for it so I can write it up properly when the time comes, and then I want to see this distribution centre or whatever it is that you've found. This sounds very interesting to me. If they are mixing, assembling, or repackaging the drugs, there it will mean a much bigger story than even I had anticipated."

Listening to Fullerton's excitement, Karl sincerely hoped that the whole thing wasn't a massive mare's nest after all. It didn't seem likely, but he couldn't help worrying about it just a little.

"Well, Kelsey says the next drop will be tomorrow. Can you make it over by midafternoon?"

"Absolutely," Fullerton said firmly. "I'll fly into Campbell River, rent a car, and drive up Island from there; it'll be the quickest way. We can keep in touch and either connect just before we go to stake the place out, or if there isn't time, we can meet up the next morning and compare notes."

The man had the eagerness of a bloodhound on the trail, and Karl found it infectious. By the time he hung up, he was more pumped for the following night's stakeout than he had been for anything in weeks.

"Wait a minute." Kelsey was standing in the door of his office, hands on hips, frowning at him. "When you said earlier that they would shoot at trespassers, did you literally mean someone shot at you?" Karl wondered if the accusation in her voice was for him, or his would-be shooter.

"Yeah, someone shot at me."

"Karl!" She took two steps forward and collapsed into the chair opposite, staring at him in horrified disbelief. "They actually shot at you?"

She appeared torn between incredulity and outrage, and Karl smiled inside, although he kept his face carefully neutral. "Yup."

"I'll kill them." She was looking distractedly around the office now, as if searching for either someone to exact her revenge upon or else a weapon to use for the job. "Those bastards! How dare they?"

"Whoa. Kels. Chill," interjected Karl, mildly alarmed at her vehemence. "I'm fine. They missed me by a mile. It was like a warning shot or something."

"You mean someone fired a gun up in the air to warn you off?" she demanded, eyeing him again. "Or someone attempted to shoot you? With a gun?"

"Well, they were shooting in my general direction," Karl hedged. "They heard me moving around in the bush. One of them shouted, 'I think someone's out there.' They fired off a couple rounds in my general direction. I hit the ground. They decided they'd just heard an animal or a bird or something, and I snuck away real careful and quiet."

"No big deal," he added, trying to reassure her or to prevent her raging out, one or the other.

"No big deal. Right." Her sarcasm was palpable, and at least a portion of her anger was directed at him now, too. "I told you to be careful!" she snapped. Surging to her feet, she spun on her heel and stalked out of the office in high dudgeon.

Karl blinked, thought about it, and decided her concern was more sweet than irritating. She *had* told him to be careful, after all. And he supposed that probably didn't include getting shot at, in her mind. Her rage at whoever had tried to shoot him also managed to evaporate any lingering annoyance at her for using him as a scapegoat with the family.

22

It wasn't until late afternoon that Kelsey broached the topic Karl had been expecting.

"So, about that empty office upstairs…" She was standing in the doorway of his office, leaning against the doorframe with elaborate nonchalance.

"Mhmm?" Karl leaned back in his chair, his arms crossed but a smile tugging at the corners of his mouth despite himself.

"Well, I was thinking," she continued rapidly, staring at the carpet with her hands thrust deep in her jacket pockets. "It's just sitting there empty, I mean, you practically never go up there, so it's basically just wasted space. And if I don't have somewhere cheap to live, I might not be able to stay in Victoria." She glanced up under her bangs to see if the shot was telling. It was. Karl straightened abruptly, no longer smiling.

"But if I could just stay upstairs for a little while as I'm looking for a new place and get my feet under me, it'd be all good. I could clean the space up a bunch. And it'd be like having on-site security."

Karl's mouth twisted with appreciative irony. The girl really did know how to get her own way.

"You don't have to blackmail me, Kels," he commented dryly. "If you think you can set yourself up there comfortably, you can stay upstairs. It won't bother me. Just don't tell anyone you're living here," he added hastily as she started beaming. "I doubt the building's zoned for that."

"Thanks, cuz!" She almost skipped over to him, throwing her arms around his neck and briefly crushing his windpipe before heading out of the office.

"I might need to keep your truck for tonight," she called over to him as she settled herself back at her desk. "There's a guy on Craigslist who's offering a bed for free if I can pick it up right away..."

***

Karl's plan to leave early the following morning was foiled by Kelsey's arrival with his truck piled high with an assortment of second-hand furniture. He helped her carry the parts of a bed, mattress, a set of armchairs, and a bookcase up the stairs. He didn't know how she had managed to secure so much in a single night, but by the time he got the lamps and the nightstands unloaded, he decided he really had to get going and headed for the highway, leaving them sitting on the sidewalk for her to collect at her leisure.

He wondered if he should try to connect with Fullerton somewhere south of Campbell River before they went north to Port Alice. It wouldn't hurt to coordinate their approach to the stakeout that night, see if they could get different camera angles of the drop, for example, and he didn't like the idea of meeting openly in Port Alice, where Fullerton could too easily be spotted as an outsider. He tried Fullerton's phone a couple of times but concluded that he must be in the air or already north of Campbell River and out of range. Eventually, Karl gave up and put his cell away; it wouldn't help any for him to get pulled over for distracted driving.

The drive north from Victoria was painfully slow. There was an accident on the Malahat that slowed traffic over the mountain to a crawl, and then large stretches of construction between Nanaimo and Campbell River. Sitting on the straight, flat Inland Island Highway, Karl wondered if he would have been better off taking the old oceanfront route, but it was too late now. He would just have to do the best he could and hope Fullerton would be waiting for him when he finally made it to Port Alice.

It was much too late by the time Karl pulled off Highway 19 and headed up Highway 30, a drive that should have been six hours having taken him closer to ten. Karl still hadn't gotten an answer on Fullerton's cell as he drove through town, but he noticed a red sedan with a rental car license plate in the parking lot of the Community Centre and wondered if this was Fullerton's and if it meant he was already in position. Then he wondered if he would have noticed a car like that in a place like this six months ago. He didn't think it was likely.

Rather than driving right up to the marina, Karl parked at the local curling rink and arena, where he hoped Kelsey's car might blend in with the vehicles of hockey players putting in a late practice. It was after dark by the time he had checked the contents of his backpack and made his way on foot to the patch of trees overlooking the main dock that he had kept lookout from before. Dropping to his belly, his bag across his back, Karl carefully army-crawled over the damp mulch to a spot where he could peer over the bank with a clear view down to the docks.

Even without the camera's zoom lens, he could tell something was wrong. Karl had never seen these men move so fast. They seemed almost frantic in their haste, tossing the bundles over the side of the boat, thumping them down on the dock without concern for the noise, although they maintained the complete lack of conversation Karl had observed before. Something had spooked them, but what? Karl would have been worried that Fullerton had given the show away, if there had been any sign of him. Maybe he had snapped a picture with his flash on? But in that case, where was he now?

When the boat started, it was with a roar, and it turned in a wide swath, its curving wake splashing loudly against the side of the dock as, with a brief lurch and a stutter, the boat sped out of the bay and around the headland, disappearing out to sea. The men who remained behind were seizing bundles two at a time and carrying them staggering up the gangway to the waiting truck, the engine already running. The driver had even jumped down from his cab and joined in carrying up the last few loads before clambering back in and grinding the gears in his haste to pull away.

Karl heard the slide and slam of the van's passenger door, then the spurt of gravel as it pulled out behind the truck, lumbering away into the night. It was definitely not a good night for trying to follow them. Karl lay, frozen in place on the cool, damp earth, while his mind spun.

23

Karl spent a restless night in the motel, too keyed up when he first got back to even think about sleep. He didn't dare go stumbling around the dock and surrounding area looking for Fullerton, in case they had a lookout watching. He could blow the whole operation, and Fullerton wouldn't thank him for that. Without the relief of his boxing gear to vent his frustration, he resorted to pushups to work off the excess energy, but that only provided a partial relief. His mind still wouldn't shut down.

He tried Fullerton's cell a few more times, then checked in with Kelsey to see if she had heard from him, but she knew less than he did, and her anxiety only added to his own. He ended up whiling away most of the night watching a marathon of old *Cheers* episodes with his mind never more than half engaged in what was happening onscreen. After finally falling asleep in the early hours of the morning, he dreamed repeatedly of bodies being dumped over the sides of boats and landing with a thump on wooden docks.

It was only a little after eight when Karl woke up with a jerk and decided he couldn't wait any longer to investigate in person. After one last call to Fullerton's cell, which went straight to voicemail, he dressed hurriedly and headed out on foot to walk to the marina. It was a beautiful, crisp, clear morning. The sun was shining, and the sky was the perfect shade of eggshell blue, with only the cleanest white clouds dotting its surface here and there. Little birds hopped about on the sidewalk and trilled from nearby trees as Karl walked past, careful to keep his pace to a casual saunter despite his desire to sprint to the waterfront and begin searching frantically for Fullerton in every bush and behind every tree.

Standing at last in the parking lot, looking down at the still waters of the little cove below, Karl wondered if he had been making a fool of himself. Maybe Fullerton's service provider didn't have coverage this far north. The red car he had noticed the night before was still parked where he had seen it, but he had no real reason for thinking it was Fullerton's, other than it being a rental. Tourists did occasionally visit these pristine coastal villages for the tranquillity and beauty that now surrounded him. Karl inhaled a lungful of fresh air, feeling the tension in his shoulders ease as he made his way down the gangway to the dock. There was no sign now of the activity he had watched the night before, and no indication that anyone was keeping a lookout for investigators.

The water of the bay lapped gently against the dock, and Karl looked around once more with a clearer eye. There was a steak floating in the water. A perfectly marbled ribeye.

"What the…" said Karl, leaning down to take a closer look. Then he saw the toes.

Except, this wasn't a foot. It couldn't be. It was too long, for one thing. And there were toes at both ends. Two at one end and three at the other. And then Karl realized. It had been split down the centre, holding together by a flap of the heel. And as his stomach churned, he leaned farther out over the edge of the dock and caught sight of the rest of what had been John Fullerton.

At least he assumed it had been John Fullerton. That was the only person this could conceivably have been, in Karl's mind, or identification would not have been possible.

It floated face down in the water, although the foot he had seen first opened upward. A portion of the skull had been sheared away, and the left shoulder and arm were missing. Deep gouges spiralled down the back and left leg, removing more sections of flesh and leaving the remaining clothing ragged and torn.

Karl retched as he dropped to one knee, reaching out to seize what was left of the plaid cotton shirt and turn the body. He gagged again as the foot flopped together, then floated apart again. It was Fullerton alright, bloated, distended, but unmistakable. And there was nothing Karl or anyone else could do for him.

Karl's hands were shaking so badly that he almost dropped his cell phone in the water, pulling it out of his back pocket. He fumbled his dialling of 911, had to stop, back up, and dial again to get it to go through. The calm, polite voice on the other end of the line asking him whether he needed the police, ambulance, or fire department confused him. He started to say ambulance then remembered that an ambulance wouldn't do Fullerton any good and changed it to police. The voice didn't seem to find this indecision remarkable and put him through to a new voice that asked him what the nature of his emergency was.

"A man's dead," Karl blurted into his phone, his voice shaking along with his hand. "He's dead in the water. Someone's killed him."

He wasn't sure why he didn't specify that it was John Fullerton who was dead. Didn't know why he made it sound as if it were some stranger whose body he had stumbled across, not someone he had started to think of as a friend, or at least a colleague. It was just easier to get the words out this way. Easier to detach his mind from the sick feeling in his gut and focus on getting to the relevant details. He would deal with the full reality later. Right now, all he could handle were the essentials.

"Are you sure that he's dead?" the cool voice was asking him, and he jerked his mind back from a mental image of the man floating below him laughing his head off with Percy Meiklejohn in the back room of the bookstore. "Can you reach him safely? Do you think you could get him out of the water? If I provided you with instructions, could you administer CPR?"

The questions didn't make any sense.

"CPR wouldn't help him," Karl replied. "Part of his head's missing."

"Okay," said the voice unemotionally, and Karl could hear rapid typing on a keyboard in the background. "Can you describe the exact nature of his injuries to me?"

"Part of his head's missing, and his arm, and...just...chunks of him are gone." Karl looked around suddenly, trying to see if any of these inexplicably missing parts of John Fullerton were floating nearby, but he couldn't see anything that seemed like that. Fullerton's pale skin puckered around the gaping hollows, the remaining flesh lining them an odd shade of purple in the water.

"Where exactly are you? I'm showing the village of Port Alice here, but there aren't enough towers in the area to narrow it down more precisely than that. Where should I send the ambulance to?

"He doesn't need an ambulance," Karl repeated, choking on the words as a large wave bumped the body against the side of the dock, causing Fullerton's head to float back and forth in the water as if he were shaking it in agreement with this statement. "He's dead. They've killed him, and it's the police who will have to deal with it now."

"The police are on their way as well." The voice was still calm. "But I need to know where to send them. Where exactly are you?"

"I'm on the dock," Karl said, forcing down the bile in the back of his throat. The keyboard at the other end of the line clicked some more.

"Is that the public dock or the commercial dock?" asked the voice and then added for clarification, "The one where the professional fishing boats tie up, or the one people use to take their pleasure craft out."

For some reason, the clarification left Karl more confused. He stared around him, at the fishing boats moored on the other side of the little inlet, at the parking lot behind him where the signs said, *No swimming* and *Use at your own risk*.

"The public dock," he replied eventually. "I'm on the public dock, and he's in the water beside it."

It felt like hours before Karl heard the scream of sirens in the distance, and another age before the first responder vehicles began pulling up on the gravel patch at the head of the walkway to the dock. He tried to straighten up from where he had been crouched at the edge of the dock, and his knees locked, almost sending him headfirst into the water beside Fullerton. He managed to catch himself with a hand on the rough wooden edge of the dock and felt a shock of reality hit him in the form of a splinter running home under his middle fingernail. With a feeling of disconnection, he made it to his feet, shaking his hand in response to his now stinging finger, and turned to meet the paramedics.

24

Karl sat in a hard, plastic chair in the reception area of the RCMP detachment in Port Hardy, waiting for someone to tell him where to go and what to do. He felt like he should tell someone that Fullerton was dead — his newspaper, or his family, or someone, but he didn't know who. He pulled his phone out of his pocket and brought up Kelsey's number.

Fullerton's dead.

Her responses followed too quickly for him to respond to them individually.

What?

Are you serious?

How?

Shit

Are you okay?

What can I do?

He answered the last one first. It seemed the easiest.

Nothing. Stay there. I'll be back soon. Just look after the office.

He added the last bit to make sure she would actually stay put. The last thing he needed was her storming into the police station. And it was true. There was nothing she could do.

***

"So, you knew the victim personally?"

"Yes, I told you, he hired me for this investigation."

Karl's conversation with the uniformed sergeant was not going the way he had imagined it would. Sergeant Mulligan was a stocky blond man whose bulletproof vest looked uncomfortably tight under his uniform. He seemed to view everything Karl told him with such skepticism that Karl was beginning to feel more like a suspect than a witness.

"In your call to 911, you said a man had been killed, you didn't say anything about knowing him then."

"I was feeling a little freaked out. It really didn't occur to me."

"And you say he hired you to investigate something in Port Alice?"

"On the Island, yes. I didn't originally know we'd end up in Port Alice."

"And when was this?"

"About...six or seven weeks ago." Karl had to wrack his memory, and he wasn't sure if it hadn't been even longer than that.

"And you've been…investigating, ever since then?" The sergeant's suspicion was starting to get to Karl.

"Yes," he insisted. "Fullerton believed that a drug-smuggling operation was being run with the Island as the drop point and distribution to the mainland by ferry. I came up here to work dock jobs, trying to find evidence that this was happening, and I found it!"

"Yes. You say there have been regularly recurring late-night unloading of fishing vessels in various ports around the North Island, which you have observed."

"Yes."

"Are you aware that it is common for fishing boats to bring their catch in by night and have crews unloading at all hours throughout the fishing season?"

"Yes, I know. I've been working on those crews. That's what I'm telling you. These are different. It's a late unload, and only some people are welcome to stay for it." He knew he was wording things badly, but he didn't know how to make this guy understand.

"If they knew a boat was going to get in later than the rest, and that they wouldn't need the full crew to get it unloaded in a timely fashion, it would make sense for them to send some workers home rather than pay them more than necessary."

"It wasn't just that. They were really aggressive about it. They didn't want anyone hanging around or watching them. I'm telling you; they were bringing in drugs." Karl's eyes were burning with fatigue, his guts churned every time he thought of Fullerton floating in the ocean, and his middle finger continued to throb.

"Did you ever actually see or come into contact with any illegal substances in the course of your," again that infinitesimal pause, "investigations?"

"Physically, no." Karl didn't think this was the right time to bring up his "shopping trip" at the beginning of the investigation. "But they shot at me!"

"When did this happen?" The sergeant sat up a little straighter and made a note on the page in front of him.

"Four days ago."

"Someone shot at you in Port Alice four days ago?"

"No, I wasn't in Port Alice at the time, I was investigating their…" Karl fumbled for the right word. Was it a distribution centre? A storage facility? A hideout? That sounded too melodramatic.

"Where they go, after they unload the late boats. With the drugs. Or whatever they're carrying," he amended quickly, rather than argue the point. "It's this old sawmill site. I was poking around, trying to see if I could find out what they were doing, and someone tried to shoot me!"

"And why didn't you report this to us at the time?"

Karl stared at him, momentarily speechless. The fact that it just hadn't occurred to him to do so didn't seem like a great answer to that question now.

"Even if someone mistook you for a wild animal, that sort of near miss with a firearm should always be reported immediately. We need to keep on top of that kind of carelessness. Hunting accidents result in several deaths a year in BC, you know. You're lucky it didn't result in yours."

"It wasn't an accident that killed Fullerton," snapped Karl. "Someone murdered *him* for poking around."

"What evidence do you have to support that statement?" asked the sergeant coolly, leaning back in his chair once more.

"Did you see him?" Karl demanded.

"Yes, I did," the officer responded levelly. "He looked a lot like the last drowning victim that was accidentally hit with a boat's propeller that I saw."

Karl just gaped at him. He had no words.

It went on for hours, and by the time they had finished, Karl was surprised that they let him leave. He'd begun to suspect that they were going to arrest him on the spot. The request that he stay in touch and not leave the Island was less of a surprise, and he was pretty sure that a failure to comply would get him arrested.

25

Karl reached Victoria in the early morning, at the hour when the city looked most like a ghost town and you could imagine how a zombie apocalypse might feel. He was bone-tired, but he didn't want to risk waking and frightening his landlady after his weeks of absence, so he headed for the office. Standing in the doorway between Kelsey's domain and his own personal space, he felt the weight of the past day and a half pressing down on him, ready to crush him, but he was just too tired. He stumbled forward and collapsed onto the couch. The familiar smell of the leather polish Kelsey used on it enveloped him, and he drifted off to sleep.

The sun was shining when he opened his eyes the next morning, and it took at least three seconds for the image of Fullerton's body, bumping against the Port Alice dock, to hit him in the gut. He stumbled up off the couch and made it to the bathroom just in time to realize he didn't have anything in him to throw up anyway. He ran the water as cold as it would go and splashed handfuls over his face. It stunned him fully awake, but it reminded him of the cold sea and he abruptly switched the water off, reached for a handful of paper towels, and scrubbed himself dry.

Ignoring the growling of his stomach, he headed back to the office. If he ate now, he really would be sick. Winding up, he planted a hard right on the bag hanging in the corner. It felt as though the relief of this physical action broke a dam inside of him, and he began to pummel the bag in earnest.

He was sweating and panting, and he wasn't sure he would be able to lift his arms the next day by the time he finished, but he no longer felt like food would make him throw up either. He picked his phone up off the desk with a hand that dripped sweat from the hairs on its back. He had a couple of voicemails. He hadn't even noticed his phone buzz over the rattle of the chain and the thump of his fists on the bag. Karl frowned at his phone's call display. Matilda. What did she want? Whatever it was, it appeared she wanted it rather badly. She had called four times and left two messages. Now that he looked at their time stamps, she was probably what had woken him up in the first place.

He held his phone to his ear, listening, still frowning.

"Karl, I hope it's all just a silly mistake, but Liam insists he saw you coming out of an RCMP detachment in Port Hardy looking like a homeless person who'd just been let out of the drunk tank and that you drove away in a horrible little orange car that he would never be caught dead in, and now they're sure you've gone broke and lost the agency and are living rough, and Kelsey won't tell me anything! Karl, please call me or call Mum and confirm that this is just a mistake or a misunderstanding. Please."

The second message had a distinctly higher pitch. "Karl, you know you can turn to your own family if you need anything, right? There's no point in being proud, just call us!"

He noticed that while "they" were all convinced of his destitute state, it was Matilda who had called. Also that, despite her insistence this was all just a misunderstanding, she was also prepared to pledge the united forces of the family to rescue him, even though she personally was several thousand miles away and powerless to act. And Kelsey wouldn't tell her anything, eh? Well, good for Kelsey.

He fired her a text. *You home?*

He heard a creak overhead and the sound of padding footsteps crossing and recrossing the floor above. He threw himself into his desk chair to wait for her. A minute later, she appeared in the doorway, headphones still in her ears, hair piled on top of her head in a messy bun, wearing sweats and an old t-shirt.

She carried two steaming mugs, their handles gripped in one hand, and a plate with a fully loaded sandwich in the other. She placed the plate and the cup full of black liquid on the desk in front of him before taking the chair opposite.

"You get that out of your system, then?" she asked, jerking her head in the direction of the heavy bag and studying him over the top of her mug.

"Yeah, I guess," he replied, reaching for the sandwich. "For now, anyway. Listen, have you heard from Matilda?"

"What?" This was clearly not what she had been expecting.

"My sister, Matilda, has she been in touch?" He took a massive bite, and the sharp taste of spicy mustard caught him in the nose and made his eyes water.

"Oh. Yeah." Kelsey shrugged and relaxed minutely. "Every so often. She messages me to check up on you."

"She does what?" Karl nearly choked on the bite of sandwich.

"She messages me to ask about you," Kelsey said matter-of-factly. "She tries to be very discreet about it, but that's what she's doing."

Karl scowled at her over the desk, thought about answering, but tore off another bite of his sandwich instead.

"Don't worry," Kelsey assured him as he chewed on the thick, delicious bread. "I don't actually tell her anything. It's pretty funny really," she added with a grin.

"Funny?" Karl took another bite and continued to chew.

"Yeah, 'cause I think it's been making her really crazy." Karl was finding it hard to scowl in the face of her increasing mirth. "She started about a month after I came to work here, just after I finally told my mom where I'd gotten a job, because she wouldn't shut up about it, so I guess our moms must talk."

Karl thought it more likely that Kris had been the one to tell his mother. Abigail had always preferred her brother-in-law to his wife, and Karl thought they'd gotten closer after his father's death and Kris's divorce, but he didn't bother to correct her.

"She sends these super obvious messages. Asking how I am, if I'm sure this is the right career path for me, how I like it, if things are busy, how you're doing. Basically, she just wants to know what you actually do and if you make any money. My mom asks the same sort of questions whenever I talk to her on the phone. I guess they're all dying to know what goes on here." She was grinning as she watched him wash down his sandwich with a gulp of the strong black brew she had brought with her.

"So, what do you tell them?" Karl asked, at last feeling sufficiently human, with a full stomach, that he didn't think he sounded accusatory.

"That things are super busy, that you're working on a big case, and that I can't say anything about it because it's confidential."

Karl snorted. "A big, confidential case hey?" He shook his head, but she'd gotten a smile out of him at last.

"Yeah, which wasn't remotely true the first time I said it." Kelsey was almost chortling at her own account now. "I think you were running around serving papers for that family law firm or something, which is really not that exciting, as I have learned since. But I wanted to make her wonder. And that's basically what I've said ever since, and I can tell it's making her totally wild. Mom too. They can't stand not knowing. It's been great."

Karl chuckled. He couldn't help it. Kelsey was so pleased with herself, and he really could imagine the curiosity his family must have suffered as a result of her game. "Did they tell you that they think I'm bankrupt and homeless now, too?"

"Oh yeah, Matilda messaged me last night. Your brother Liam was driving one of his trucks up to Port Hardy and saw you. Apparently, he didn't think much of my car." She sniffed disdainfully at this lack of taste in Liam's part, and Karl had to smile again as she continued.

"Tilly was much less polite with her questions than usual; she practically came out and asked if I still had a job or if this place had gone under." She waved a hand at the office in general.

"But I just said what I always say, we're busy, big case, can't talk about it, confidential. Of course," she added meditatively, "this time it was true."

Karl felt the half smile slide off his face.

"Anyway," Kelsey hurried on. "Right after that my mom called and when I let her go straight to voicemail, my dad tried."

"Kris called?" Karl was incredulous now; he thought his mother must have stepped in to raise that level of concern.

"Yeah, I bet he was pissed when I wouldn't pick up for him either." Kelsey's satisfaction at the thought of her father's irritation was clear. "Eventually, I just turned my phone off after I heard you get in. Or I'm sure they'd have kept me up all night trying to find out what's going on."

Karl took this in, looked at Kelsey thoughtfully for a moment, then drank the last of his coffee in one gulp. The few hours of sleep he had managed the night before and the workout on an empty stomach were starting to catch up with him now that he had eaten. He didn't think the coffee would be enough to keep him awake, and he desperately needed a shower.

"I guess I better tell her everything's fine, or we'll have Liam banging down the door next..." Karl pulled out his phone, found his sister's number and selected the "message" option. He didn't have the energy for a real conversation.

Everything's fine.

He sat staring stupidly at the phone. Everything was definitely not fine, but he wasn't about to explain that to Matilda. Or, via her, to the rest of his family. He tried to think.

I was driving Kelsey's car because...

What reason could he give for driving Kelsey's car instead of his own vehicle that they would accept without question?

…because she needed to pick up a new couch, so I lent her my truck.

I think she's a little insulted at Liam for saying it was ugly, lol.

He added the last bit for good measure to prove how ridiculous their concerns were. He watched the message send and hoped it would reach her in time to prevent a family invasion of the agency. He definitely wasn't up to facing any of them right now.

"Can you hold the fort here today?" he asked, rubbing his hands over his face.

"Yup, no problem," Kelsey replied, pushing herself to her feet and beginning to collect his dishes.

"Thanks for the sandwich," he mumbled, looking around for his bag.

"Mhmm." She acknowledged this as a matter of course as she headed back to her own desk and to work.

Karl managed to make it back to his basement without falling asleep at the wheel, but that was all that could be said for his driving that morning.

26

When he returned to the officc late the following afternoon, Kelsey was waiting for him.

"Two background check requests came in yesterday afternoon. I took care of them."

"That's great," Karl replied. "Thanks for looking after everything around here," he added.

"No problem. Also, I set up an appointment for you with a reporter called Alex Dyson. Apparently, he worked with John Fullerton. He's coming over on the first ferry tomorrow. I told the assistant person who called to set it up that you could be here at eight, is that alright?"

"Yeah, I can do that." Karl hesitated. "Did she say what he wanted?"

"Only that he wanted to discuss the investigation you'd been working on for John. The assistant obviously didn't know much, so I just made the appointment and left it at that."

"Okay, thanks."

He wasn't sure how much he should say to a stranger about John's death or the circumstances surrounding it. He didn't yet have it all straight in his own mind, and he was sure the police wouldn't want more shared than necessary. On the other hand, maybe a coworker could fill him in on some of the background details he'd missed the chance to get from Fullerton.

***

When he arrived at the office the next morning before eight o'clock, he was surprised to find Kelsey sitting at her desk, sipping a steaming latte and reading the news online.

"You're here early," he commented.

"I want to see what this hot-shot reporter is like," she replied, still squinting at her computer screen. "Apparently, he's a total protégé, graduated university really young and way ahead of the curve in his career. The assistant who made the appointment made him sound so great, I thought it'd be worth getting up to see."

She sounded nonchalant, but Karl suspected a more serious interest than she was letting on.

"Apparently, you don't want to see him well enough to put your glasses on," he commented sardonically.

"Shut up," Kelsey rejoined, still not bothering to look at him. "Go to your office and shut your door. I'll show him in when he gets here."

Chuckling under his breath and shaking his head, Karl did as she ordered once he had made himself a cup of coffee and sat down to check his emails while he waited.

After a few minutes, he heard voices in the outer office but stayed where he was, as instructed. Kelsey knocked at the door more quickly than he'd anticipated and opened it without waiting for his response.

"Ms. Dyson to see you," she said briskly and stepped aside.

Ms. Dyson? Karl's eyebrows rose in surprise.

A petite blonde with deep blue eyes and curly hair pulled back in a ponytail stood in the doorway. She wore jeans and a t-shirt with hiking boots, and she gave off an aura of serious competence. As Karl rose from behind his desk, her eyes widened slightly and her eyebrows rose a fraction. Her shoulders drew back, and she pushed a wisp of blonde hair behind her ear before stepping forward and holding out her hand.

"Mr. Larsson?" She sounded bemused. "For some reason, I thought John's contact on the Island was an…older man."

"You're probably thinking of my grandfather." Karl's smile was brief, his handshake quick and firm. "He founded the agency, and he worked with John in the past. I only took it over recently, and this was the first investigation I've worked on with John. Have a seat. Would you like a coffee? Water?"

"I'd kill for a coffee right now. The stuff they serve on the ferry is disgusting." She smiled as she took a seat, setting her satchel on the ground beside her chair.

"Cream, sugar?" he asked, preparing to make a trip to the kitchen.

She shook her head. "Black's fine, thanks."

He could feel her eyes on his back as he strode across the outer office, and he took more care than usual not to spill any on his way back to her. Returning to his chair, Karl felt more secure with the bulk of the desk between them and was able to say with genuine sympathy how sorry he was about Fullerton's death. Her mouth tightened and her eyes brightened in a distinctly unnerving way, but she held herself together, sipping her coffee before replying.

"Look," she said after a tense pause, during which Karl held his breath and prayed she wouldn't burst into tears on him. "I realize as well as you do that John must have screwed up somehow to get himself killed like that."

This thought had not occurred to Karl before, but he maintained a politely sympathetic exterior while considering the merits of the suggestion. It seemed probable, now that she put it to him.

"But the thing is," she continued, "he wasn't a stupid man. And he wasn't careless. He's worked in some of the toughest areas of the world. In active war zones. Gone into places where the press wasn't even legally allowed to be. It's not like he didn't understand the risks."

She was speaking rapidly, staring fixedly at a water stain on the surface of Karl's desk the entire time, struggling to explain something that was clearly very important to her but difficult to articulate.

"He was obsessed. The whole drugs racket was like a mania for him. He couldn't keep perspective on it. He wouldn't have gotten caught snooping if it had been any other type of story." She finally looked at Karl directly, her eyes insisting that he needed to believe her.

"What was so significant about the drug trade that it would make him feel that way?" Karl asked. "There are other topics just as serious. War. Human trafficking."

"For sure, and he would have agreed with that, technically." She nodded rapidly, the curls in her ponytail bouncing. "But drugs were a personal issue for John."

She must have realized how that sounded, because her mouth twisted in annoyance at her own inability to explain.

"His son died of an overdose," she stated baldly, watching Karl as she said it. "It was years ago now, but it really messed John up. Ricky was only nineteen. And he was a good kid. No one saw it coming. It was just one of those things. He and a couple of friends smoked a joint that was laced with something that shouldn't have been there. Ricky died, and one of the other kids ended up with permanent brain damage. It was awful."

For the first time, Alex looked like she really might cry, but she blinked hard and continued.

"John was a single dad. His wife was killed in a car accident when Ricky was thirteen. He'd given up traveling the world, chasing all the crazy stories, to stay home and raise his son. And then, just like that, Ricky was gone too." She waved a hand in illustration, staring into her coffee as she reflected on the past.

"John wasn't the type to let his feelings out. Face them. Deal with them. He just threw himself into the work, kept busy, and kept it all bottled up. But every time there was a drug-related case, he'd go a little crazy. Get obsessive. Start taking too many risks. Pushing the bounds of legality. The *Post* literally shipped him overseas to work as foreign correspondent after the last time, because it was that or fire him, and he was too good to fire. I mean, the man had a nose for news. And god, could he write."

Karl let her talk, watching her face, finally getting the picture of Fullerton that he had wanted and never had the opportunity to form for himself. He noticed that her right eyetooth was slightly crooked, and she twined and twisted her fingers around each other when she was fighting her emotions. He thought that Fullerton must have meant a lot to her and wondered what their relationship had been. Just colleagues, or something more?

"I just want you to understand," Alex continued, "where John was coming from. He was great at what he did, and if he says there's a story here, then there probably is."

"I would have thought his death sort of proved that," Karl replied at last. "Although the police don't seem to agree."

"Maybe." Alex sounded unconvinced. "But don't be surprised if it turns out that they took anything you told them a lot more seriously than you realize. The RCMP don't like to show their hand on an investigation. Not to civilians. Not if they can help it."

Karl found this possibility more comforting than he would have expected. At least it made him feel less like a fool meddling where he didn't belong and more like a bona fide detective again. Alex wanted to hammer out the details of the situation and decide what to do next right away, but Karl needed time to think. He still wasn't sure how much he was prepared to commit to, so he said that he had previous commitments for the rest of the day. Alex said she could find a hotel for the night and promised to return bright and early. They could make plans then.

She was clearly determined to see the investigation go ahead, and she had the paper's backing to make it happen.

***

Karl sat in the near dark office hours later, reading John Fullerton's archived articles on the paper's website. He had been shutting out the lights, ready to head out at the end of the night, when the idea occurred to him. He needed to understand the man, get inside his head. Alex would be back in the morning to discuss next steps, and Karl really wasn't sure yet what he thought those steps should be. Her description of an obsessive grieving parent who took unwise risks in order to prove a point worried Karl. Fullerton had gotten himself killed. He could accept that. But could he accept following in the man's footsteps? Taking the same risks, with so little reward for his efforts, even if he did succeed?

The soft glow from the streetlights gave shapes but no details to the furniture around him. The only thing clearly visible was the screen, its eerie glow bathing him in a circle of pale light. Scrolling back past the articles Fullerton had written during his time overseas, Karl found a series from a year and a half earlier on the drug trade in satellite cities around Vancouver, Burnaby, Richmond, Surrey, and Port Coquitlam. Fullerton didn't come across as crazy in his news pieces, however obsessed he might have been. He was clearly passionate, but factual too. And Alex was right, the man could write.

The accounts of individual families torn apart by the addiction of a single member, juxtaposed against the statistics of school age children trying, using, or addicted to these substances was powerful, and Karl could feel his own anger growing against the people who made them available, or worse, pushed them on to kids too young to recognize the risks. Kids like Ricky. He knew from experience just how easily an adult could find whatever they were willing to pay for, but that was a different matter. What Fullerton described was intentional targeting of schools and playgrounds. Hook 'em while they're young, he said.

And Fullerton had said that Odin's Tears was worse. More addictive. More deadly. Thinking of Gabe Ross's family, he could no longer sympathize with the man's decision to participate in something that was destroying other people's lives, just so he could give his children what he hoped would be a better life. It was like sacrificing babies on the altar of some ancient god to ensure a good crop for the rest of the village. The end did not justify these means.

Whatever Fullerton might have done to get found out; he didn't deserve to die like he had either. Alone, in the cold salt sea. His body mangled without thought or care. Or had it been? Karl suddenly wondered if hitting the corpse with the boat had been intentional, in the hope of producing just the sort of damage he had seen and of covering any evidence of the murder, leading to the exact situation the police had outlined to him. He could feel his shoulders tense, and he knew that this case wasn't over for him. He couldn't leave Fullerton's final investigation unfinished, whatever it cost him to continue.

27

Karl sat behind his desk, his right ankle resting on his left knee, leaning back in his chair and facing the two women across from him. The united front they represented was a little disconcerting, but he reminded himself that he was boss here and ploughed ahead with his recital of the plan formulated in his mind the night before.

"I haven't stayed more than a few nights in any one town all summer, so I don't think the fact that I came down here for a couple of days will be noticed, unless they've got someone keeping lookout in every little village and hamlet, which I doubt. Even finding John's body doesn't necessarily make me suspicious; someone was bound to, and unless they have someone in the RCMP on their payroll, they won't know that I knew him."

"Do you think they do?" Kelsey's eyes were wide at the thought.

"No," said Alex flatly. "Even if a member wanted to be dirty, the RCMP is so procedure-oriented and has so many checks and balances in place that getting information out of them is like getting a charity donation out of my Great-Uncle Charlie. I'm not saying it's never happened, but I've never seen it. And believe me, I've tried. Everything is either public information and scrupulously open and above-board, or it is extremely unavailable. They might know that Karl had been there for questioning, if they were watching the detachment, but that's it. And like you say…"

She nodded to Karl now. "You found the body, so of course you'd have to answer questions. It's only natural."

"Exactly," Karl agreed. "I really don't think they see me as a threat. They're used to my face, and a lot of them know me well enough to say hello, at least. As far as they know, I'm a drifter, out of work and short on cash, just trying to make a few bucks to get by. As long as there are fish to haul, I'm covered."

"I've described myself as a photography student working on a nature portfolio before now when I wanted to slide under the radar," said Alex. "It's always worked, and it gives me a good excuse to poke around and take a lot of pictures, so long as it looks like I'm pointing my camera in the direction of something natural. If I happen to catch someone behaving badly in the shot, well, too bad for them."

Kelsey grinned. Karl could tell how much she admired Alex, and he wasn't sure he liked it. He felt happier when her grin faded and she turned a worried gaze in his direction.

"What if they do get suspicious, though?" she asked, and she didn't try to hide her anxiety. "I mean, if they had no problem with killing John, how much more likely are they to go after you, if they find out about you? I mean, he just showed up. He could have been nobody as far as they knew, but you've been around all this time. They would have to realize that you know a lot and could cause a lot more trouble for them. What if they kill you too?"

Her voice was suddenly younger and more vulnerable than Karl was used to, and he was abruptly reminded that she was not yet twenty and her future was wrapped up in the agency as much as his own right now.

"The fact that I've been around this long is why I don't think that'll happen," he assured her. "These guys have talked to me, they've accepted my account of myself, they think they know me. I really think there's very little chance that I'll get spotted as an outsider at this point, otherwise I wouldn't be taking the risk."

He told himself it was true. This was a calculated decision, not a casual gamble. He told himself it would all be fine.

"What if they figure out you're a detective, though?" Kelsey insisted. "What if they look you up? It would be smart of them, especially if they were going to let you join their crew."

"If they look me up, they'll find out I'm exactly what I say I am, an out-of-work roughneck. There's not much else for them to find."

"Um, hello, what about this agency?" she demanded, wide-eyed.

"My first name's not on anything to do with the agency, not on the website or anything like that, and they don't know how I spell my last name. Larsson with two S's isn't that common in these parts. I really don't think they're likely to make the connection."

Alex nodded her agreement, but that didn't help his own personal assurance much.

"He's right," she told Kelsey. "Besides, disappearing now would make them much more likely to suspect him than continuing in the role he's established already. And I'll be nearby, keeping a discreet eye on the situation in case he does get into any trouble. Even out there, there are RCMP in all the bigger towns. I can always call them in if anything gets out of hand."

Trying not to think about the possibility that he had waited too long to call in the RCMP when he should have, Karl forced himself to focus on the logistics of coordinating the investigation.

"The question now is, will they continue the schedule they've been following, which Kelsey worked out so nicely?" He shot her a grin and was rewarded with a straightening of her shoulders at this recognition of her success. "Or are we back to step one?"

"I don't think it's really step one," Kelsey interjected. "If they used a recognizable pattern before, they probably will again. Get two or more drop dates and locations, and I think we could work it out. People aren't nearly as original as they think they are."

"Okay. Good," said Karl. "Personally, I think my best bet is to go back to working my way from town to town, trying the different docks in turn, keep to the pattern I was following before, and hope I come across the right crew before too long."

"I'd like to check out the date and time that would have been next on your schedule," Alex said to Kelsey. "Just in case. I agree it's a long shot." She addressed Karl now. "But I don't want to miss the obvious just because it is obvious."

"Sure, fine," said Karl, thinking that it couldn't hurt for them to tackle the thing from two different angles. They could only be in two places on any given night regardless; let her pick her spot, and he would pick his. In the end, their odds were the same.

They began discussing the information that Karl had collected to date, and the sort of evidence they would need to bring to the police in order to convince them of the validity of their case. By the time they were reviewing the camera and survival gear that each of them would be taking along when they headed up Island, it was lunch time and Kelsey was dispatched to Subway for sandwiches and cookies, or in Alex's case a wrap.

"I think we should bring Kelsey in on this," Alex said offhandedly as she checked the contents of her backpack.

"What do you mean?" asked Karl, still focused on the map he was poring over. "She *is* in on it. She knows everything that goes on around here. She'll be available for any support we need, if that's what you're thinking."

"No, I was thinking we should get her out in the field with us." Alex glanced up at him. "If two of us staking out possible drop points doubles our chances of catching them, then three would triple them."

She clearly thought that this was an obvious point and one he should have realized for himself.

"No," Karl replied flatly, looking her directly in the eye. "No way does Kelsey come out there with us."

"Are you serious?" Alex straightened in her chair, leaving the backpack at her feet, and crossed her arms, facing him squarely.

"Yeah, I am," he replied. "It's too dangerous. I was shot at. Fullerton is dead. Kelsey is not coming with us. Period."

"Don't you think she should have a say in the matter?" Her voice rose in disapproval.

"No, I don't. She's nineteen. She's inexperienced and impetuous. Also, she's my family, and it's my business, so it's my call. I am not putting her in that kind of risk."

"I think you're being unreasonable," Alex said hotly. "Kelsey's not…"

"You weren't there," Karl interrupted her. "I am not about to pull her mangled body out of the water like I did with Fullerton. Not happening. Drop it, or we're both off the case and good luck finding anything on your own."

Karl knew he sounded mean, but he was too disturbed by the possibility to leave room for argument. The mental picture that had flashed across his mind at the question chilled him. Alex's nostrils flared, and her lips thinned, but she recognized an immovable object when she saw one and bent over her pack without further comment.

Karl was in the kitchen making himself a fresh coffee when Kelsey returned with their sandwiches. He was on his way back to the office when he heard Alex comment, "Quite the protective big brother you've got."

Kelsey's confusion was natural. "I don't have a brother… Oh, you mean Karl. He's my cousin."

Alex snorted. "Huh, none of my cousins ever bothered about my well-being like that."

"What do you mean?" Kelsey began, but Karl pushed the door open abruptly, cutting that conversation off before it could go any further. He did not feel like discussing the risks of field work with Kelsey. He knew exactly what she would think of his mollycoddling her, if she heard about it.

Alex's eyes followed him as he crossed to his seat, and the irritation she had shown at his earlier obstinacy seemed to have evaporated.

28

For the sake of continuity, Karl loaded up Kelsey's little Tercel when he headed back north the following morning. He knew Alex would be going the same direction, kitted out in her nature photographer get-up and ready to play her part in the hunt, but he didn't wait for her before hitting the highway. It wasn't as if they were going to drive in a convoy, and their ultimate destinations were different, even if the route was the same most of the way.

What he really needed was to get back into the crew. Get talking to the guys he already knew. Make the right connections that would get him included in the operation itself. That was the only way Karl could see of getting definitive proof of their activities and Fullerton's murder. And he needed to get it soon. The fishing season was almost finished, and with it his cover would be gone. His plan was to start in Kelsey Bay and work his way in a systematic arc around the north island communities he had worked before, spending only one night in each place in the hope that, even if they had changed their schedule, as he expected, the smugglers would at least still spend a day or two in each town before bringing in their illegal cargo, as they had before.

With Alex checking the locations that would have been next on Kelsey's original schedule, it was possible their paths might cross, but they had agreed not to recognize each other if that happened. Karl, the established local transient, and Alex, the new nature photographer in town, had nothing in common and couldn't interact safely in public. Any contact, except for emergencies, would be funnelled through Kelsey.

He started with Kelsey Bay, since a switch to the east coast of the Island seemed possible after the crew's run-in with Fullerton. It was a picturesque village, with no hotel near the bay but a little place with camping, cabins, and rooms to rent a few kilometres away in the Sayward Valley. The problem from Karl's perspective was the three-man RCMP detachment in the village, less than a minute from the dock and much more active than the other locations he had observed operations at before. He wasn't surprised, therefore, when he didn't recognize the late shift on the docks that night, although he was disappointed when he was turned away without work for the first time that summer. The work was drying up more quickly than he had hoped, and the local fishermen seemed to prefer hiring teens from the village rather than bringing in a stranger now that they didn't need the extra manpower as badly.

He made his way north, trying Telegraph Cove again the following day and briefly poking around Beaver Cove before moving on to Port McNeill. At least he had no trouble getting work there. He had just fallen asleep at the end of the night's shift when his phone began to buzz on the hotel nightstand. He reached for it, expecting to see Kelsey's number, but it was Alex's name, and he felt a jolt of panic at the possibility that something had gone wrong. His "hello" was sharp as a result.

"They were here!" Alex's voice sounded positively gleeful in her triumph. "Right on schedule, exactly when and where Kelsey predicted. It went down exactly the way you described it.

You may be right about keeping that girl in the office; she's a genius at predictive modeling. I'd like to see what she could do with sports stats."

Karl frowned in the darkness. They hadn't changed their schedule at all? Just showed up at the next scheduled drop point as if nothing had happened? It didn't make any sense to him. Had killing Fullerton not concerned them in the least? He didn't like it and it made his reply harsher than he intended.

"Why are you calling me directly? Why didn't you run this through Kelsey like we discussed?"

It sounded like an accusation the way he said it, and Alex responded, clearly stung. "I just thought you would want to know as soon as possible. No point in dawdling around on the east coast of the Island now that you know they'll be in Tahsis in three days."

This made Karl even more irritated, as if she were rubbing in the fact that her hunch had paid off while his had been entirely wrong.

"Right, I'll be there then. In the meantime, don't call me directly unless there's a real emergency. Kelsey could have told me where to go in the morning."

He hung up before she could answer, then lay in the dark feeling like a jackass. What was his problem? Yeah, she'd scared him, but he was glad, really, that nothing was wrong. And as it turned out, playing both hunches had paid off, and they were much farther ahead on the case then he would have been on his own. So why did he react so poorly? Was it just because she was the first attractive female to come into his orbit since his divorce?

He didn't know, and he didn't like thinking about it, but that didn't make it go away. He lay awake for a long time, thinking about Alex and kicking himself for being an idiot.

***

Karl arrived in Tahsis the day before Alex had indicated. He wanted to be in place in advance of the drop. He was also hoping to connect with Gabe Ross again, if possible. So far, he was Karl's best connection to the operation, and Karl wanted to cultivate that link while he had the chance. So, when Karl saw Gabe's Ford in front of the Westview Marina, he congratulated himself on his foresight. He might not have guessed right about their schedule, but he did know their behaviour patterns.

Gabe was nowhere in sight when Karl entered the bar, but that didn't bother him. He wanted to let Gabe come to him, rather than give the impression that he was seeking the other man out. Taking a seat at the bar with open stools on either side to give Gabe room to join him if he liked, Karl ordered a stout and idly watched the Lions game that was playing on TV. He preferred the NFL to CFL; the extra down made the game move faster, but it was something to do while he waited. His patience was rewarded when Gabe emerged from the bathroom a few minutes later and joined him at the bar.

They exchanged nods, and Gabe ordered his usual as he sat down. Neither man spoke until Gabe had a beer in hand and had taken his first drink, then he glanced over at Karl.

"You working on the dock tonight?" he asked.

"Hoping to," Karl replied, hunching his shoulders and grimacing slightly at his drink. "Last couple towns, I tried didn't have enough to go around, and I came up empty-handed."

It was only partially true, but he was going for an impression here.

"If it doesn't look like there's enough work to go around here, I might try Port Hardy next. They're a bit bigger, might have better luck there." Karl projected dejection, with a hint of desperation, and Gabe took the bait.

"I have a bit of a side gig I might be able to get you in on," he said after checking that the bartender was busy at the other end of the bar.

"Yeah?" Karl let himself perk up, show the sort of enthusiasm that was natural for this news.

"It's a little different, though. You'll be dodging more than just the CRA for this cash."

"Hey, there is no bad money in my books right now," Karl replied, putting real angst into his voice.

"Even if it's a little shady?" Gabe asked, giving Karl his sidewise look. Karl paused long enough to seem like he had to think about this. That it was a serious consideration he was making up his mind about.

"If the money was right, I think I'd commit murder right about now," he finally ground out.

"Right." Gabe didn't seem to find this answer too over-the-top. "Let me make a phone call, see what I can do."

He slid off the bar stool and through the crowd, his beer left standing on the bar next to Karl's. Karl glanced casually over his shoulder to see Gabe pushing through the bar door to the parking lot, his phone already out, dialling. Passing Gabe on her way into the bar was Alex. Karl cursed under his breath and turned his back on her. Praying that she wouldn't spot him and decide to say hi, he focussed his gaze on his beer and his attention on sending out stay-away vibes. Whether Alex felt his vibes or not, she didn't approach and after several long moments Karl risked another glance over his shoulder. She was sitting at one of the tiny tables over by a window, placidly surveying the place without any sign of recognizing him.

Karl breathed a little easier and returned his attention to waiting, mentally crossing his fingers that he might get in where it counted. He had intentionally tried to give an impression of weakness over his weeks under cover. Not physical weakness, but a lack of moral courage, a lack of basic guts. Physically strong, a bit gutless, not a criminal but desperate enough to be open to crime as an option. That was what he had tried for. Now to find out if he had succeeded.

"Okay." Gabe was back, sliding onto the stool beside him without looking his way. "I talked to the boss. You're in. Meet us Thursday at the Ucluelet dock, not the one in the harbour, the dock by the Eagle's Nest Pub. You know the one I mean?"

"Yeah," Karl replied, his eyes on his beer. "I've worked there before."

He managed to refrain from blurting out, *What about tomorrow night?* in time, since officially he didn't know anything about the next night's shipment.

"Good, be there for five."

Gabe drained the last of his beer and slid off the stool and through the crowd, out the door without anyone else noticing him go. Karl gave him a couple minutes head start, then loped out after him without looking in Alex's direction.

29

Karl understood, now, why Alex had called him directly before. He was dying to tell her the news, to celebrate his success, but he couldn't very well break his own rule after he'd been so bad-tempered about it before. On the other hand, he couldn't bring himself to run it all through Kelsey, leaving the interpretation up to her. In the end, he settled for a group text. It was bending the rules, but he would apologize to Alex when he got the chance.

I'm in.

I've got an invite to join the late crew Thursday night in Ucluelet.

Kelsey reacted first.

Excellent!

Then she rethought the matter.

Or is it?

Is that safe?

Will you be doing illegal stuff?

Like, go to prison if the police find out, illegal stuff?

It's amazing news, Alex interjected. *We need to make plans. Kelsey, give me a call.*

She had said it was amazing news, and she was following his rules, but Karl was still annoyed that they would be making plans without him. He was the one going out on a limb here. It was a quarter of an hour before he got a private message from Alex.

Can you meet me in Campbell River?

Do you think that would be safe?

I'd like to have a face to face before you go further undercover.

Karl appreciated the reminder that he was "undercover." It felt less nefarious than joining a drug-running operation otherwise would. Although he doubted the police would see the distinction if they found him in a compromising situation. The mental picture of landing in prison with the same crew he had infiltrated flashed through his mind, and it wasn't pretty.

Okay, he texted back.

Tomorrow? she replied.

Yeah. Meet me at the Riptide. 8:00.

Karl realized that he sounded like a domineering male, but once the message was sent, he couldn't think of any way to soften it.

Will do, came back a few seconds later, and he shrugged. If she wasn't upset, it was probably for the best.

***

She was sitting at a table in the corner when he arrived. She looked much more elegant than she had in the Tahsis pub, wearing a long, flowing skirt, her hair curling softly over her shoulders. Karl would have been more comfortable sitting at the bar, but he wanted to make amends for the way he'd behaved the past few days, so he joined her with a smile.

"Hey," she said.

"Hey," he replied. He was about to launch into the apology speech he'd been planning on the road down Island, but she spoke first.

"I hope it's alright. I ordered us a round of Macallan 18. It was John's favourite, and he kind of got me hooked on it. It seemed appropriate."

Karl wasn't sure about appropriate, but it was hard to argue with a good Scotch. Besides, he was still determined to make his apology.

"Look," he began. "I'm sorry about the way I've been…"

"Don't worry about it," she interrupted before he could get the first sentence out. "John was the same way when he got deep into a big story. It gets to you, this lone wolf stuff. I'm used to it."

Karl gaped momentarily, then closed his mouth with a snap and nodded briskly. "Alright then," he replied. "What do you have in mind for our plan of attack?"

Letting her take the lead on this planning session seemed like a better apology than words would have been anyway.

Before she could answer, a waiter arrived with their drinks, the golden liquid swirling around cold black stones rather than ice cubes.

Alex took her glass and raised it to Karl. "To John."

Karl returned the toast, and they drank. The whiskey went down smooth and warm and burned in his gut. She was right; it was good. When she gestured for the waiter to pour another round, he didn't argue, not even when she told him to leave the bottle.

"You know," said Alex, leaning her elbows on the table and turning her glass between her hands. "John taught me everything I know about this business."

Karl sipped his whiskey, letting her talk.

"I was this bright-eyed intern, fresh out of university. He must have seen something in me." She shrugged. "He took me under his wing, showed me the ropes, introduced me to all his contacts, took me along when he did interviews, taught me how to write them up."

She looked up, her face stiff, her eyes bright. "You know, to this day I have never handed in a piece to my editor without having John read it first."

She thought about that for a moment then finished her drink in one sip.

The evening's conversation did not go the way Karl had intended. He wanted to establish a plan of attack for his undercover mission, but somehow they never got off the topic of John Fullerton and what he was like as a journalist and as a man. At one point, Alex was laughing so hard, there were tears running down her face.

"After that, whenever John would get going on a case, like really get going, someone would say, 'Look out, he's gonna go full Johnny!'"

Karl laughed too. He couldn't help it. Even though they made him wish more than ever that he'd gotten the chance to know Fullerton properly, he liked hearing these stories about the man. They felt like validation of his decision to stick to the case.

It was after 2:00 a.m. when Karl walked Alex back to her motel. He wondered for a moment if she would invite him in. They had connected more this evening than at any time on the job so far, but she just said, "Have a good night. I'll see you in the morning."

He nodded and turned to walk away as she closed the door. He wasn't sure if he was disappointed or relieved.

***

When he reached Alex's motel the next morning, Kelsey was there.

"Check it out." She was overloud in her excitement, and Karl winced, feeling the aftereffects of the late night and the whiskey. Fullerton might have loved the stuff, but Karl wasn't sure it agreed with him. He didn't even want to know what time Kelsey must have left Victoria to get to Campbell River this early.

"What?" he asked unenthusiastically.

"We've got a wire for you to wear!" Kelsey was painfully excited, almost bouncing on the edge of Alex's bed, where she sat, an assortment of electronics spread out on the coverlet around her.

"A wire!" she exclaimed. "Like in the movies!"

Alex came out of the bathroom as Kelsey said it, towelling her hair dry after a shower. The wire idea didn't seem to be news to her.

"I don't know," Karl objected. "Aren't hidden recording devices illegal for anyone other than the police?"

"Technically they are for the police as well, if they don't have a court order to use one," Kelsey agreed. "Unless one of the parties involved, i.e. you, consent to the recording."

"Wait, what?" Karl was definitely confused now. "I can consent to my recording with an illegal device?"

"If you're a legitimate party to the conversation, then it's not illegal," insisted Kelsey. "You can't go around planting bugs and listening in on other people's conversations. But if someone tells you something directly, says something to you, then you can record that. You can choose to consent to the recording of any conversation that you are personally, directly involved in."

"It's really not that complicated," she insisted when Karl continued to look skeptical. "If someone tells you something, then you can do whatever you want with that information, including recording it. Trust me! I read all the relevant acts and a bunch of precedent cases; I know what I'm talking about!"

"Really? You read the act and all of that?" It was Alex's turn to look surprised.

"You have no idea how boring it can get around the office when I'm running things alone," Kelsey informed her. "I mean, if there are jobs coming in to keep me busy it's alright, but I can't handle more than two slow days in a row. If I didn't give myself research assignments, I'd lose my mind.

"Besides," she added with an impish grin, "I gotta make sure my boss," she jerked her head in Karl's direction, "knows the law. If I don't watch him, he does things like go out and buy a whole whack of drugs on the weekend for 'research purposes.'" She made air quotations with her fingers.

Alex laughed heartily at this idea. Karl forced a laugh of his own but shot Kelsey a warning glance. She responded with a brief lift of one eyebrow before tossing her head and continuing.

"All joking aside, we agree Karl can definitely wear a wire if he's recording conversations he is a part of, and we will let you review anything interesting that he gets for your story, *but* anything incriminating will be handed over to the police."

"Absolutely," Alex agreed. "I want them caught and the drugs stopped as much as I want the story. All evidence goes to the police. Just not to any other journalists, right?"

Kelsey nodded in emphatic agreement, but Karl wondered if it was true that Alex cared as much about keeping drugs off the street as about getting her scoop. Fullerton had, he was sure of that; journalism was a means to an end for him, but Alex... Karl wasn't so sure about her. He wondered if there was a Canadian version of the Pulitzer.

30

Karl and Alex took separate routes north again while Kelsey returned to Victoria and the agency to wait for Thursday. Karl showed up at the Ucluelet dock Wednesday night, following his established routine of getting into position early. Gabe and a few of the other late-shifters were there, but other than exchanging a nod of greeting at the beginning of the night, Karl had minimal contact with them. The big foreman, Roy, wasn't there at all, and Gabe didn't show at the pub that night.

Karl didn't expect to hear from either of the girls until after the night's work, so he was surprised to see Kelsey's number on the call display when his phone rang the following morning.

"Kels, what's up?" he asked.

"They're not likely to find out about the agency, hey?" Her voice sounded slightly hysterical. "They won't figure out how we spell our last name, hey?"

"What do you mean?" Karl demanded, adrenaline suddenly coursing through his veins. "What happened?"

"Oh, nothing much." Her laugh was definitely hysterical. "Just some huge goon," she spat the word at him, like it was a curse. "Waiting in the office when I came down this morning."

"What?" Karl's stomach twisted into a hard, painful knot. She was supposed to be safe. He had left her behind where she would be safe. "Are you okay? What happened?"

"Oh, I'm fine," she replied breathlessly. "He was just standing there, reading the names on the licenses on the wall."

Karl's stomach, which had relaxed slightly at the news that she was fine, cramped again. His license was on that wall. With his name on it.

"I took down your and Mordecai's licenses and locked them away when you first said you were going undercover, just in case," she continued, and Karl mentally blessed her foresight. "But when I walked in he just looked up, all casual, and said, *Hey, is Karl around?*"

"I seriously thought I might have a heart attack. I just blurted out, *Who are you and how did you get in here?* I was so mad at myself for leaving my pepper spray upstairs in my other purse. But he just played dumb and was like, *The door was open*, which it wasn't. I definitely locked up last night, no way I would forget that. And then said *I'm just looking for Karl*, but by that time I was pretty sure we had never worked with him before, and I said *Karl who?* Like I had no idea what he was talking about and thought he was crazy. And he said, *Karl Larsson. Isn't this his place?* And I was like, *No! This is my place!* And pointed at my license and the business license that were still hanging there on the wall. And he looked back at them, as if he didn't already know exactly what they said, and said, *Oh, my mistake*, and just left! Like there was nothing weird about it at all."

She had told this story in such a rush that Karl couldn't have gotten a word in edgewise even if his pounding heart would let him speak, but she had to stop for breath now, and Karl managed to say, "Whoa. Good thinking. Thanks."

"Yeah, fine." She was slightly calmer now that her story was out. "But you gotta get out of there, Karl. You and Alex. They've made you. You aren't safe."

Karl thought about this for a minute. "No. No. I don't think that's true," he said at last. "They were checking. Making sure. But your response was good. In fact, it was perfect."

"You can't go through with this now," she exclaimed. "You just can't. What if that guy didn't believe me? What if they do something to you? What if they torture the truth out of you?" The hysteria was back and rising fast.

"They won't. Kels, think about it." He was more confident the more he thought about it. "If I don't show up, just hours after one of them was there... By the way, what did the guy look like?"

Her breath puffed out, and she drew in another one, steadying herself. "Big guy. Really big. At least as tall as you, maybe taller, and broader. Dark hair. I dunno. I was too freaked out to pay attention to details. I was mostly looking everywhere but at him."

"Roy," said Karl. "That would be Roy. It makes sense," he added. "He wasn't there last night when we were unloading. But think about it. If I disappear right after Roy talks to you, they'll know there's a connection. But if I still show up on schedule after he's talked to you, then it'll confirm there's no link between us. That I have nothing to do with Larsson Investigations. Really. This is a good thing."

She snorted loudly at this, but he thought she was coming around. At least her breathing wasn't coming in gasps anymore.

"I'll be fine," he insisted. "But I don't want you taking any chances. I want you to install deadbolts on the street door, one at the top and one at the bottom, heavy ones. And I want you to run three-inch screws into the frame at twelve-inch intervals all around the casing, because most doors are easier to kick down than their locks are to break…"

"So I'll be safe in my Fort Knox and you'll be hanging out in the lion's den?" She was back to being sarcastic. Karl thought she would be fine, mentally at least.

"I mean it, Kels. I don't like the idea of Roy being able to just walk in like that."

"Oh, I'll do it. I just don't think it's fair that I have to be so careful, but you can take all these risks."

Considering this attitude, Karl was thankful that the idea of her joining them in the field had never been suggested to her.

***

Against Karl's better judgement, he agreed to meet Alex in Ucluelet before the rest of the crew arrived that night. She insisted it was important they connect in advance, instead of going in separately like he and Fullerton had done, under the circumstances. If she was going to back him up effectively, she said, they needed to coordinate their movements. Kelsey had seconded this opinion so forcefully that Karl felt unfairly outnumbered. He suspected Kelsey's nerves were getting the better of her.

Karl wasn't in the best mood when he left his hotel that afternoon. The tape used to attach the wire was tugging at his chest hair, and it was very uncomfortable. He twitched his shoulders irritably against his seat as he drove to the rendezvous, subconsciously trying to ease the itch that was developing under the binding. He was fairly certain an evening sweating his way up and down the docks wasn't going to help this any, and he wouldn't be able to take off any extra layers for fear the wire would show through. He didn't know what he was supposed to do if anyone asked to check him for wires. He was surprised Kelsey hadn't thought of this.

Alex was waiting for him in the parking lot overlooking the dock, where they had agreed to meet. Karl didn't expect anyone from the crew to be around for another hour at least, but he still glanced around nervously as he pulled into the lot. It wasn't a very open spot, and he didn't really think they were likely to be spotted, but it made him nervous nonetheless.

Karl pulled Kelsey's car up alongside her and rolled the window down without getting out.

"I'm supposed to meet Gabe down there," he said tersely, gesturing to the lot below. "It's earlier than we usually get here, so he might take me from there to wherever they meet up. The late crew typically arrive together, in the van. We'll have to come back here to unload the boats, but you might have a bit of a wait."

"Right. I'll cover you from up there." Alex pointed up the brush-covered incline beside the parking lot to where tall trees towered, blurred against the late afternoon sky. She reached behind the seat of her Jeep and pulled out a long black case, clearly heavier than its plastic cover made it appear from the way she hefted it, with a solid lock on either side of the handle. Moving with a brisk efficiency that was mesmerizing, she unlocked the case, pulling out a rifle with the word *Remington* stamped into the stock, pulled the bolt back, checked the chamber, then fitted a serious-looking scope onto it, as if she did this every day.

"Cover me? With a gun? Are you joking?" Karl looked askance at the rifle she now slung over her shoulder as she rooted in her glove compartment, coming up with a box of cartridges. The box read *7mm - 08 Remington*, and she slipped it into her pocket without checking its contents.

"Only in case of real trouble. Believe me, I do not want a firearms violation on my hands, never mind murder. But I don't intend to let you end up like John either. Officially, I was never here, but if someone does pull a weapon on you, just make sure you aren't between him and that hill. Besides," she added. "I can see what's going on a lot better through the scope."

Pocketing the box and zipping her coat up under her chin, she pulled a dark toque down over her light hair and started climbing the gravel incline of a short side road, her boots sending a small hail of pebbles down behind her with each step before turning off to scramble through the underbrush.

Karl was more afraid of Alex shooting him than of any drug boss right that minute, but he didn't have time to argue — he needed to get into position.

31

Karl parked on the gravel shoulder across from the head of the dock. Locking the car, he leaned casually on the hood, his hands jammed in his pockets, trying to look relaxed and inconspicuous. He almost wished he smoked, just to have something to do with his hands. He didn't have long to wait. A white van that he recognized but pretended not to pulled up a few minutes later, but there was no flat deck truck behind it.

Only Gabe and Roy climbed out of the van, crossing the gravel to where he waited.

"What happened to the truck?" Was Gabe's only greeting.

"Couldn't make the payments." Karl's voice sounded tenser than he'd intended, but he didn't think it hurt to be nervous. Gabe just nodded and jerked his head for Karl to get back in the car.

"Um, where are we going?" Karl asked, his heart rate increasing at this unexpected turn of events. He had told Alex that they might leave, but it hadn't occurred to him that he might be expected to drive.

"You'll see," Gabe replied, climbing into the back seat when Karl popped the car's door locks. Roy slid in beside Karl and held out a hand.

"Phone," was all he said.

Desperately hoping there wouldn't be any tell-tale texts on it, Karl unlocked his phone and handed it over. Roy didn't seem interested in the phone's contents, however; he just punched an address into the maps app and handed it back to Karl. Looking at the address, Karl realized that they would be leaving the main town site, but not the Ucluelet peninsula. Maybe they would meet the rest of the crew there. He popped the car into gear and turned in the direction indicated.

They ended up near the tip of the outcrop, in a dead end with only a couple of private drives branching off it. It was a nice neighbourhood. The homeowners had probably paid a hefty premium for their own private piece of paradise. Roy pointed to one of the drives disappearing between evergreen shrubs and tall cedar trunks. Karl turned in.

The house at the end of the short lane was lovely. Classic west coast architecture, weathered just enough to look like it belonged to the landscape and with a gorgeous view of the tidelands and the channel beyond. Was this a crew member's home? A second hideout? Karl parked facing the house and put on the emergency brake, then turned to Roy, waiting for an explanation. Roy smiled thinly at him.

"The homeowner's away for the week," he told Karl coolly. "And both the neighbours work. There's no fancy burglar alarm. All you gotta do is get in, find all the jewellery in the house, and bring it and the fancy vase on the mantle back here."

Again that thin smile. "And we have a pretty good idea what jewellery is in there, so make sure you get it all."

Karl stared at him then glanced back at Gabe. Both of them were calm, serious, and unsmiling now. Karl didn't know what to say. He couldn't exactly argue that he hadn't signed up for this. After all, he had never been told what he was signing up for. He certainly couldn't ask about drugs, when officially he had no idea there were any. He could feel his heartbeat throbbing in his throat, but somehow the blood didn't seem to be getting to his brain, which remained unhelpfully blank.

After a couple of very long seconds, the fact that he didn't have many options penetrated the pounding. It wasn't likely he would be allowed to say, *I've changed my mind*, and trying to escape these two looked like the quickest way to end up in that wickedly sparkling ocean. He took a deep breath and looked back at the house.

"Right," he said and opened the car door. Roy pulled out a phone of his own, propped it on the dashboard, and flicked on the camera app. Karl got out of the car.

It's just a test, he told himself. *They want me to prove myself, then they'll trust me for real. Just get through this and I'm in*, he thought. But he had thought he was in before, and now he was here, standing in a stranger's driveway, about to break into their house. Which he was pretty sure was a felony. Karl did not want to go to prison.

Forcing his shaking legs forward, Karl approached the house and tried the front door. It was locked, of course, and he schooled himself not to look back at the pair waiting in the little orange car. Instead, he began to make his way around the house, systematically checking each window and door that he came to, hoping for a miracle. He didn't get one. By the time he got back to the front door, he knew what he had to do, because picking locks didn't happen to be a skill he possessed.

Wrapping a sleeve of the sweater he wore around his hand, he picked up the nearest large rock bordering the drive, studied the front of the house briefly, then approached the tall, narrow sidelight that flanked the front door. Firmly, and without haste or unnecessary violence, Karl broke the window, knocking away any glass shards left clinging to the frame with the rock before slipping through the gap. His work boots crunched on the scattered glass as he stepped carefully across the foyer, his ears straining for any sound, but the house was silent. He wasn't surprised. Roy and Gabe wouldn't have come with him if they hadn't been sure of their information.

Karl glanced through arched doorways into kitchen, dining, and living areas, and spotted the vase on the mantle. It was lidded, and he was suddenly, sickeningly certain that it contained ashes. It was too much like the urn in Percy's back room for him to mistake it for anything else. Karl turned away from the living room. There was a door that he thought must lead to the garage, but he doubted anyone would keep their jewellery in their garage or the mudroom, so he turned toward the stairs leading to the second floor.

Brushing the shards of glass off his boots on the bottom step, he made his way upward, careful not to touch anything. Reaching the landing, he carefully balanced the rock he still carried on the banister, wrapped his sleeves more firmly around both hands, and began testing doors. Two of the bedrooms were clearly intended for guests, the pillows and mattresses stripped bare, comforters folded at the foot. Their closet doors stood open, and their shelves were stacked in one case with Christmas decorations, in the other with yarn. Karl reclosed each door, glanced into the open bathroom, then pushed open the final door.

The master bedroom felt entirely different than the two spares. It was warm, cozy, and lived in. The bed had been made, but imperfectly. The bottom edge of the quilt hung a little crookedly over the foot. A tall dresser was topped with an old fashioned jewellery box, while its lower, wider counterpart held a further assortment of rings, bracelets, brooches, and necklaces in china dishes among the brushes, makeup, and hair products, all reflected in the large mirror that hung above it. The room smelled like old lady perfume and talcum powder, and Karl was reminded forcefully of his grandmother. He had liked his mother's mother.

Karl realized he didn't have anything to carry the jewellery in, but he didn't want to take more from this home than he could help. He lifted the jewellery box down, squeezing it hard between wrapped hands to avoid dropping it, and emptied each tiny drawer out onto the bed. Pulling the hem of his sweater out in front of him and holding it like a hammock, he began scooping everything that looked valuable off the top of the low dresser, adding the pile from the bed last. It was enough to make his sweater sag and stretch. If even half of it was as expensive as it looked, the collection was worth more than the agency made in a year.

Karl looked around the room one more time and checked inside the closet, which was full of the sort of clothes that his grandmother had worn, and dropped awkwardly to one knee to check under the bed. He was pretty sure he had it all. All except the urn, that is. Leaving the empty jewellery box lying on the bed, he made his way downstairs. Entering the living room, he noticed the pictures sitting at either end of the mantle, flanking the urn. One was a black-and-white wedding photo, at least fifty years old. The other was more recent. A smiling, white-haired couple held hands and stared back at him.

Karl felt sick. Taking a firmer grip on his sweater with his left hand, he wrapped his right arm around the urn, hugging it to his shoulder as if it was a baby, and turned to leave, trying to ignore the faces in the picture. It was a lot harder to slide through the broken sidelight with the load he carried, and his sweater snagged on a small glass shard he had missed before. For a gut-twisting second, Karl thought he was going to lose his grip on the urn, but his sweater tore free and he hurried across to the Tercel, his heart pounding again.

Roy leaned across and pushed the car door open for him, then took the phone he had propped on the dash and slipped it into his pocket. As Karl slid awkwardly in behind the steering wheel, Roy watched him with something that might have been disgust.

"You couldn't grab a pillow case?" he asked. Karl looked at him, anger suddenly vying with the fear in his gut.

"You really need some old guy's ashes?" he shot back. Gabe snorted from the backseat. Karl twisted in his seat.

"Can you take this, please?" he demanded, and Gabe accepted the urn with twitching lips. Karl noticed that he didn't seem worried about leaving fingerprints. They weren't planning to return these ashes.

"So what do you want me to do with these?" he asked Roy, who was looking mildly amused now as well.

"Back to the van," he told Karl, and seemed to find Karl's driving one-handed, while holding on to his sweater with the other, even more amusing, although not as much as Gabe. Karl just hoped Gabe wouldn't spill old man ashes in the backseat of Kelsey's car with all his laughing. He didn't think Kelsey would appreciate it, somehow.

When they got back to the parking lot facing the dock, Roy said "wait here" and went to the van, returning with a small duffle bag that he placed on the passenger seat next to Karl. Karl awkwardly poured the contents of his sweater into the bag. Gabe was still laughing at him from the backseat, especially when he had to unhook a couple of mismatched earrings and a brooch that had gotten snagged from his sweater. Karl shot him a dirty look, but that just made him laugh harder.

"I tell you what," he told Karl with a final chortle. "You can keep the ashes safe."

Karl accepted the urn without comment while Roy zipped the bag closed and slid the seat forward to let Gabe out of the back.

"You coming?" Gabe glanced back at Karl, one hand on the passenger door, about to slam it shut. With a deep breath, Karl stepped out of the car, knocking his door shut with an elbow and only locking it once he had tucked the urn carefully in the crook of his left arm. He followed Roy across to the van, and after a quick survey of the available options, wedged the urn firmly in a door pocket. Gabe strolled up behind him, still chuckling under his breath.

"Come on." He slapped affectionately Karl on the shoulder. "I need a drink, and I bet you could use one too." Turning to Roy, he added, "We'll see you at the usual time?"

Roy nodded, and Gabe turned to lead the way back to the Tercel. Karl realized that his mouth was unusually dry and decided a drink might be a good idea. Neither he nor Gabe spoke until they were sitting at a booth near the back of the half empty bar, a beer in front of each of them.

Gabe grinned across at Karl and raised his beer in a salute. "Nicely handled."

Karl snorted. "Did everyone in that late group have to do that?" He thought this was a safe question, since he had previously asked about staying late and been rebuffed. They must realize that he knew something more was coming, since Gabe had referred to returning at the usual time.

"Or something similar," Gabe admitted. "You can't be too careful in this sort of business."

"Which is?" Karl asked.

"You'll see," was all Gabe would tell him, and Karl decided it was better not to push. At least he seemed to be truly "in" at last.

32

When they returned to the dock at the usual time, Roy had already arrived with the rest of the late crew. Karl climbed out of the car after Gabe and sauntered over to the men congregated around the van. A few of them glanced his way, but no one commented. They must have known somebody new would be joining them. Karl worried that he might be overdoing the casual act but reminded himself that anyone would have nerves under the circumstances. And he definitely didn't need to fake these nerves. Not after all the shocks of this day.

Other men Karl had worked alongside before but who were not included in the late shift arrived one by one over the next half hour. By the time the first trawler pulled up, Roy had started turning away men looking for work. Karl stood on the edge of the group, his hands hanging loosely at his side, ready for action but trying to remain calm and conserve his energy for the night ahead. When the first tub of fish came over the side, Karl was there to catch a handle. Gabe grabbed the other, and they balanced the tub easily between them as they headed up the walkway, work boots thumping on wooden planks.

Gabe stuck to Karl's side for the rest of the evening, and Karl was glad to have the company. The smaller man worked tirelessly, but he was unhurried and steady about it, providing some stability for Karl's nerves. When the rest of the workers were paid off and sent home, Gabe was one of the few remaining who didn't immediately light a smoke. Which meant he was also one of the few who didn't flick their cigarette butts into the water when the low chug of a boat's engine reached them an hour later.

The sound was a relief to Karl, who was feeling antsy again. Waiting in the dark, with only the lapping of water against the dock to break the stillness, reminded him of finding Fullerton, and he did not want to think about that now. When the boat chugged into view, he breathed a sigh of relief and straightened, more than ready to get on with the job.

The bundles that were passed over the side this time were almost as large as the fish bins, but they were lighter, wrapped in plastic tarping and tied with rope to keep them secure and protected from the water. Rather than carrying a bundle slung between them, Gabe grabbed the ropes of one and heaved it single-handed out of the way and off to the far edge of the dock. The next bundle came over the side, and Karl followed suit. Before long there was a steady circling chain of men moving the bundles with surprising speed and ease.

Karl wondered why they kept so many on their crew when less than half the men could have unloaded this shipment in under an hour. As it was, they had the boat emptied and on its way in little more than twenty minutes. Then began the more tedious task of carrying the individual bundles up the gangway to the waiting truck. Once or twice Karl caught himself glancing in the direction of Alex's lookout. He was relieved to note that there was nothing on the dark hillside to indicate they had a watcher.

Once all the bundles had been stacked on the truck's flat deck, a tarp was thrown over them and the whole load was secured with ratchet straps. Gabe again jerked his head for Karl to follow, and they piled into the back of the van, along with the others. There were no seats other than the driver's in the van. The men crouched haphazardly together, a hand pressed against a window, the roof, or the floor to steady themselves. Karl supposed they wouldn't all fit into the usual number of seats in a van this size.

The van pulled out after the truck, and Karl forced himself not to check whether Alex was preparing to follow. He didn't see any lights behind them as they pulled out onto the highway, but he thought that was rather a good thing. His legs began to cramp early in the trip, and he would have preferred to sit on the floor of the van, but no one else was. By the time they turned off the highway and bumped their way over the gravel track several kilometres into the forest, he wasn't sure he would be able to straighten his legs to get out of the van.

When the van stopped, Karl looked around hopefully, but forest still surrounded the van, with no end of the narrow track in sight. Roy threw the van into park without turning the vehicle off, and Gabe jumped out, disappearing into the trees. Karl glanced around, but no one else seemed at all interested in this procedure. It was almost five minutes before Gabe returned. Roy glanced at him as he pulled himself up into the van.

"All good?" he asked.

"Yup," Gabe replied.

"Both?" asked Roy.

"Yeah," Gabe replied. Roy jerked a nod, put the van in drive, and continued up the rough track without further comment. They arrived at the sawmill less than a minute later.

Karl's legs cramped as he stepped out of the van, and he paused to stretch them, but he seemed to be the only one who felt this need.

Without any hesitation or conversation, the crew began to unstrap the load from the back of the truck. The big foreman pulled out a bunch of keys and unlocked the heavy padlock on the large sliding door, pushing it open with a groan of wood rubbing against metal. He disappeared inside, and a minute later Karl heard the hum of a generator, and the interior of the building lit up. No one spoke until the last bundle had been carried inside and the big door closed with another groan.

"Okay, everyone." Gabe stood in the middle of the room facing the rest of the crew. "As I'm sure you've noticed, we have a new man on board, replacing Williams. Hopefully he'll prove a little less jumpy."

A few of the men snorted at this, like it was a joke, but most were stone-faced and silent.

"This is Karl. He'll be helping us bring in and repackage shipments, and he'll step in to make deliveries to the mainland whenever we need him to. Any questions?"

A couple of them shook their heads. Roy said, "You're the boss," and the rest nodded their acceptance.

"Then let's get to work," said Gabe. Everyone except Karl began to move. Karl stood frozen in place, staring at Gabe.

"You're the boss?" He couldn't help the incredulity. It just slipped out. The little man grinned at him. He seemed to be waiting for Karl to get the joke. Karl forced a smile in return, but it was the last thing he felt like doing.

"Can't blame me for not wanting to advertise the fact, can you?" Gabe asked, still grinning. "Come on, I'll show you how things work here."

Around them, men were already beginning to cut open the bundles with utility knives or pulling on white coverall suits, gloves, and face masks. It was as if a whole room full of dock workers were suddenly turning into lab techs before Karl's eyes. It was surreal. Even more so when Gabe walked over to a nondescript cabinet in the corner, punched a code into the keypad on its front, and opened the heavy swing door to display a row of rifles. Taking out a pair that looked very similar to the one Alex had covered Karl with, except that their scopes were already in place, Gabe handed them to the large foreman and another, smaller man whose name Karl didn't know. Grabbing a couple boxes of shells off the top shelf, he slapped one into each man's hand then turned to relock the cabinet as they slipped back out the sliding door into the night.

Karl stared after them then jerked his attention back when Gabe said, "Sort of inherited these when my old man died. Better taste in guns than women. Had no clue what to do with them. Just left them stashed in the basement for years. Wasn't until after I got into this business that I remembered how much he hated registration laws. Realized the benefit of having a couple untraceable backup options." Gabe winked. "Now, at least they come in handy.

"So, like I said." Gabe finished relocking the cabinet and turned to lead Karl around the large interior of the former sawmill. It contained at least a dozen wooden tables, set up with various instruments and paraphernalia that Karl couldn't identify. What remained of the mill equipment was heaped haphazardly in a back corner, rusty and abandoned. Karl followed, still feeling as though none of this could be real.

"We bring the stuff in, in bulk. We repackage it for distribution, then we deliver it to various retailers both down Island and on the mainland."

"What exactly is this stuff?" Karl asked, looking at the powder being carefully poured into the top of a pill press.

He turned toward Gabe, desperately hoping the tiny recording device strapped to his chest could pick up the other man's voice. It didn't seem to occur to Gabe that there could be any reason to hedge.

"The technical name is just a list of components and about a mile long, but it's called Odin's Tears on the street."

Karl felt a ripple of excitement mingled with fear run down his spine at this confirmation, but he needed to make it seem like this was news to him. Like he had never heard of the stuff before. "So, drugs?"

"Sure," Gabe agreed easily. Then, perhaps in response to the look on Karl's face, he added, "Hey, I'm not a bad guy, okay? I got a family, I got kids, and I've taught 'em never to touch this crap." He gestured around at the packets of dark powder now being stacked on tables for processing. "What I am is a businessman. And business is all about supply and demand. There are people demanding this stuff in a big way, and I gotta pay for things like braces and college and alimony. So if I can make my packet delivering what people are asking for anyway, then I will."

"Fair enough." Karl looked around again, taking it in, letting Gabe think he was just adjusting himself to the facts.

"But nonviolent, right? I mean, you're not hurting anyone, are you?" Karl jerked a thumb toward the cabinet in the corner, then glanced at the door the two lookouts had exited through. "I wouldn't want to actually hurt anyone." Karl made this protest half-heartedly. He didn't want to hurt anyone, but that didn't mean he couldn't if they really needed him to. He'd just need to be paid a lot more for that. That was the impression he was going for, but his real goal was a confession, if he could get one. He wanted more than just proof of drugs to take to the police. He wanted to hand them Fullerton's killer. And sooner rather than later. He didn't want to get his own hands any dirtier than they already were. The last thing he needed was to go to prison for his involvement in this mess.

"Don't worry about those guys." Gabe gestured toward the door. "The only thing they need those popguns for is scaring off a bear, or maybe a cougar. Those are the only intruders we ever get up here. We keep a lookout just to be safe, but no one's ever come snooping around this place, and no one's ever likely to. It's been empty for so long, I doubt anyone even remembers it's here."

"So, no killing," Karl repeated, looking Gabe straight in the eye.

"That sort of thing is avoided if at all possible," Gabe replied with another grin. It was too ambiguous for Karl's purposes, but there wasn't much he could do about it at the moment.

"Come on, grab a paint suit, you can package pills. It's easier than pressing them. We can teach you that another time."

They both grabbed the flimsy white suits — which Karl saw on closer inspection were the type worn by house painters to protect their clothes on the job — began to pull them on. Karl had a momentary struggle trying to decide whether to pull off his wool Stanfield, risking Gabe getting a peek at his wire, and leaving it on, which could muffle the recording. In the end he decided he was more concerned about being outed as a spy than he was about the actual spying, and he zipped the white suit up over everything he wore.

It was uncomfortably bulky and too warm, but he didn't have the luxury of worrying about that at the moment. Gabe was snapping on blue latex gloves and a disposable industrial respirator, and Karl followed suit. Gabe led him over to one of the tables and pointed at a large basin heaped full of little charcoal pills that had just been deposited there by another masked and suited figure.

"Ten pills to a little baggy." Gabe pointed to the boxes of bags waiting at the end of the table. "Ten little baggies to a big baggy. Make sure you press out all the air and that each bag is fully sealed."

He left Karl to it, moving off to check on the others' progress. With a surreal feeling, Karl began counting pills. Now that he was here, he just couldn't believe it. Couldn't believe that he was actually counting out tablets of an illegal substance that would be distributed to drug dealers and sold to…he stopped himself there. He didn't want to think about who might end up taking these innocent-looking pills. *We'll get the police involved before they reach the street*, he told himself.

33

Karl worked through the early hours of Friday morning in a fog of unreality. The air inside the sawmill was chilly and damp, and over the course of the night it became infused with a fine dust that floated around the working men, making them look like strange scientists in a movie about invading aliens or viral outbreaks. Only in this case they weren't fighting to save lives; they were preparing to destroy them.

Watching the others stuff completed packages into a variety of the temperature-controlled delivery bags with popular restaurant names on them, Karl had to forcibly suppress the guilt he felt for being a part of this. *I'm just trying to stop it all*, he told himself. *My participation isn't voluntary.* This wasn't strictly accurate, but he went with it anyway. As the hours passed, Karl began to develop a crick in his neck from bending over the table so long, counting out little pills and sealing them in little baggies. Then his lower back began to stiffen. The physical discomfort slowly drove any question of guilt from his mind. He just wanted the night to end.

By the time Roy rolled back the big front door and the early morning sun poured into the room, Karl was stiff, sore, and exhausted, mentally and physically. It had been too dark the night before to notice much about the large open lot in front of the building. Now, Karl saw the row of vehicles lined up along the edge of the gravel. He realized that they must have been wrapping up on the morning when he had come through the woods to investigate. He had caught the tail end of the night's operation. Any later, and he might have missed them altogether.

One by one, the men stripped off their masks, gloves, and suits and headed out to climb into their cars, pull them up to the front door, and pack their personal payload into the backs. By the time the big foreman had thrown a couple of hockey bags into the back of the van and driven out of the lot, the place looked surprisingly vacant again. The dust had settled, and the equipment sitting on the tables could have been abandoned for years as far as anyone could tell by looking at them.

"Come on." Gabe gestured toward the last vehicle in the lot, a pickup that had been nice a few years ago but was starting to show its age. "I'll give you a ride back to your car."

Leaving his suit in a pile with the others, Karl followed his old drinking buddy, and new boss, out of the building, waited while Gabe relocked the padlock on the front, then slid into the truck's passenger seat.

He didn't know what to say to this man who, until a few hours ago, he had thought he knew and understood. Gabe wasn't so reticent.

"Well, what do you think?" he demanded, throwing the truck into gear and manoeuvring out of the parking lot and down the rough gravel track. Karl noticed that he hadn't loaded any of the bags into his own vehicle. Apparently, he didn't play the role of mule himself.

"Very slick," Karl replied. "Very quick. Very smooth…Impressive," he added after a beat. He needed to seem impressed. He needed the man to brag.

"It's taken a little while to get that way," Gabe acknowledged self-deprecatingly. "But we've been building efficiencies, working out the kinks. Believe me, it's taken some work."

Just like any other business, Karl thought. The puff of air through his nose might have been taken for amusement, but that was the last thing he was feeling.

"You and me, we're in the same boat," Gabe continued. "We know what it's like to succeed, to really rock our life, and then to have all of the good things we've worked for yanked out from under us. We got more to prove than most of those guys. They've all been deadbeats forever. They don't really understand hustle or what it feels like to be successful. They just want to make their drinking money, and they don't care how they do it. Fair enough. They're useful to me. I'm not complaining. But you could do well in this business. I'd like to have a right-hand man I can count on to look after things if I'm ever indisposed. Show me you're worth the trouble, and that could be you."

Karl wondered if Gabe gave every new guy this speech. And what, exactly, Gabe expected him to say in return. He wondered too, if he pressed the matter, whether Gabe would admit to the visit to Kelsey, and if there had been any more to his vetting than that and the break-in. How much did Gabe know about him, really?

"What made you decide on me?" he asked with real curiosity. "Why bring me in, rather than someone else?"

"Other than the fact that you clearly needed it more than most?" Gabe looked at him sideways. "I may have done a little background research."

Karl looked over at him and jerked his eyebrows in inquiry.

"You're Eric Larsson's son, right?" It wasn't exactly a question. Gabe was sure of his facts, and Karl couldn't help the slight flinch, realizing how close they had come to finding everything there was to know about him and his business.

"How'd you know that?" he asked, trying to be cool about it, but his voice wasn't entirely level.

"Googled you." Gabe laughed. "There's not much hidden on the Internet these days."

He glanced over at Karl again, trying to gauge his reaction. Karl stared straight ahead, and Gabe returned his attention to the road and continued.

"You mentioned a brother with a trucking company around here. Only one it could be was Larsson Transports. And from there it was easy to find an obituary with both your names listed as Eric's sons. And it's not as if I haven't heard of Kris and Eric Larsson. I've been around the coast long enough. I've heard the rumours. I understand Kris keeps a lower profile these days?"

This was a rhetorical question too, technically, but Gabe sounded curious, so Karl shrugged and answered evasively. "I never got along that well with my uncle."

"Fair enough." Gabe nodded. They had reached the highway, and he looked both ways before pulling onto the tarmac, heading toward town. "Like I said before, I wouldn't want to work for family myself. But I figure if you're Eric's son, and Liam's brother, you probably know how to keep your mouth shut at least."

Karl wondered what Liam had been up to for Gabe to include him in this analysis but decided he was better off not knowing.

The truck's tires whirred on the highway, and Karl thought about what he had heard. It didn't explain the visit to the agency or how they had connected him with Eric without connecting Kelsey with Kris. Then again, neither Kelsey nor Kris liked to advertise their relationship, while Karl's mother had posted a picture of the whole family with his father's obituary. He'd had a stupid look on his face because Liam had goosed him just before the photographer snapped the shot. He'd been annoyed at his mother for choosing that particular photo at the time, then he felt guilty for the feeling when he knew he should be grieving.

Gabe glanced over at him and seemed to sense his mood, because he added in a lighter tone, "Roy even checked out some detective agency in Victoria with the same name."

Karl had been waiting for this admission and schooled himself to glance up with mild surprise on his face and nothing more.

"Some young chick, probably playing detective with Daddy's money." Gabe laughed. "You don't have a cousin named Kelsey or anything like that, do you?"

"No," Karl said with careful neutrality.

"Didn't think so," Gabe replied. "I can't see Kris Larsson backing a detective agency, can you?"

This was also rhetorical, but Karl replied anyway. "No." This was easier to affirm.

"Well…" Gabe reflected for a moment. "Not an honest one, anyway. I suppose it could be useful to have a detective in the family, if they had their priorities straight…"

He thought about it for a minute then shrugged. "Anyway, she said she's never heard of you, and if you've never heard of her, then…" He shrugged his acceptance of the implications. "Just a funny coincidence, but we have to be careful in this business."

Karl nodded, but he couldn't help wondering if that shrug was one hundred percent genuine. They rode in silence until Gabe pulled into the dock lot in Ucluelet and parked beside Kelsey's Tercel.

"Next drop is on Tuesday," he said, turning to look fully at Karl now that he didn't need to watch the road. "Meet up at the processing shed at seven, ride down to the dock together."

Karl raised his eyebrows at the description of the sawmill as a processing shed but just nodded.

Gabe continued, "I'll work out which deliveries you can take going forward. That way you get a bigger piece of the action."

Karl nodded again, reaching for the door handle.

"You understand." Gabe put a hand on Karl's arm, stopping him before he could open it. "I'm trusting you here. I brought you in because I figured you're trustworthy. Because I figured you need this as much as I do."

Karl looked back at him. The guy sounded sincere, but Karl hadn't missed the implications of his initial test or the pictures Roy had taken.

"I do," he replied. "I appreciate you giving me a chance, and I won't forget it."

He reached his right hand around and offered it to Gabe. They grasped hands briefly, then Karl opened the door, slid out of Gabe's truck, and turned to Kelsey's car. He felt his skin crawl at the thought of the enemy at his back, but he flipped the truck door shut, and Gabe pulled away, leaving Karl alone. His hands were suddenly shaking so hard that he had to grasp his right hand with his left just to get Kelsey's key into the lock to open the car. He wanted to get out of town. Now.

He considered leaving his things at the motel and heading south right then and there but thought better of it. Keeping up the appearance of normality was important for a little longer.

34

Alex was waiting for Karl, sitting on the edge of his bed, when he opened the door of his motel room.

"What are you doing here?" he hissed as he quickly pulled the door shut behind him and checked that the curtains were fully closed.

"Don't worry," she replied. "No one saw me come in."

"How did you get in?" he demanded, looking around for some sign of forced entry and fervently hoping she hadn't gone to the manager for a key. That wouldn't be a giveaway or anything.

"Jimmied the bathroom window," she replied calmly. Looking through the door into the bathroom, Karl thought that she would have to be a gymnast to get through that window but didn't comment.

She forged ahead. "So, let's see that wire. What did we get?"

"Well, they're dealing with Odin's Tears alright. Ross named the stuff himself." Karl hoped this fact would be enough to balance out his own activities earlier in the evening. "We have proof of that, at least. If the mic caught it, anyway."

He stripped off his Stanfield's sweater and began unbuttoning the flannel shirt he wore underneath.

"It's a pretty powerful little unit," Alex said. "Unless something went wrong, we should be able to hear everything you did."

Throwing the flannel shirt onto the bed, Karl went into the washroom to take off the cotton undershirt that he wore over the wire, pushing the door closed enough for privacy. Pulling the t-shirt over his head, he removed the wire with quick painful yanks, setting the whole contraption on the toilet seat while he examined the damage to his chest hairs before putting the shirt back on and exiting the bathroom.

Alex held out an eager hand for the bundle. When he passed it to her, she fiddled around with the unit, extracting something that looked like a phone's sim card and plugging that into a slot on the side of her laptop. She plugged in a set of headphones and began to listen intently. Karl sat on the other bed, relaxing back into the pillows as she skipped through his night, seeking out clear conversation points. At last, she pulled off the headphones and sat looking at him across the space between the beds.

"This is perfect," she said at last. "You couldn't have done better."

Karl allowed himself to feel the glow of pleasure her words gave him. He felt like he'd earned it after the night he had just put in. He only hoped the police would see things in the same light.

Alex continued, "All we need to do now is go up and photograph the site, and we'll be ready to go to print."

"You're kidding me, right? I told you they shot at me the last time I poked around there uninvited, didn't I?"

"Sure," she replied. "But no one will be there now. You said it yourself, they're all off making deliveries."

"Ross could have gone back," Karl insisted. "It's too risky."

"If he's there, we'll see his truck before we get too close."

It was a logical argument, but it didn't make Karl any happier. The shaky feeling in his gut might have been the result of hunger and sleep deprivation, but the hours spent in close proximity with men he knew were killers hadn't helped any.

"I need pictures for my story," she continued. "And it's not like the police are going to grant me access once you've turned this over to them. Once it's declared a crime scene, I'll have no chance."

"It's a crime scene now. Just because the police haven't cordoned it off yet doesn't make it less of one."

"And I will be very careful not to tamper with any evidence," Alex insisted. "I just want to get a feel for the place and take a few pictures, not mess anything up."

Karl just shook his head.

"Look, I'm going up there. A story without images loses half its impact," she said. "If you want to run back to Victoria without me, go ahead. I'll meet you there."

Karl wondered what she would say if he offered to go straight to the local detachment and let them catch her at their crime scene. On the other hand, he wanted to present a united front when they went to the police. He had been to the sawmill already, had even been inside and handled the drugs there. Going back now couldn't make things any worse for him, could it? And her paper was his current employer.

"Okay, fine, but we go in, you take your pictures, and we get out. And copies of everything we get go to the police."

Her mouth tightened at this last caveat, but she gave a brief nod of satisfaction at his overall capitulation.

***

They drove up in Alex's Jeep, leaving Kelsey's Tercel parked at the arena. Karl directed her through the crisscrossing back roads built over the years by various logging companies, intent on reaching their allotments and extracting their valuable timber. Since most of this area had been replanted after it was logged many years before, it was heavily wooded and the asphalt old, rough, and cracked. Alex drove much more aggressively over this surface than Karl would have done, but he clenched his jaw and refrained from commenting.

Karl's backpack was full of the survival equipment he had carried the last time. He had the detailed map and his compass ready. He wasn't about to take any chances. He was glad that he hadn't mentioned these preparations to Alex, however, when she gave his compass an amused glance as he checked it, confirming their direction relative to the road. He noticed that she had not bothered to bring anything other than her camera equipment, and he disapproved of her lack of caution. He sincerely hoped that the survival gear would not be required. He was even less interested in being lost in the wilderness with Alex than he would have been on his own.

The hike through the trees was silent, except for their footsteps falling on the thickly covered forest floor and the occasional rustle as they pushed past a branch or fern. Neither of them had forgotten their argument, and Karl still wasn't happy to be here. He was pleased to find that approaching the sawmill did not give him the sense of panic he had feared. Apparently, surviving a night inside decreased the threat of its exterior. He gestured for Alex to move behind him as they got closer and proceeded slowly, careful to avoid any fallen logs or similar pitfalls.

She had been right, of course. There was no sign of anyone around. No vehicles. Nothing at all, except a few tire treads in the gravel to indicate that anyone had been there recently. It might have been abandoned for years, except that Karl had seen it full of activity only a few hours before. He suppressed a yawn at the thought of that long night and wished he could have replaced the coffee he had grabbed before leaving the motel with a solid eight hours of sleep. He stepped out from under the cover of the trees and looked around, noticing details he hadn't seen before.

There were weeds growing through the gravel on the lot. The dark green paint was peeling away from the sides of the building in places, leaving exposed patches of reddish-brown rust. The only thing shiny and new in sight was the large padlock holding the doors shut. Karl really didn't see why Alex had wanted to make the hike for a picture of this. It didn't strike him as particularly newsworthy.

Alex walked past him, her hiking boots crunching on the gravel, pulling a pair of thin leather gloves out of a pocket as she approached the large door to the sawmill. Karl didn't catch what she planned to do, even when she dropped to one knee and studied the padlock closely. Only when she pulled a small pouch from her pocket, selected a slim bit of metal, and inserted it into the lock did it dawn on him. Karl started toward her abruptly.

"Hey!" he shouted. "What do you think you're doing?"

She glanced over her shoulder at him briefly, her ponytail swinging, then returned to her task. "What do you think?" she asked with a hint of impatience in her voice as she continued to prod inside the lock.

"This is not what we discussed," he insisted. "Picking locks definitely falls into the realm of tampering with the evidence."

"Only if you do damage or mess up any fingerprints."

"And." The padlocked popped open, and she grasped the shank between finger and thumb, twisting the whole thing off in one quick motion. "I am doing neither."

"I think any form of breaking in would count as tampering in the eyes of the police," Karl pointed out.

"Which is why we won't mention this part of it to them." Alex's jaw was tight, her eyes flashing.

She pushed against the edge of the door with the side of her palm, and it rumbled sideways. Hanging the lock back on its eyelet, she slipped through the gap into the building.

Karl couldn't believe what he had just witnessed. She had made it look so simple. He wasn't sure if his rage had more to do with the risks involved or how much he could have used this skill a few hours earlier. He told himself that she was just asking for trouble, but there wasn't much he could do about it now. He looked around the empty lot then approached the door slowly, peering inside without entering.

Alex was making her way around the large open space inside, placing each step with care, not touching anything, her hands busy with the camera hanging around her neck. She paused to get a shot of the pill presses lined up on one row of tables. It was weird, looking around the dim interior, shot through with the occasional sunbeam that had found a crack in the metal siding, but otherwise shadowy and unlit.

Karl stepped back; he had already spent more time here than he liked. The flash of Alex's camera lit up the interior several more times while Karl stood in the parking area, hands jammed into his pockets, scowling at the black hole that was the doorway. Alex emerged a few minutes later, flashing him a satisfied look before turning to close up behind herself. If his scowl bothered her at all, she didn't show it.

"All set," she said brightly and began to walk toward the part of the forest they had come through. Karl gritted his teeth and followed her. She marched briskly uphill between the trees, her arms swinging, her ponytail bouncing. Karl didn't bother trying to overtake her. His longer legs made it easy to keep pace, but he was content to follow, preferring to delay a conversation he was certain would only frustrate him further. They made it back to her car and managed to drive all the way into Port Alice in silence, Alex maintaining her air of cheerful satisfaction, Karl steeling himself for the confrontation ahead.

She pulled up next to Kelsey's little Tercel and turned to smile brightly at Karl.

"Well, I think that's it for me," she said. "I'll be heading back to the mainland and see if I can't get this story written up in time for tomorrow morning's release."

"No," Karl replied flatly.

She raised her eyebrows at him, her hands tightening on the steering wheel.

"No?"

"No," he repeated. "You're coming with me to the RCMP detachment in Port Hardy. You will corroborate my account to them, and you will be providing them with copies of everything you have collected. You will then return to the mainland and publish your story when they say you can."

Her eyes narrowed, all satisfaction gone. "That wasn't part of the deal."

"Yes. It was," Karl replied. "That is exactly the deal that I had with Fullerton, and it is the only way I am letting you use any of the data that I've collected."

The details of his arrangement with Fullerton had never been stated so explicitly, but she didn't know that.

"You collected that information while in the employment of the *National Post*," she said angrily. "It belongs to the paper."

"It belongs to me until I sign it over to the paper confirming the accuracy and validity of its contents. In writing. Signed in the presence of a notary."

The last was Fullerton's requirement if he was going to cite Karl as a source in his story, a very anonymous source, but Karl was fairly certain that she would have a hard time pushing things through if he flat-out refused to share anything at all. Even if the paper could take him to court and get access, it would take time and ruin her big scoop.

She glared at him, and Karl returned her look coolly. He always found confrontations easier once he was in the middle of them. It was the waiting he hated. It was a long minute before she replied, and he could watch the intervening thoughts playing out across her face. He waited. He had time.

"Fine," she snapped at last. "I'll come to the detachment, I'll report, we'll hand over copies. But you better hope I still make my deadline, because I have no problem withholding your fee for the maximum time period permitted."

This might have worried Karl more if he'd been waiting on the paper to pay his bills, but the agency had enough in its account to get by for the moment, so it wasn't as big a threat as she seemed to think. Karl wondered if it was a tactic she often used with her sources.

"I guess we'll see how it goes," he said, finally opening the passenger door of her Jeep and climbing out. He grabbed his backpack off the floor and said, "I'll see you in Hardy," then slammed her door and turned to unlock the Tercel. She pulled out of the parking lot more violently than necessary, but he wasn't worried about keeping up with her. Let her wait for him at the detachment. It'd be good for her to have some time to cool off.

35

Although they could have gone directly to the local RCMP detachment in Port Alice, Karl wanted to turn his evidence over to the skeptical sergeant who had interviewed him after Fullerton's death. He wasn't sure if he had been sent to Port Hardy on that occasion because it was a larger detachment and they had more resources, or simply because everyone from Port Alice had been busy on the crime scene, but he felt better walking in and asking for someone he had dealt with before, even if they hadn't been particularly encouraging.

When he pulled into the detachment parking lot, he saw Alex sitting in her vehicle, apparently working on something on the passenger seat. Taking a deep breath, Karl unfolded himself from the Tercel's driver's seat and walked over to the Jeep. She was entirely engrossed in the laptop she had set up on the passenger seat and jumped when he rapped on her window. He gestured toward the detachment, eyebrows raised, clearly asking, *Are you coming?* She rolled her window down, annoyed.

"Give me five minutes. I need to finish backing all of this up." She grimaced. "They're almost certain to take the originals."

Karl knew that she blamed him for this but couldn't believe that she thought it would be any different. Of course they had to give their findings to the police first. What did she think he was? He sighed and headed into the detachment. They would probably have to wait for the sergeant to see them anyway; she could join him when she was ready.

The civilian member manning the detachment's front desk took Karl's information and directed him to the waiting area while she tried to track down the sergeant Karl had spoken with before. As Karl sat in the stiff plastic chair, he thought about Gabe Ross and three kids who wouldn't get the braces and the dance lessons he wanted for them. Kids who wouldn't get to know their father at all as they grew up when he went to prison. Gabe's words kept ringing in his ears, *I'm trusting you…because I figure you need this as much as I do.* Betraying that trust shouldn't feel like such a big deal after the kind of vetting he'd gone through to earn it, but Karl wasn't happy.

He looked out the glass entrance door of the detachment toward where Alex was parked. She was just climbing out of her Jeep, slinging a bag over her shoulder, ready to join him. Someone pushed the door open, and the shifting glass made the light ripple across her face like water. A picture of Fullerton floating in the bay rose in Karl's mind, and for a moment that image crowded everything else out of his brain. Fullerton, not Gabe, was the victim here.

The reporter had lost his only son to a batch of tainted weed. Written dozens of articles exposing the danger and damage of the drug trade. He had done it all in an attempt to prevent other parents going through what he'd experienced. He had died for it. And there wasn't a thing Karl could do about it. With the lesser, easier to prove charges, Fullerton's death might never be brought home to anyone. Gabe, or someone on Gabe's crew, had murdered Fullerton, Karl was sure of that. Even when he shook the man's hand, that fact burned in the back of his mind. Yet he,

Karl, couldn't prove it. Gabe's trust hadn't gone that far. And now, would they ever be able to prove it?

Karl looked up. Alex pulled the glass door toward herself and walked into the waiting area just as the sergeant Karl was expecting rounded a corner from somewhere inside the detachment's halls. They both looked at Karl, and he got to his feet to introduce them.

***

It felt like forever before the door opened and Alex exited the meeting room without the bag she had been carrying. She shot Karl a dirty look and walked over to the vending machine against the wall, fishing in her pocket for the requisite coins. Karl was certain her hope of making the morning deadline was long gone, and the satisfaction this thought gave him provided the boost he needed to stand tall and walk through the door the sergeant was holding open for him.

They sat opposite each other, and the sergeant gave Karl a long, hard look.

"So, you *were* hired to investigate this drug ring."

It was a statement, not a question. It sounded as if he hadn't really believed Karl until Alex confirmed it.

"Yes," Karl replied.

"And you took it upon yourself to go undercover and not only discover the processing and transport operation being run out there, but also to participate in it as a means to prove it."

"That's right," Karl replied.

"Right," said the sergeant, scratching the bridge of his nose. "You'd better give me the whole story, in your own words."

He prepared to take notes as Karl gathered his thoughts.

***

"So, now I suppose I have to come to Victoria with you and get your notarized statement about my copies," Alex snapped.

They were standing in the parking lot outside the detachment, and the sun was already disappearing behind the mountains surrounding Port Hardy. Karl had forgotten that part of his blackmail to make her go to the police with him, but he supposed it wouldn't be a bad idea. If he dragged her back to Victoria, he could insist on getting copies of everything they had given the police to complete his case file. And he didn't mind forcing her to stay a little longer at this point. Her impatience irritated him. He had thought she cared about Fullerton, but now her mind seemed to be entirely fixed on her story. He wondered if Fullerton would even be mentioned as its originator, or if he would merely add a convenient splash of gore to the account.

"If you want to use my findings, then yup," he said flatly. Without bothering to wait for her response, he added, "I'll see you at the agency in the morning," and turned and walked away.

***

By the time Alex arrived at the agency the following morning, Karl had already called the law office that he served papers for most frequently and arranged to meet with a solicitor who could notarize his agreement with the paper. He had also printed out and filled in the form that Fullerton had provided to him weeks before. Kelsey must have heard him slamming doors on the printer when it jammed halfway through the process, because she appeared rather earlier than usual.

"How'd things go with the police?"

He'd filled her in on his night's adventure while driving from Port Alice to Port Hardy the day before.

He'd only gotten as far as, "Alright," when Alex walked in, clearly disgruntled, but also, Karl thought, a little surprised to find them both in the office already. He got the impression she had planned to be waiting for him when he arrived, and he was pleased not to give her the satisfaction.

"The lawyer who will be notarizing is expecting us at nine," he informed her before she could complain or even say hello. "There's coffee in the kitchen, if you'd like some before we go."

Alex gave him a nonplussed look then retired to the kitchen to fortify herself. Kelsey looked at Karl.

"What's wrong with you?" she hissed under her breath. "What have you done to upset her now."

"Insisted on following the rules and keeping to the right side of the law," he snapped back, although he kept his voice down. Kelsey raised her eyebrows, but she didn't have time to inquire further because Alex returned with a steaming mug in her hand and settled herself in the chair opposite Kelsey's.

Ignoring Karl, who was standing in the doorway to his office holding the forms in his hand, she leaned confidingly toward Kelsey and asked, "Do you still want me to show you how to pick locks?"

Karl turned abruptly and returned to his desk, setting the forms on it and busying himself pulling up an unrelated file on his computer. Kelsey, on the other hand, leapt her feet.

"Yes," she exclaimed. "Do we have time?"

"Oh, sure," Alex replied. "It won't take long. It's really not that hard."

Kelsey grabbed her key ring from her desk, saying, "Can we do deadbolts as well as regular locks?" She paused briefly on her way around her desk.

"Karl, don't you want to learn this too?" she asked, looking in at his door and rattling her keys encouragingly. "Knowing how to pick locks could be pretty useful as a detective."

"I'm good, thanks," he replied. "You have fun."

Alex's eyes narrowed at his indulgent tone, but Kelsey just shrugged and led her down the stairs to the outer door. Karl made a mental note to get Kelsey to show him how it was done as soon as Alex was out of the way and began sorting through his backlog of emails to pass the time.

At a quarter to nine, the women returned from their housebreaking activities and Karl scooped the papers up off his desk, ready to get things over with. He wasn't entirely thrilled to hear Kelsey gushing about how it would be "so good to know, even if I just lock myself out or something," even though he intended to take full advantage of her new expertise.

"Shall we?" he said to Alex. She, in turn, gave Kelsey a quick hug and a gift of her lock-picking set, which resulted in Kelsey ecstatically hugging her again. Karl barely managed not to roll his eyes. For someone who was so impatient to be away, Alex didn't seem all that worried about being on time to the lawyer's office. He had intended to walk the few blocks to the building where their offices were located, but when Alex jumped into her Jeep without asking if he wanted a ride, he shook his head and climbed into his truck.

Completing the documents at the lawyer's office took very little time, and before Karl had a chance to usher her out, Alex was holding out her hand to him.

"Thank you for your services, Mr. Larsson," she said as they shook briefly. "The *Post* appreciates everything you have been able to do for us." And she was out the door and across the parking lot to her vehicle before he could reply.

Karl took a deep breath and paused to thank Janelle for arranging the notarization for him on such short notice. She at least seemed pleased to have the opportunity to work with him again and mentioned some papers that would be ready for serving in the next day or two. He left the office a few minutes later, relieved that the case was finally over. Of course, the police could contact him for further details at any time, but he hoped he wouldn't need to testify. In any case, regardless of when the arrests were made, the trial was sure to be a long way off.

Returning to the office, he found a note from Kelsey saying that she was running errands and would be back later. Karl checked the time on his phone. Alex would be at the ferry by now, impatiently waiting to get back to Vancouver to write up her big story. Only, it wouldn't bring Fullerton back. It wouldn't even do much to keep drugs off the street. If Fullerton's old stories hadn't made any difference, what could this one do? Change a few shipping routes. That was about it. Karl sighed and ran his fingers through his hair. What he needed was a run, a hot shower, and a good night's sleep. Tomorrow he would pick up those docs the lawyer wanted served and get to work tracking down the intended recipient.

36

Karl ran to work the following morning, pleased to find that his time hadn't gone down at all while he'd been away. Apparently, hard physical labour didn't hurt a person's fitness. Karl grinned at the thought that he would never have to haul fish again as he let himself into the agency and bounded up the stairs.

He was sitting in his office chair, catching up on emails, when the office phone rang.

Kelsey wasn't at her desk yet, so he punched a button and picked up his extension.

"Hello, Larsson Investigations," he said automatically.

"Larsson, you son of a bitch!"

Karl froze, shocked by the venom in Alex's voice. He knew it was her, but he didn't know how it could be.

"Uh," was all he managed to get out.

"How could you?" she screamed down the phone line. "How dare you? I met every one of your stupid conditions. I deserve this story. I earned it. How the hell could you screw me like this?"

Karl just sat there, holding the phone away from his ear, at a complete loss to know what was going on. As she sucked in air to have another go at him, Sergeant Mulligan walked into the reception area, along with another officer, and Karl realized that his mouth was hanging open and Kelsey wasn't there to greet them. Closing his mouth abruptly, Karl said, "I've got to go," into the phone and hung up without listening to what she was screaming now.

"Officers." He pushed himself to his feet and came around the desk, unsure of his position in the eyes of the police. "What can I do for you?"

"Are you alone in the office?" Mulligan asked, glancing around. Karl realized that he had no idea where Kelsey was at the moment.

"Um, my assistant seems to have gone out," he faltered. Were they going to arrest him? Take him to jail for participating in the manufacture of an illegal substance, even though he had been the one to tell them about it? His throat felt dry.

"I'm sorry to drop in unannounced." Mulligan didn't sound very sorry. "But it was urgent that we speak with you."

He turned to the uniformed officer at his side and said, "Mr. Larsson, this is Sergeant Archer."

Archer held out his hand, and Karl stepped forward to shake, reassured by the gesture but still uncertain what was going on.

"Would we be able to speak to you in private, Mr. Larsson?" Sergeant Archer asked, glancing around in the same way that Milligan had a moment ago. Karl wasn't sure how much more private the empty agency could get, but he hurried to grab an extra guest chair from in front of Kelsey's desk and shut the door to his office on his return.

Karl rounded his desk and felt a little better taking his seat with that barrier between them. The two officers settled opposite, apparently quite comfortable with the situation.

Archer got right to the point. "We'd like your help, Mr. Larsson."

"With what?" Karl picked up a pen and began spinning it slowly between his fingers, just to give his hands something to do. Archer glanced at Mulligan, who replied.

"I didn't want to say anything until I had a chance to check with Sergeant Archer here, but he's been leading a team investigating the possibility that the Island might be being used as a drop point for a while now."

Karl stared at him. He couldn't believe his ears. Mulligan had practically sneered at the idea when Karl first came to him. He had made it sound as if the possibility was laughable, even ludicrous.

"You understand," Archer cut in. "This is extremely confidential. Operations like this take months to set up, and we need solid evidence on all the major players before we can move on any of them."

He glanced at Mulligan again then turned back to Karl. "The thing is, you've blown the whole case open." The way he said it, Karl was not sure whether this was a good thing or not.

"You used tactics that we couldn't have, of course," Archer continued. "But if an informant comes to us of their own free will, we can use the evidence they provide, as long as the RCMP were not involved without proper authorization at any point."

"That's why I made sure to give you everything I had," Karl hastened to say. "So that you could use whatever was useful."

"And we appreciate that," Archer assured him. "Your willingness to work with law enforcement is part of the reason we've come to you now. You see, Mr. Larsson, we think you could continue to be useful to our investigation."

Karl stared at him, uncomprehending. "Useful? How?"

"You're already in their crew." Archer spoke as if explaining it slowly would help Karl understand more easily. "You've successfully infiltrated their operation."

When Karl continued to stare at him, Archer frowned slightly and leaned forward to emphasize what he was saying. "It could take us months to get an undercover officer in, and at this time of year that officer wouldn't have the opportunities you did for getting near the principal individuals involved."

Karl remained silent, and Archer's mouth twisted in annoyance.

"The fishing season is almost over," he said. "This crew won't be able to use it as a cover for their operations, so they are likely to become much more cautious. If we are going to pick them up, we will need additional details regarding their schedules, their suppliers, the dealers they are selling to. We need a man on the inside."

He finally leaned back, fixing Karl with a hard stare. "And you're already in place."

Karl looked back and forth between them for a moment, aware of what they were asking of him but not wanting to believe it.

"But I'm out now," he finally said, knowing it sounded lame. "I came home, I turned my findings over to the *Post*."

"We have contacted that news agency and required that they quash the story for the time being."

Karl's eyebrows rose. That explained Alex's call.

"It's common practice when the release of a news story could compromise an open investigation," Mulligan assured him.

"So," Karl said, trying to avoid the implicit request. "When I first came to you, after Fullerton was killed, you already knew all about the operation?"

Mulligan had the good grace to look uncomfortable, but his response was defensive. "As Sergeant Archer said, it's an extremely confidential case. We don't typically encourage amateurs to go stumbling into the middle of an active crime ring. We prefer that people like you leave situations like this to the professionals."

Karl clenched his teeth at the condescension in the man's tone. Archer hastened to smooth things over.

"Generally, this is true; however, you have handled yourself surprisingly well considering the risks of the situation. The fact that you maintained your cover after the reporter's death is probably the biggest thing going in your favour right now. It's unlikely that you are suspected of having any involvement, either with the reporter or the police, or you never would have been invited to join their operation. This is what makes you invaluable to us at this stage."

Karl wondered if he had a choice in the matter. Would the RCMP continue to view him as an informant, a potential ally, if he refused to cooperate now? Would his involvement in criminal activities suddenly be considered much more serious if he didn't go along with this plan?

"Was an autopsy done on Fullerton?" he asked, continuing to deflect the conversation. "Did you know that he had been murdered when I first talked to you?"

"Yes," Archer responded before Mulligan could say anything this time. "The death was identified as suspicious from the outset, and the investigating coroner confirmed that Fullerton suffered from at least two stab wounds, probably made by some kind of utility knife, prior to entering the water, and definitely prior to being struck by the boat's propeller."

Karl's stomach lurched at the memory this statement recalled but controlled himself sufficiently to ask, "Would you have told me this if you didn't want my help with the investigation now?"

Mulligan frowned, but Archer continued calmly, "The details of Fullerton's death are being kept under wraps until they can be released without compromising the investigation. Since you are already involved, I don't feel it is too great a risk to provide you with the basic facts as we know them so far."

Karl took a deep breath. This was what it came down to. He was already involved. He was on the inside. He was essential to their investigation. Whether he liked it or not.

"If I continued in this case, how would that work?" Karl finally asked, and he could hear the resignation in his own voice.

"You would be acting as a police agent," Archer informed him, sitting up a little straighter in the guest chair, his voice becoming more business-like and less conversational. "You would receive an agreed-upon weekly payment, plus expenses, directly from the RCMP, during the remainder of your involvement in the investigation, with an additional lump sum at the end if specific arrests can be made as a result of the information you provide."

After studying Karl's face for a moment, Archer added, "I believe you will find the compensation that the RCMP is prepared to offer in this case comparable to what the *Post* was paying you."

Karl realized this might be his only chance to make sure the case covered its own expenses, since he hadn't actually gotten anything from the paper beyond his initial retainer and some operating expenses from Fullerton. From what Alex had said about delaying payment before leaving the Island, it could be a very long time before he got the promised bonus from her paper, if ever.

"Because of the sensitive nature of this case and the importance of maintaining confidentiality until arrests can be made, you will not be able to involve any of your contacts with the news agency or inform any of your staff, family, or friends of your participation," Archer added, accepting Karl's agreement as a foregone conclusion.

Karl wasn't surprised that he wouldn't be able to work with paper any longer, and he wasn't about to break his heart over it, but staff, family, and friends were all pretty well tied up in Kelsey these days, and he didn't like the idea of keeping her in the dark.

"I only have one staff person, and she is completely trustworthy. She's been essential to my work on the case so far, and I would prefer that she at least know the basics of where I am and what I am doing, if I do go back under cover," he said, inserting that 'if' as firmly as he could manage. "I can vouch for her discretion, and she might be of further use to the investigation, too. She's the one who came up with the system for predicting the crew's drop dates and points after all."

"It's not a matter of vouching for anyone. The circle involved needs to be as limited as possible," Archer stated. "Also, we've reviewed the method used to identify drop points, and while it has been useful, it involves a high degree of guesswork and supposition."

"It's never failed yet," Karl interjected.

"Regardless. The serious crimes unit will be providing you with professional support and observation on this case going forward. The help of a nineteen-year-old receptionist will not be required, regardless of your familial loyalty."

Karl's jaw clenched again. Despite his attempt to keep things friendly, Archer was really no less condescending than Mulligan. Although he would have liked to tell both of them exactly where they could shove their opinions, Karl bit his tongue and remained silent. Staying on the RCMP's good side seemed wise, and at least Kelsey wasn't around to hear their comments.

In the end, Karl signed the paperwork they had brought with them, apparently confident that he would agree to their proposal. He could just imagine Kelsey's reaction to the waiver absolving the RCMP from any liability in the event that he was injured or killed in the course of the operation, but he signed anyway. He also provided them with the details of when and where he was to meet the crew for the next drop. They were politely optimistic about the outcome of the sting and kept their condescension under wraps now that they had achieved their point. After informing him how to meet up with his support team for outfitting and further instructions, they each shook his hand again and left through the empty front office.

Kelsey didn't get back until after three o'clock. Karl was beginning to worry when he heard her footsteps on the stairs.

"Where've you been?" he called as soon as she walked through the door. He was sitting at his desk, trying to think through what he would need to arrange in order to disappear for several weeks without arousing suspicion.

"Court," she replied, tossing her leather jacket and purse onto her chair and coming over to stand in the doorway to his office, hand on hip, looking tired. "I had to give evidence at the initial hearing for that family law case I took care of a month ago.

"I told you about it yesterday," she added, raising her eyebrows at him.

"Oh, right." Karl thought he might remember hearing that, somewhere between her recriminations about Alex. He didn't want to remind her of that portion of their conversation, so he hurried on.

"Do you think you could manage things here for the next couple of weeks?"

"Probably, but why? The case is over. Do you have a new one already?"

"No," he hurried to assure her. "I just thought it'd be nice to take some vacation time. You know, get away. Relax. I don't think I'll be gone for more than two or three weeks."

"Seriously? You just barely got back. And you're leaving again? It's lonely around here when you're gone. And I won't even have the case to work on. It'll totally suck."

She folded her arms across her chest, pouting now.

"It's been a tough case, and I could really use a break," Karl told her. That wasn't a lie anyway. "It's only for a couple of weeks, and I'll be back before you know it. And you can totally run the agency however you like," he added to placate her. "Work whatever hours you like, as long as any work that comes in gets taken care of."

"I do that anyway," she informed him. He was sure this was true, and he wasn't going to argue about it.

"You know," he said, trying a different tactic. "Part of the point of having someone else working here is so that I can take vacations, get away once in a while. Covering for me is sort of your job."

"I know!" He thought for a moment that she was actually going to stamp her foot in frustration, but she refrained. "And it's fine. Just don't be gone too long, okay?"

Karl smiled at this. "I'll try," he assured her.

37

Since he had to keep Kelsey in the dark about his new activities, Karl couldn't use her car any longer, and since he had told Gabe Ross that his truck was repossessed, he couldn't show up driving that either. As a result, he spent the evening searching buy/sell and trade sites and making phone calls. It took longer than he had hoped, but by the following morning he had found a functioning Dodge Caravan for under a thousand dollars. He picked it up for cash, telling himself that the silver minivan would be as difficult to keep track of as Hansen's Sunfire had been. He spent the better part of the next day arranging to license and insure it, carefully keeping away from the neighbourhood of the agency.

Reviewing the clothes he had been wearing during his months on the North Island and the remaining contents of his wardrobe, Karl concluded that a trip to Value Village was in order. He stopped by the thrift store that evening to supplement his existing transient's costumes with a few more similarly battered ensembles. Standing in line to pay for strangers' castoffs, Karl was amused at the thought of what his family would say to this.

The van started when Karl was ready to go the next morning, but the climb up the Malahat seemed to take its engine to its limit, and he could hardly maintain a speed ten kilometres below the speed limit until he was cruising down the far side of the mountain. By the time he reached the RCMP detachment in Courtney to meet the serious crimes unit led by Sergeant Archer, Karl was sure he could smell the engine overheating, and the fact that no warning lights had appeared on the dash was no longer comforting him.

Karl checked his reflection in the car's rear-view mirror. He had trimmed his beard, and he didn't think it looked as scruffy as it had at first. It was beginning to fill in nicely, in his opinion. He wasn't a fan of his hair this long and sloppy, but it fit his current persona, and the face in the mirror was reassuringly different than his usual look. Hoping that the officers he was about to meet wouldn't judge him too harshly for his shabby appearance, he locked the car and did his best to walk confidently through the detachment's front door and up to the reception desk.

There were two people ahead of him in line waiting to speak to the desk officer, and the person currently leaning over the counter was making a pitiful attempt to explain why their accident really had been the other driver's fault, while the woman behind the desk attempted to convince them to take a seat and fill out the collision form. Eventually, after repeating this request at least a dozen times in the same measured tone, the officer finally got the poor driver to sit down with a pen and begin writing, muttering under his breath the entire time.

By the time the other two people in line had presented their problems and been helped, both with similar vehicle accidents they had definitely not been responsible for, it was already ten minutes past the time Karl was supposed to meet Archer. He was just stepping up to the desk and had opened his mouth to ask for the man when Archer strode around a corner, looking irritable, spotted Karl, and said, "There you are, at last.

This way!" He turned back the way he had come without waiting for Karl to follow, and Karl had to hurry to catch up with him.

Archer led the way through windowless halls to a conference room full of at least a dozen people, some in RCMP uniform, some in plain clothes, some clearly dressed for specific roles on the team. Archer's introductions were brief and largely uninformative. Karl tried to keep track of names but got lost after Lars, Robbie, Micah, and Shane. Karl refused an offer of coffee and took a seat at the table. Archer strode to the front of the room and continued a discussion he had obviously interrupted to go find Karl.

Running down a list of tasks to be done, Archer handed out assignments to everyone in the room. Everyone, that is, except Karl. There was an electronics expert, who would be providing Karl with a much more discreet and, Karl hoped, more comfortable wire to wear, as well as a tiny camera that she claimed would be invisible. Karl was a little nervous about this idea but tried not to show it.

Besides the electronics expert, there was a kid who looked younger than Karl who would be looking after Karl's vehicle. There were several officers who would be monitoring Karl in shifts and available to answer a confidential phone line at any time of the day or night, in case he needed support or just to report in. Other members of the team were already looking into tracking down available records for the sawmill, the boats Karl had identified, and any of the individuals he'd managed to photograph. They all seemed to have a good grasp of what was expected of them, and the meeting wrapped up not long after

Karl arrived, with the various individuals heading off to carry out their assignments.

Karl would have asked Archer what he was supposed to do now, but Archer was deep in conversation with a uniformed officer, and Karl didn't see an opening to interrupt as they gathered their things and left the room. He sat at the table, looking around the now empty conference room, and wondered if he had missed something. After a minute, he got up and helped himself to a cup of coffee from the machine on the counter. It was lousy coffee, but at least drinking it gave him something to do. He was halfway through his second cup when the youngest officer came bounding back into the room. At least, Karl assumed he was an officer. He had a badge of some kind on the shoulder of his mechanic's coverall.

"Hey, sorry we didn't get the chance to meet properly earlier. I'm Robbie." The young man held out his hand and Karl shook it, relieved to have someone acknowledge his presence at least. "Archer's briefings are always a bit intense; he doesn't waste any time, you know?"

"I noticed," Karl replied, making Robbie grin.

"So, what are you planning to drive?"

"I picked up a used Dodge Caravan. I was driving my cousin's car for a while, but since she doesn't know I'm still on this case..." Karl's words trailed off. He suddenly wondered if he had wasted his time and money. Maybe the police had their own vehicle that they wanted him to drive. But Robbie nodded approvingly.

"Great, that'll do fine," he assented easily. "I'll be placing a tracking device inside the dash, somewhere no one will ever find it, don't worry. Then I'm going to give it a once-over and make sure it'll run properly for the duration, if that's alright with you?"

It was a rhetorical question. Being stranded by a broken-down vehicle wouldn't help the case one bit.

"Right. Sure." Karl relinquished his keys and explained where he had parked, and Robbie hustled off to look after these mechanical matters. Karl waited some more.

The electronics expert, Shane, stuck her head in after another half an hour and said, "Oh, there you are. Can I borrow you for a few minutes? Is this a good time?"

Karl rose, abandoning the dregs of his third cup of coffee, which was cold anyway. "Yeah, for sure, what do you need?"

"I need to get you wired up so that we can record your interactions and track your movements while you're undercover," she told him, leading the way down the hall. Karl followed, feeling self conscious about the squeak of his shoes with each step.

She led him into a small, windowless room with too many monitors lit up at once and a variety of electrical wiring and bits and pieces that Karl didn't know the name or function of. She slid into the only available chair and began hunting for something through the paraphernalia heaped on all available surfaces. Karl began to pull his off t-shirt in preparation for the wire being attached.

"What are you doing?" Shane asked and Karl froze, his t-shirt halfway over his head, then quickly pulled it back down.

"I thought you were going to put a wire on me."

"We don't literally put wires on our informants anymore." Shane sounded amused. "It's unreliable, not to mention dangerous. It's a good way to get an informant killed, actually. All I need is your phone."

Karl hastened to dig the phone out of his back pocket and handed it over, his face red. Still amused, Shane took the phone, spent some time fiddling with the settings, removed the sim card and inserted it into some sort of computer add on, returned it to the phone, then spent some time with the phone attached by a cord to her computer, pecking away at the keyboard and squinting at the screen. Her manner reminded Karl forcibly of Kelsey, despite the difference in their appearances. He leaned awkwardly against the wall, his hands jammed in his pockets, and wondered how things were going at the agency.

"Okay." Shane's voice brought him out of his reverie with a start. "Your phone will act simultaneously as a tracking, listening, and recording device. All you have to do is keep it turned on and on your person at all times."

She held it out to him, and Karl took it, studying it briefly. It didn't look any different to him. "I thought my car was going to be tracked." He slid the phone into his back pocket.

"Yeah, we'll be tracking both, but the car is primarily a backup measure because tracking a phone is so iffy that far north. But don't forget, if your phone dies we not only won't be able to track you on it, we also won't get any recordings from it." Shane gave him a mock stern look. "So try not to let your phone die, okay? Makes my life much easier if it doesn't."

"Right." Karl couldn't think of anything more clever to say, and he didn't know where he was supposed to go from there. The tiny room was beginning to feel distinctly overfull with just the two of them staring at each other. Shane didn't seem to notice this; she just turned back to her computer, poked a few keys, and then said, "Ali needs you next."

"Right," Karl repeated, looking around as if he might somehow discern the route to Ali on the walls of the office.

Shane looked up and laughed. "Come on, I'll show you the way," she said, pulling the door open and leading him off down yet another hallway.

Ali turned out to be a Corporal Alison Munroe, who provided Karl with a phone number to memorize and instructions on how often to check in, how to signal if he was in trouble but couldn't speak, and a dozen other details of protocol that seemed excessive to him. Archer joined them near the end of this briefing and added his two cents.

"The important thing is to behave naturally," he said gravely, frowning down at Karl from his half-leaning perch on the edge of the table. "You've got to be one of the crew. You need them to believe that you have never spoken to the police, would never consider speaking to the police, that you are as much a part of their world as any of them. It's important to get in the right headspace if you're going to blend in."

Karl stared back at him, exasperated. He had been doing this for a while now. He didn't feel like he needed tips from Archer, who would stand out like a sore thumb in that crowd, but he bit his tongue, reminding himself that he had to work with this man for weeks to come, and he might need him very badly one day soon.

By the time he walked out of the detachment, Karl felt more than ready to return to criminal life. At least he knew where he stood with those people, and they sure didn't nag as much as the police.

***

The fishing season seemed to be drawing to a close, and Karl ended up kicking his heels around Port Hardy for the weekend with no work and not much else to do either. After catching a news story on the local channel where an old lady begged the thief who had broken into her home to return her husband's stolen ashes, Karl didn't feel much like sitting in his hotel room. He felt sick watching her sob, *Keep the jewellery, I don't grudge it, just let me have my husband's remains, please!*

He ran over to Coal Harbour for a day just for something to do. Something that didn't involve watching cable television in his motel. He liked the shabby small-town feel, surrounded by all that natural beauty, better than the more commercialized tourism of places like Telegraph Cove. No one cared that the saskatoon and blackberry bushes crowded the ditches and encroached onto the roadways here. Wandering along Harbour Road, Karl even found a few late blackberries to pick. They were deliciously sweet, but the seeds got stuck in his teeth, and eventually he turned back the way he had come. The woman's sobs kept echoing in his mind. Her grief at losing this last link to her loved one was a stark contrast to the casual discard of his grandfather's ashes by the family. He needed to get back to work. Waiting around too long could make him crazy.

38

On his way to the sawmill Monday evening, Karl paused at the spot where the van had stopped, but only for a moment. It occurred to him, even as the vehicle slowed, that if there were cameras around, he didn't want to be seen looking for them. He pulled into the gravel lot at ten to seven. Gabe and Roy were the only two there ahead of him. They stood in front of the sawmill door, talking while they waited. The white van was parked at an angle next to the building. Karl wondered if it was Roy's personal vehicle. He pulled the Caravan in beside Gabe's truck, climbed out, and headed over to join them.

Gabe squinted toward Karl as he crossed the lot, shading his eyes against the late afternoon sun with his hand. "What happened to the pumpkin?" he called.

Karl said, "Huh?" then looked over his shoulder to where Gabe nodded and realized what he meant.

"Transmission blew on me," he replied as he joined them. "Spent every last dime I had on this piece just to get here."

Gabe grinned at him. "Well, that won't be a problem anymore," he said, pulling an envelope from an inside pocket and holding it out.

"What's this?" But Karl could feel the stack of bills inside, and he knew the answer before Gabe said it.

"Last shipment's pay. I always pay my crew the day of the next shipment whatever they're owed for the last one. Keep them coming back, see? No one wants to miss out on getting paid for work they've already done."

Karl thumbed the envelope open and checked the contents. It had to be at least as much as he'd made in a good week hauling fish. He looked up to find Gabe watching him.

Gabe laughed at his expression. "We don't do this for peanuts, you know," he told Karl, slapping him on the shoulder.

Roy looked at Karl like he thought there must be something wrong with him. Karl supposed it was odd not to be worried about payment after helping to process a shipment of drugs. He'd just wanted to get away as far and as fast as possible the last time he'd been here. And here he was, back again, indefinitely.

It wasn't long before the rest of the crew began pulling up. Karl was starting to recognize faces and even put names to a few of them. Bob was the guy who stammered. Torey's arms were covered in faded tattoos. Karl thought that the short guy with the bow legs might be called Jake, but maybe it was Jack. They varied in height, build, and age, but they all had the same used-up, worn-out expression on their face. These men had lived hard, and they were tired.

They loaded into the back of the van, Roy driving as usual, and Karl settled himself cross-legged on the floor. He figured if he was stuck with this gig, he might as well be as comfortable as possible. The unload went more or less the same as the previous one had, except that this time the load seemed bigger to Karl, and the process took longer. He wondered how the size of a drop was determined, but no one else seemed to notice or care about the difference. Karl fell into the rhythm of the work, focusing on fitting in and not drawing attention to himself.

Karl caught and shifted his share of the bundles then hauled them up to the truck with the same steady trudge of the rest of the crew. Back into the van and back to the sawmill. Unloading the bales and pulling on suits, gloves, and masks. Karl thought it should feel strange to be this familiar with the illicit routine already, but he was just getting on with the job like everyone else. He looked around, saw his former position at a packaging station open, and spotted a tall stool standing against a wall. Snagging the stool on the way by, he settled down to work in greater comfort than he had experienced the first night and thought he caught an amused glance from Gabe when the other man passed him a few minutes later.

The hours dragged by, the work was as tedious as before, but thinking about the wad of cash currently sitting in his pocket, Karl could imagine most people would be willing to put up with a bit of tedium for that kind of payout. The first rays of the morning sun were starting to peek through the cracks in the mill's siding when Karl finished counting out and zipping up his last bunch of pills.

This time he was also one of the delivery crew, stripping off his coverall, mask, and gloves, loading his appointed Skip the Dishes bags into the back of his van, and memorizing the list of names and addresses Gabe had for him before returning it, just like everyone else.

***

Driving down the highway, Karl's heart beat more rapidly than usual, and his palms felt slick on the steering wheel. He was carrying several hundred grams of a highly controlled substance clearly packaged for distribution in the back of his van. The bags containing them might be covered by an old blanket during transport, but Karl still felt exposed. The fact that he was technically working for the police while delivering these packages didn't help his nerves much, now that he was doing it. Delivering drugs. Like an actual drug dealer. Somehow, it felt worse than processing them. This was the real deal.

Every town, village, and small city he came to on the road to Nanaimo made Karl's pulse jump and his nerve endings tingle. He followed the speed limit religiously but still drove with one eye on his rear-view mirror. The one time a police vehicle pulled up beside him at a stop light, Karl literally stopped breathing until the light changed color and they turned right while he drove straight. Between the lack of oxygen and the increased heart rate, he wondered if he might just pass out at the wheel, but he made it to the ferry terminal somehow.

Karl could feel a bead of sweat trickle down his temple as he pulled up to the booth and handed the attendant cash with a hand that trembled slightly. He hadn't been this nervous since his wedding day, and that situation had not turned out well for him.

"Lane 6," said the attendant, passing Karl his ticket. He put it on the dashboard and drove in the direction she pointed. He spent the next hour sitting in the sweltering vehicle, the windows rolled up and the doors locked, despite the fact that every other passenger waiting in the lot was either out of their vehicle, strolling up to the terminal building to buy coffee and ice cream, or else sitting with their windows, and occasionally car doors, wide open to catch whatever breeze was available.

When the announcement came to begin loading, Karl's shirt stuck to his seat as he leaned forward to start his engine, following the vehicle ahead of him toward the large white vessel. He had to force himself to take slow deep breaths as he pulled up the ramp, following the BC Ferries employee's gestures, inching forward until he was a foot from the car ahead of him then lurching to a stop when she held up her hand. He hated the idea of leaving the van and its contents unsupervised, but the sign on the wall said all passengers must leave the vehicle deck, and he didn't want to arouse suspicion. After carefully checking that the van was fully locked, he made his way up to the passenger deck and found a seat at a "business station" far enough from the cafeteria that he didn't have to smell grease the entire crossing.

The ferry's horn blew overhead, and Karl heard the shrieks of surprise from less experienced riders on the outer deck. It was the first time that he had been off the Island since taking over the agency. Staring over the fluffy grey heads of two seniors already nodding off in the seats by the window, he watched the terminal fall away as the vessel pulled into the strait and headed for Vancouver. He realized with surprise that he felt bereft, as if he were being torn from his home, even though he would be returning the very next day. It was the first time in his life he'd felt that way about a place.

Two hours later, the Dodge bumped over the ferry's offramp, and Karl breathed a sigh of relief. He couldn't believe it.

It had been every bit as easy as Fullerton described. No questions, no police, no security, not even the suggestion of a search. It occurred to him that this might be due to the RCMP operation currently monitoring his every move, but Gabe's crew had been doing this for months, maybe years for all Karl knew, and it didn't sound like any of them had been caught.

Karl had clear instructions from the police not to behave suspiciously in any way while in possession of illegal substances. He was to make the deliveries exactly as instructed, giving Gabe and the rest of the crew no reason to doubt him, in case they had someone watching the new man on the team. As a result, Karl headed directly for his first appointment, determined not to be a minute later than necessary.

He parked across from the address Gabe had given him and mentally double-checked the address to be sure he was at the right place. The sign said *Tri-City Realty Pro*, which was right. Karl just hadn't expected to make his drop somewhere so clean and shiny. The glass and steel storefront gleamed, the business name outlined in channel letters above. A row of home sale brochures lined the lower part of the window, each of the houses depicted nice enough to impress even his mother.

Karl climbed out of the van, popped the back door, and grabbed the first duffle inside, locking the vehicle before jogging across the street. A little bell tinkled as he pushed the door open. The reception area inside was small but maintained the impression of gleaming professionalism projected on the exterior. The counter was white marble and wood and the guest chairs were white leather. There were more brochures of houses for sale on the walls, along with a large, glossy portrait of an attractive woman in her early fifties with short, stylish grey hair wearing a well-cut suit. The name Gloria Steinman followed by *CREB Realtor of the Year* was printed on a little plaque below the picture.

The original of the portrait walked through the door from the back of the office, apparently summoned by the sound of the bell. Karl shifted the duffle bag nervously from one hand to the other.

"Hello." The woman's smile was warm and professional. Karl could believe that she was realtor of the year with a smile like that. "Can I help you?"

"I'm, uh, I have a delivery for...Lollipop?" Karl replied. It was the first contact name he'd been given, and he felt idiotic saying it to this polished professional.

"Of course." The smile didn't falter for a moment. "Come right through."

She led the way past a small kitchen nook and into a single, large office at the back of the shop. The modern black-and-white theme had been carried through to the office furniture, and the only pop of color in the room was an abstract painting hanging behind the desk. Gloria Steinman closed the office door behind Karl and turned to smile at him, holding out a well-manicured hand.

"I'm Lori," she said, shaking his hand firmly. "Nice to meet you."

Karl didn't know what to say. There had to be some mistake. He was torn between hoping that she hadn't noticed how sweaty his palms were and wondering how in the heck he was supposed to get out of this one. Lori added, "Would you mind just putting the bag on the desk for me?"

Karl stared at her for a moment longer then did as she instructed. With cool familiarity, she unzipped the bag and began counting the packets of pills inside. When she had satisfied herself that the order was correct, she unlocked a drawer in a black filing cabinet and proceeded to pack them into a voluminous Michael Kors purse and a cardboard tube inside a lululemon yoga mat bag. Karl watched all this in awed fascination. Once she had relocked the cabinet, Gloria Steinman checked the phone lying on her desk and gave Karl a long look.

"Gabe says I can send payment back with you," she said. "He seems to think you're reliable."

Karl didn't have an answer to this, so he kept his mouth shut. She shrugged.

"I guess he knows what he's doing," she said, and reaching into a desk drawer, she pulled out a bundle of cash. It was several times larger than any amount Karl had laid eyes on at one time in his life. She held it out to him, eyebrows raised, and Karl jumped, realizing she expected him to take it. Hastily seizing the saran-wrapped fortune, he clumsily attempted to stuff it into the now empty compartment of the food bag while Gloria Steinman produced a second packet of cash. Karl finally managed to get both packages into the bag and get it zipped, straightening to find Gloria smiling in obvious amusement at his discomposure.

"You're new, huh?" She was teasing him now.

"Uh, yeah." Karl tried to put on a nonchalant air, but he knew it was pointless. "Still learning the ropes."

"It's Karl, right?" Gloria asked, looking him over.

"Yeah," said Karl, shifting from one foot to the other.

Gloria nodded, still smiling. "Tell Gabe he can send you back any time he likes."

Her smile was coquettish as she opened the office door and led the way back to the front of the shop, her walk slower and more sinuous than before.

"It was nice to meet you, Karl," she said, holding out her hand again, her fingers lingering briefly in his as they shook.

Karl crossed the street in a haze of disbelief. That was how a drug deal went down? That was what a drug dealer looked like? He wondered briefly if he might have accidentally landed in some sort of alternate reality. But no, the crappy Dodge Caravan was still parked where he had left it, and the engine required two attempts before it would start. This was real. It was just really weird. Karl shook his head and pulled away from the curb, heading for his next drop and feeling distinctly uncomfortable about the mass of cash now keeping the drugs in his bags company.

The class of establishments to which Karl delivered devolved over the course of the next couple hours, until he began to feel reassured that his previous ideas about drug dealers hadn't been entirely wrong. By the time he left the last package at a dingy apartment on the fifth floor of a building without any elevator, Karl was feeling the effects of going without sleep. The stairwell stank of piss, and he decided he would give just about anything for a hot shower.

39

Technically, Karl could go either to Jakob's house or his mother's condo to stay the night, but he couldn't face an evening of deflecting questions and covering up his police cooperation. In the end he opted for a modest hotel room near the Tsawwassen ferry terminal. Only after he had checked in and showered did Karl call the police contact number from the hotel phone.

The phone rang twice before it was picked up and a cheerful voice said, "Hello, Ali speaking."

Archer had told Karl that his contacts would always be prepared to maintain his cover whenever he called in and would go along with any story he needed to pass off, in case of emergencies. Such an informal greeting from Corporal Munroe still caught him off guard, and he found himself suddenly unsure of how to proceed. He had planned a very succinct report in his mind, driving to the hotel. Short and to the point so that he could get to sleep already.

"Hi... This is Karl Larsson. I'm calling to report?"

"Hi, Karl," Ali replied. "Are you alone? Can you talk?"

"Yes." Karl was finding this whole conversation almost as weird as the one with Gloria Steinman.

"Great," said Ali. "How was the last twenty-four hours? Are you in a secure location? Will it be possible for you to …"

Karl's phone buzzed on the nightstand. He picked it up and saw Gabe Ross's name on the call display. "Uh... Ali? I gotta go," he told her.

"Is everything alright?" The instant concern was nice to hear, even though he knew it wasn't for him personally.

"Yeah, just another call I should take," Karl replied. "I'll call you back."

"No problem!" She was back to being bright and cheerful, and the line went dead.

Karl answered his phone. "Hey."

"Hey yourself," said Gabe. "How did the drops go?"

"Okay, I think," Karl answered, stretching out on the bed, one arm behind his head. "I found all of them. Three of them gave me payments. They said you'd told them to, but the others didn't say anything, so I didn't ask about payment. Was that alright?"

"Absolutely," Gabe replied. "I have different arrangements with different contacts. You did exactly right. Gloria has already requested that you be her regular 'delivery boy,' as she put it."

Karl could feel himself redden as Gabe laughed down the line. "Yeah, she's…interesting," he said.

Gabe just laughed some more. "Don't worry," he told Karl. "She won't eat you. Unless you want her to, that is."

Karl didn't know what to say to that. His face was feeling distinctly warm, and the heat was spreading down his neck. "So, where do I bring all this cash?" he asked, to change the topic.

Gabe chuckled at his reticence. "Meet me in Hardy tomorrow, 3:00 p.m. at Bear Cove Park."

"Isn't that a bit public?" Karl asked nervously. "What if someone sees us?"

"What? Sees a couple of dudes having a laugh while one of them returns the other guy's hockey equipment?" Gabe laughed. "You need to learn to relax, man. I've been doing this for a while. No one looks at you funny if you don't act like something funny is going on. Just be cool. It'll be fine."

He was still laughing as he hung up, and Karl supposed that he must know what he was talking about. He sat up, picked up the hotel phone, and redialled Corporal Munroe.

"I'm supposed to deliver the cash to Ross tomorrow at the Bear Cove Park in Port Hardy," he told her. Somehow it was easier to talk about Gabe Ross to the police if he only used the man's last name. Calling him Gabe felt too personal.

"Tomorrow?" He could hear the sound of nails clicking on a keyboard. "And you're at the Coast Tsawwassen Inn now?"

"Um…yes." Karl was a little perturbed that she knew this when he hadn't told her, until he remembered the trackers in his car and phone.

"Okay, what's your room number?" she continued. "We'll have officers there in one hour to photograph and tag the bills."

"Won't that make them suspicious?" Karl asked, thinking longingly of sleep.

"Our people know what they're doing," she informed him. "They'll be careful. Room number?"

He gave it to her and collapsed back on the bed, hoping he could get an hour's sleep in before anyone arrived. He was jolted awake forty minutes later when two men in plain clothes walked into the room without knocking. He had been asleep for ten minutes.

By the time they finished the process and rewrapped the bundles of cash with careful precision, Karl was so wired that he didn't have a hope of sleeping. After they had gone, he lay in the dark, staring at the ceiling, contemplating the situation he was in. This shipment, at the very least, was going to hit the streets. People were going to purchase these drugs. Drugs that he had helped process, had delivered himself. It was possible, even probable, that one or more of those people would overdose, might even die as a result of taking them.

The fact that the whole operation could potentially prevent a great many more deaths in the long run didn't alter this immediate fact. He wished he could tell Kelsey about it. He was sure she would have an opinion on the topic, and even if he didn't agree with that opinion, at least it would help him to clarify his own. He had an entire RCMP Serious Crimes Unit backing him, but Karl still felt isolated without Kelsey waiting up to hear how things had gone and what he had found out. It was going to be a long few weeks.

***

Two weeks and five shipments later, Karl no longer felt sweaty and panicky every time he passed a police cruiser or security vehicle with drugs in his van. He had stopped blushing at Lori's teasing innuendos or worrying about being spotted handing the cash over in public places. He was starting to realize the truth behind the saying that you can get used to anything, given time. Smuggling drugs, it turned out, wasn't any more exciting than packing fish, although it was a great deal more lucrative. Or it would have been, if Karl had been allowed to keep the cash Gabe paid out each time they met for the previous haul.

Unfortunately for Karl's bank account, every bill went straight into evidence, collected by the same nameless officers who arrived to photograph each payment before Karl passed them along. At least Karl was getting used to sleeping through their activities once he had called in his report for the night, only turning over and going back to sleep when they walked in on him unannounced.

The leaves on the maples and aspens were beginning to change color, spotting the mass of dark green forest with oranges, yellows, and occasional reds. The air was chilly off the water in the evenings, especially during late nights unloading. Karl wondered if he would be working through the winter at this job and how he would explain his absence to Kelsey if that happened. The rhythm of the work was easier now that they were only shifting drugs and not fish most nights.

As fall closed in, it became dark enough to bring the boats in earlier, and Karl was starting to recognize the faces of the boat crews that they worked with regularly. He no longer bothered to track which boat was which or wonder where they came from or where they went. All of that was up to Archer and his team. Karl just nodded to the men he recognized and got on with the work.

40

The next load came in on a sodden night that left no hope of staying dry on the dock. The thick, low-hanging clouds made killing the dock lights practically superfluous, visibility was already so close. The steady drizzle wasn't so bad, but the twisting, whirling wind forced it under hat brims and up sleeve cuffs, and the receiving crew were unpleasantly damp by the time the boat arrived. Everyone was in a hurry to get the night over and done with as quickly as possible.

The crew on the boat passed bundle after bundle over the side to the men waiting below. Karl took his turn catching and stacking the ones that fell to him. The last bundle was on the pile, and the boat's captain was reaching for the rope anchoring them to the dock when Gabe held up a hand.

"Hold on a second," he said. "There should be one more package here."

Karl was standing on Gabe's right, and he could see the moment of hesitation before the captain shook his head.

"That's all of it. That's all we were given to deliver," he said, his voice insistent. Karl thought he might just throw off the bowline and try to run for it.

"There should be another package," Gabe repeated, threatening now. Out of the corner of his eye, Karl saw Gabe's right hand slide back under his jacket. The boatman's hands came up, and for a moment Karl thought he was surrendering before Gabe had even pulled a weapon on him. Then, seemingly out of nowhere, a shotgun was in the boatman's hands. He swung it down to point directly at Gabe's chest.

Gabe froze, still reaching for the small of his back, but Karl reacted without taking time to think. He stepped forward and to the right, reaching up and seizing the barrel of the gun with his left hand as he did so and jerking it toward himself. The boatman hadn't had time to get his finger on the trigger, and the move directed the muzzle away from Gabe's chest and over Karl's shoulder, jerking the other man off his feet. Still gripping the barrel like a kubotan, Karl drove his fist into the man's face as it fell toward him, hard enough to snap the man's head back and make him lose his grip on the shotgun.

Karl stepped back and swung the stock of the gun up under his right arm so it pointed at the man now slumped against the gunwale, dripping blood down the side of the boat.

"Don't you know carrying concealed weapons is illegal in Canada?"

It was the first thing out of Karl's mouth, and he had no idea where it came from. Ross gaped at him for a moment, then his face broke into a grin. He began to laugh. A full, hearty, jovial laugh that seemed to come from the bottom of his stomach and shook him all over. Karl had never seen a thin man belly-laugh like that before. Gabe removed his hand from under his jacket and slapped Karl on the back, almost doubled over with mirth.

"Keep this clown covered," he finally said when he'd laughed himself out. "I'm going to check the boat."

He jerked his head for Roy to follow him and climbed aboard the vessel. The other crew member didn't say anything.

Apparently, the fact that Karl had a gun pointed at his captain was enough to keep him under control. Karl had no idea if the shotgun was loaded, but he wasn't about to take any chances. Not only would he risk killing someone, he was pretty sure he could injure himself if he fired it in this position. He kept his finger off the trigger, wrapping it around the outside of the guard to reassure himself. He tried to hold the heavy weapon steady, even though his guts were starting to churn at the thought of what he had just done.

Gabe and Roy came up the steps from the ship's hold a minute later, carrying the missing bundle between them. They tossed it down to one of the guys waiting below, then Roy levered himself over the side of the boat, landing with a heavy thunk on the dock's wood surface. Gabe turned to the captain, who had straightened up and was trying to dab away the blood dripping from his nose.

The two men stood facing each other for a long moment, Karl still covering the captain. Without warning, Gabe surged forward, driving a fist in the captain's stomach, the full weight of his wiry body behind the blow. As the man keeled forward, Gabe shifted his weight back, grabbed a fistful of hair, and brought his knee up hard into his opponent's face. If the captain's nose hadn't been broken before, it was now. Gabe let him fall to the deck, moaning, his hands over his face, and turned the other crew member.

"I will be informing Deglas of this," he stated coldly, and the flicker of fear in the man's eyes told Karl that this was all the revenge Gabe would need to take. He vaulted over the side of the boat, landing next to Karl, and turned to stand beside him as if presenting the boat with a unified threat. The crew member stepped over his captain to throw off the bowline, started the boat, and pulled away from the dock without a word.

Gabe turned to Karl and held out his hand with a smile. Karl passed him the shotgun and shoved his hands into his pockets to hide their trembling.

"Nice job," Gabe said, and Karl jerked a nod in return.

"Let's go," Gabe called to the rest of his crew, and the men jumped into action, grabbing bundles and beginning to make their way up the ramp. Karl picked one up in his turn and fell into line with the others. He wondered if this was how they had responded to Fullerton's murder. Frozen silence, then getting on with the job as soon as the excitement was over. He felt distinctly unwell. He suddenly wondered how many times his grandfather had found himself in life-threatening scenarios in the course of his career, and how he would have handled the situation if it had been him instead of Karl on that dock.

<h1 style="text-align:center">41</h1>

After this incident, there was no longer any question; Karl was not only in—he was on the inside. The outward dynamics of his situation remained the same, but beneath the surface Karl's status had shifted. Gabe treated him like a friend rather than an employee. The rest of the crew looked at him with something akin to awe. Even Roy showed a grudging respect in their occasional interactions. With Gabe's official approval, the gang had been ready enough to accept him as a member from the start, but now Karl found he spent fewer nights drinking alone or with strangers. His opinion was asked, his presence was invited, he was worth knowing. It should have made life more liveable, or at least less lonely, but it didn't improve his mood.

The fact that he was helping to put a deadly drug on the streets continued to haunt him on the nights he wasn't too exhausted from the work to think at all. Lying awake in impersonal hotel rooms, waiting for the next drop, Karl's frustration came to the surface. He was supposed to be a detective. He was supposed to find out if something criminal was happening and who was responsible for it, collect the evidence and pass it along. That was what he had signed up for. Not this week after week living like a criminal, just waiting.

Karl wasn't even sure what he was supposed to be waiting for. Surely the police had the evidence they needed by now. What was he still doing out here? Kelsey was beginning to send daily *where are you, when are you coming back* messages, but Karl didn't know what to tell her except *soon*. He didn't even know if it was true, but there wasn't much else he could say. He was in this until Archer said otherwise, and that wouldn't be until the case was wrapped up.

Kelsey worried Karl too. Competent as she was, Karl didn't like leaving her to operate his business entirely alone for this long. At least at the beginning of the case, when they had been in regular contact, she could ask his advice or get approval on major decisions. What if she did something that could put his license at risk? What if another case put her in danger while he was away? The thought of Roy letting himself into the agency, with Kelsey unsuspecting and unprotected upstairs, made him sick every time he remembered it.

It was this thought that finally drove Karl to ask the question that had niggled at the back of his mind for so long. He and Gabe sat side by side at the bar of the Grillhouse in Tahsis, tucking into cheeseburgers and coffees in anticipation of the night ahead of them.

"Who was Williams?" Karl asked abruptly then hoped he wasn't pushing his luck. Gabe seemed to trust him absolutely since Karl's rather spectacular defense of him on the dock. But he didn't want to risk putting Gabe on his guard. Too late to take the question back, Karl covered his flush of nerves by taking a large bite of burger and chewing on it.

"Who?" Gabe stopped with his burger halfway to his mouth and gave Karl a hard, sideways look.

Karl swallowed then sipped his coffee. "Williams," he repeated. "When I first started, you said hopefully I was less jumpy than Williams. I just wondered."

Gabe's mouth tightened, but after a moment he relaxed again. He set the burger back down on the plate and scrubbed his fingers with a paper napkin. He took his coffee cup and held it between both hands.

"Might as well tell you. Someone will, eventually," he said. "Williams was a twitchy little addict. I don't know if you noticed, but most of the guys on my crew like their booze a little too much, but they don't use the stuff we move. I try to make a point of that. Addicts are a whole different bundle of issues from drunks. A drunk might not show up one day, and there's a risk with some that they'll shoot their mouth when they're really into their bottle, but that I can watch out for, predict before I bring a guy on board. Addicts…"

He shook his head, apparently at a loss to describe it. He took a long swig of his coffee and glanced around to check that no one was close enough to overhear them. The bartender was serving a couple of women at the far end and didn't look likely to come back their way any time soon.

"We had a bit of trouble about a week before you started."

Karl felt a shot of adrenaline hit him and had to consciously prevent himself straightening in his seat. For the first time in weeks, he thought of the listening device built into his phone and wondered if it was still working. The second he thought of it, of course, he felt the urge to check his phone, but forced himself to leave it where it lay, face down on the bar in front of him. If it was ever going to get the chance to record something useful, this was it.

"Some reporter from Vancouver came poking around," Gabe said casually. "We had to deal with him."

"How did you know he was a reporter?" It was the only question Karl could think of that didn't give his foreknowledge away. At least, he hoped it wouldn't.

Gabe snorted derisively. "Had his press ID on him. Camera, listening gear, the works.

"You said at the beginning that you don't like violence," he continued, and Karl knew Gabe was looking his way again but kept his gaze fixed on the burger in his hands. He felt he had proved his willingness to use violence when necessary. This shouldn't be an issue. He took another bite instead of answering.

"Neither do I," Gabe continued. "All anyone has to do to get along with me is to deal with me straight and keep their nose out of my business. I am more than happy to live and let live. But I couldn't just let the guy take our pictures, scope our drop, blow up the whole operation. I couldn't."

Karl gave a half nod, indicating that he was listening, implying that he could see Gabe's point.

"So, we had to dispose of him," Gabe said. "We didn't really have a choice."

"Yeah? And how does one do that?" Karl kept his tone neutral, not too curious, just flat. He reached for the ketchup, pleased to see that his hand was steady, without a tremor.

"It wasn't that hard. Williams was already all hopped up that night. Twitching like the little rat he was. I told him if someone didn't off this guy, there wouldn't be any more product coming in for a long time. Never get between a junky and his next fix." Gabe was grimly satisfied with his own solution. Karl wondered how many questions it would take before Gabe decided he was getting a little too curious, but he had to know. Glancing around in turn, he lowered his voice.

"So, Williams killed this reporter?"

"Partially," said Gabe. "Not especially well. He took a utility knife to him like it was some kind of shiv. Not the cleanest or quietest way to handle things. We knocked the reporter in the water to shut him up and keep him from bleeding all over the damn place, but that didn't sort Williams out. He wouldn't shut up, kept bouncing around, squawking about *what had he done* and *oh my god*, and *maybe we should call someone,* or *maybe we should just get out of there,* until Roy gave him a clip to the chin and put him down."

Karl tried to think about the best way to answer this. What would Gabe expect him to say to a revelation of murder? He dipped a fry in the ketchup.

"So, the reporter went in the bay, and Williams got to take a nap…" He intentionally made it sound macho, like he really didn't care much either way about this whole story, then left the sentence hanging. Gabe picked it up.

"Williams had been a problem for too long already. When the boat came in, we put him on it and made the other look like an accident. Don't ask how," he added when Karl flicked a glance his way. "It won't have been pretty, although I didn't stick around to look."

Karl, who had seen exactly how not pretty it had been, felt his gut twist and forced himself to eat another fry, without ketchup this time.

"The boat took Williams and the reporter's gear out into deep water to dispose of them. They know what they're doing. I don't expect anything to surface in that department."

Gabe chuckled at his own pun, and Karl forced a snort of what might have been laughter. He had never felt less like laughing in his life, but he did feel a deep satisfaction at being proved right about Fullerton's death. He couldn't wait to check in with Corporal Munroe that night.

When he heard her casual, "Hello, Ali speaking," several hours later, he didn't even bother to greet her in return.

"Someone is listening to all my conversations, right?" he asked urgently. "They are being recorded, aren't they?"

"That's right," she confirmed. His demanding tone didn't seem to phase her any, but then neither had anything else in the weeks he had been checking in.

"Then you heard what Ross said about Fullerton. About how they killed Fullerton and one of their own guys. We were talking really quietly, and there was background noise. I wasn't sure it would come through clearly enough."

"Oh yes, those phones have surprisingly sensitive microphones in them. It's the reason we were able to let you keep using your own device. And Shane is very good at cleaning up background noise. I don't think there is any issue with the recording, although Sergeant Archer would prefer you not to be so direct with your questions. That kind of behaviour could blow the whole operation, you know."

Karl gritted his teeth at this and managed to swallow the first retort that came to mind, saying instead, "But you have what you need now, right? You can arrest them for murder and smuggling, and I can get out of here, right?'

"Soon." Ali was soothing now, which didn't make Karl any happier. "We're working with our counterparts down south, and we will be making arrests once we have everything lined up to make a clean sweep of the operation. With the number of agencies involved, you have to allow for additional time to coordinate, but I can assure you, it won't be much longer."

Karl had no choice but to accept this verdict, but he didn't feel a great deal of confidence that her definition of *soon* matched his, and he didn't like what this job was doing to him. When he was busy, working with the crew or talking to Gabe, he could almost believe this was who he really was. The kind of man he'd never wanted to become. Even the regular contact with Corporal Alison and the messages from Kelsey were beginning to feel unreal, like odd glitches interrupting daily life rather than the links back to his real life.

42

Five weeks into his tenure with the crew, unloading yet another shipment from the back of the flatbed truck and hauling the bundles in through the big sliding door, Karl wondered if Archer even knew how much longer this operation would take. Was this going to go on indefinitely, with Karl's existence suspended in the limbo of coordinating agencies? Even Kelsey seemed to have given up on him. She hadn't texted in almost a week.

"Here." Gabe jerked his head for Karl to follow him over to the gun cabinet in the corner. "Why don't you and I take the watch tonight?"

Karl had noticed that this task went to someone different each time, but he was still surprised to be assigned. Even more so that Gabe would join him. Gabe punched in the combination code and swung the door wide, and Karl did a double take. There, on the shelf in the top of the cabinet, sat the urn from his test robbery, next to a pile of ammo boxes.

Gabe pulled a rifle out of the case, passing it to Karl, along with its box of shells, before grabbing one for himself and leading the way to the door. Karl wondered why he bothered with a rifle. He was pretty sure he was right about Gabe's concealed carry habits, but perhaps Gabe didn't like to advertise that aspect of his equipage, even to his own men.

Besides that night on the docks, Karl had handled a weapon exactly once before in his life. He had been to a particularly redneck bachelor party in Edmonton that included several hours at an indoor range. The place, called the Wild West Shooting Centre, was in West Edmonton Mall. Everyone at the party had been expected to shoot their share of guns, with the size of weapon chosen acting as a measure of their individual manliness. In Karl's opinion, this experience was not enough to make him competent for guard duty, but he didn't have a whole lot of choice in the matter. Gesturing him to follow, Gabe slid the large door back a foot, stepped through, and waited for Karl to follow him before closing it behind them.

Karl casually slid the box of cartridges into his pocket and checked, as he remembered the instructor at the range insisting upon, that the chamber was open and empty. It was as much as he could do. He cradled the gun in the crook of his arm as casually as he could and paced alongside Gabe as he wandered across the gravel lot. Neither of them smoked, so in a way it was nice to have the guns to occupy their hands as the two men reached the end of the gravel and turned to look over the quiet, moonlit scene. Clouds scudded across the night sky, covering the lot in moving shadows. Moonlight occasionally glinted off a car window before being extinguished again by the shifting wind.

Standing in the shadow of the trees at the far end of the lot from the mill, Karl saw the dark shapes moving first. At first he thought they were more cloud shadows. Then he saw the clear outline of a man. The shadow raised his arm and gestured, bringing several other forms running forward in obvious formation. Karl gasped involuntarily, and Gabe jerked around, searching for the cause and finding it instantly. His hand gripped Karl's arm, and he stepped slowly, softly, backward, deeper into the cover of the trees. The wind died for a moment, and in that time they could hear feet crunching up the gravel track to their right before it was muffled by a new gust. Karl watched in awe as more than a dozen armed officers, bulky with tactical gear, burst into the lot and fanned out to cover the front of the building.

He turned his head to look at Gabe and saw the same shock he felt mirrored on Gabe's face, close as it was in the dark, mingled with a rising fury as the implications of the situation hit home. Gabe's hand tightened on Karl's arm, and Karl felt a shot of fear pause his heartbeat for a moment as Gabe lifted his gun, but it was only to sling it over his shoulder before raising a finger to his lips. Karl managed to jerk a short nod and didn't resist as Gabe cautiously pulled him another step into the forest, away from the sawmill and away from the encircling line of armed men.

What were they thinking? He had told them about the armed lookout, had warned them there would be men outside the mill. How had they let him and Gabe get behind their ring like this? He heard more steps on the gravel of the track as additional officers arrived to join the advance rush. He should alert them, let them know somehow that the leader of the gang wasn't in the building they were surrounding. That he was standing here, under the shadow of darkness with Karl. But he couldn't. Gabe would kill him if he suspected for a moment that Karl had sold him out, and besides, the sound of the wind would make it difficult to be heard.

They had frozen again at the sound of the new footsteps, and Karl could just make out the forms carrying some sort of equipment into position, their heavier footsteps crunching the gravel loud enough to be heard over the wind. Or was it fading away again? Abruptly and without warning, the night was lit up by a pair of brilliant spotlights trained on the mill building, and a voice spoke through a megaphone, shattering the silence.

"This is the police. You are surrounded. Put down your weapons and come out with your hands up."

There was a long pause, with no movement visible from either the men inside the mill or the officers surrounding it. Karl thought, *They can't lay down their weapons. They haven't got any. They're all locked up.* But even as he thought it, he remembered Gabe handing a rifle to him and pushing the cabinet door shut with his free hand. Not locking it, just pushing it to.

But they won't know that, Karl thought. *They won't know the gun safe is open. They're going to push the door open and come out with their hands up any second now.*

"I repeat, come out with your hands up."

The scene seemed frozen in time. Brilliant light surrounded by blackest shadow. Silent. Expectant.

Karl didn't see the big door move, didn't hear the rumble it usually made, but he did hear a distant voice shout, "Are you crazy? No!"

Then shots rang out from the mill. One pinged off the metal of the spotlight, and suddenly the air was full of the sound of gunfire. The police had formed a semicircle around the building, their weapons carefully trained to ensure they couldn't hit each other. Karl couldn't imagine what it must be like inside as the racket of bullets tearing through metal siding assaulted him.

"Come on," Gabe growled at him, and Karl realized this was their opportunity. They had to get out of there. He was turning to follow Gabe when he heard the pause in police firing, a moment of silence as he began to move, and then new shots coming from the mill.

Karl had taken exactly two steps when he felt a thump like a baseball bat hitting him in the back of the right thigh. With a yell as much from shock as pain, he stumbled. His leg gave out under him, and he crashed to the forest floor. The rifle he was carrying flew out of his hand, landing at Gabe's feet as he turned to look back to where Karl lay.

Karl would have expected the sounds of concentrated firing to make all other sounds imperceptible, but it didn't prevent him hearing the shouts from the gravel track.

"What was that?"

"Did you hear that?"

"Is there someone in the trees?"

"Was that one of ours?"

Karl stared up at Gabe's silhouette, standing taut and poised a couple of yards from where he lay, clutching his strangely numb right leg. Karl waited for him to run. He only hesitated for a moment. In three strides he was back at Karl's side, grabbing Karl's arm, hauling him upright with unnatural strength, pulling Karl's arm over his shoulder and dragging him, half running, half hopping between the trees and away from the shouting voices.

Karl's heart was pounding in his throat. He was disoriented and off balance. Gabe's gun banged painfully against his elbow, worse than his leg registered at the moment. He could hear someone crashing through the bush behind them, but they were heading off at an angle. If they kept going that way, they would miss Gabe and Karl entirely, and what could Karl do about it? Gabe's right hand had Karl's wrist in a vice-like grip, and his arm around Karl's waist was the only thing keeping Karl upright. And Gabe was better at moving quickly and quietly through the dark forest than their pursuers.

The crashing behind them paused, the gunfire in the distance went silent, even the wind slowed. It was Karl's best chance. Swinging his injured leg forward hard on his next hop, he brought it around in front of Gabe's near leg, tripping him as he tried to take his next step and bringing them both toppling to the ground. With a cry of simulated pain, Karl writhed where he fell. With relief, he heard the shouts and crashing steps of their pursuers turn toward them.

They were getting closer, and Karl could hear Gabe cursing in the dark beside him. He was twisting where he lay, trying to free the rifle strapped over his shoulder and, unlike the one that Karl had dropped, Gabe's gun was loaded. Karl moaned, clutching at his leg and rolling sideways onto the butt of the gun so that it pinned Gabe to the ground, the barrel driving his shoulders into the undergrowth.

"Karl, you need to roll off of me." He could hear Gabe's low growl as he struggled to push off the taller man's weight. "Buddy, I need you to roll over."

But it was too late. Flashlights found them on the mossy, needle-strewn ground, and several voices at once ordered them to freeze. Karl threw up his hands, holding them before him in a warding motion as if to prevent them from firing on him, the butt of Gabe's gun still digging into his spine as he felt Gabe go still. Karl was bemused at the sight of blood on his flash-lit hands and wondered where it had come from. Then he was yanked off of Gabe and thrown on his stomach, his arms twisted behind his back and cold metal closed over his wrists. Turning his head, he saw Gabe's face pressed forward into the leaves of the shrub he had landed on, while other hands cuffed him in turn. Karl wasn't sorry he couldn't see Gabe's expression as the man was pulled to his feet and marched back the way they had come.

43

Karl lay where he was for what felt like a long time, listening to distant shouts, breathing in the smell of damp earth and rotting logs. His leg was still partially numb, but he could feel his pulse beginning to throb in his thigh. One of the officers standing over him was holding a crackling conversation on his radio. It sounded to Karl like they were discussing the merits of waiting for the paramedics to arrive versus carrying him out between them.

This discussion kept Karl so distracted that it was some time before he realized the shooting had stopped. He could hear the occasional order barked out and the sounds of movement, of men running or thumps and grunts from what he assumed were captives being forced to the ground, but no more gunfire. It wasn't much later that he heard the sound of additional vehicles arriving and saw the red, flashing lights of ambulances driving past on the road to his left. Eventually, the two officers guarding him seized him firmly by his arms and lifted him to his feet between them. They made their way to the gravel roadway, which was closer than the lot, and an ambulance met them there.

The back door of the ambulance opened, and two paramedics jumped down, quickly pulling out a stretcher between them, then slamming the door shut again. The ambulance continued up the track toward the sawmill. The paramedics stood clear of another ambulance and a first responder truck that followed, then moved to unfold the base of the gurney and prepare it to receive Karl. One of the officers holding his arms undid the handcuffs, Karl was spun quickly around, and his wrists were recuffed in front of him now. He was lifted bodily onto the comfort of the stretcher and firmly strapped in place.

One of the paramedics pulled out an odd, crooked pair of scissors and proceeded to slice Karl's right pant leg open to the hip, while the other began an embarrassingly thorough examination of the rest of his body, poking and prodding him with gloved fingers. The first paramedic examined Karl's now dully throbbing thigh, but when Karl strained forward to see it, the officer standing beside him pushed his shoulders roughly back on the stretcher. After a brief consultation, the paramedics slapped a large cotton pad onto Karl's leg, wrapped it with a tensor bandage, and then strapped his legs to the stretcher for good measure. Karl was beginning to feel like a trussed chicken, but he didn't think complaining would be helpful at the moment.

Between them, the two paramedics and two officers managed to roll the stretcher up the rough track to the lot in front of the sawmill, where a flurry of activity was going on. The wind had died out completely, and the clouds covered any moonlight that remained, but it didn't matter. The entire area was lit with the headlights and flashing red and blue strobes of police and emergency vehicles. Karl was parked unceremoniously beside an ambulance, apparently waiting to be loaded at his rescuer's convenience. The skin on his exposed leg was chilly, and he could feel goosebumps coming up along it, everywhere except the hot area beneath the bandage.

Karl saw a couple of paramedics bending over Roy, lying on another stretcher. They straightened and shook their heads at an officer he thought might be Archer. He moved away through the swarm, and they covered the body with a blanket. Karl wondered if it had been Roy who started the shooting. It seemed likely. At least he was likely to be blamed for it, now that he wasn't available to defend himself. Karl couldn't see Gabe anywhere, although he twisted his head around to look for him. Many of the crew were still lying face down on the gravel, but some were being packed into police cars, and a few of those cars were starting to pull away.

Eventually, Karl was loaded into the back of the ambulance and they left the lit-up scene, driving into inky darkness. The ambulance ride took hours, first over the rough gravel track and then down the winding Island highway. The driver didn't bother to turn on the siren, and Karl was grateful. He relaxed into the embrace of his bonds and let the sway of the turns lull him to sleep. A uniformed RCMP officer rode with Karl, feet braced on the rocking floor, half sitting on the small counter, his back wedged against cupboard doors. If he knew that Karl wasn't a regular criminal, he gave no indication of it.

Apparently, the hospitals in Port Hardy and Port McNeil couldn't handle the number of gunshot wounds suffered by Gabe's crew, and Karl, at least, ended up at the North Island Regional Hospital in Campbell River. Since his injury wasn't life-threatening, Karl was parked in a cool, earth-toned hallway in the emergency department and left to amuse himself as best he could by studying a piece of Indigenous artwork on the wall. It appeared to represent the spirits of several birds and animals all crammed into a circle with a man at their centre. Karl wondered idly if this was intended to represent the Earth.

It was midmorning before he was wheeled over to the surgical unit, his wrists still handcuffed, and inspected by a surgeon. The hospital staff discussed his injury and its treatment over his head without bothering to consult him, concluding that it would be simpler to put him under for surgery than to wait for an officer to come and guard him so that he could be uncuffed while they worked. Karl thought about informing them that he didn't actually need police supervision because he wasn't actually a criminal, but the idea of being put under and taking a nice long nap was too attractive, and he let himself drift away as the lights above the operating table began to spin. His last thought before everything went black was how much like Gabe's crew they all looked in their matching green scrubs, masks, gloves, and hair nets.

By the time Karl woke up in recovery, the handcuffs were gone. His credentials must have been verified, because there was no officer on guard, and he had a room to himself. A nurse bustled in and out every half hour or so to check the state of his mended wound and make sure his oxygen levels were sufficient. Other than that, he was allowed to sleep in short, uncomfortable spurts. The chemically induced unconsciousness required for surgery had not been as restful as he hoped.

Archer stopped by, briefly, later in the day. Karl was awake but still groggy and tired. He didn't bother to sit up properly when Archer came in, just stared at him stupidly from where he lay, propped against his pillows.

"I just wanted to check in, see how you're getting along." Archer was as brisk as ever and didn't seem to require any reply from Karl.

"Thanks for all your help on this case. We wouldn't have gotten Ross if it hadn't been for you." Archer held out his hand, and Karl shook it but couldn't bring himself to acknowledge the implied compliment. After all, it wasn't true. They wouldn't have gotten Gabe if Gabe hadn't come back for him. Gabe's capture had been entirely the result of his misplaced loyalty to Karl, and Karl didn't know how he felt about that. Archer shook Karl's hand with finality and seemed about to leave, but he hesitated.

"You know," he said, almost reluctantly. "We know who your father was. Who your uncle is. The police noticed when you took over the agency in Victoria. Some thought I was crazy, bringing you in on this case, but..."

He hesitated again, didn't seem to come up with anything more to say, and turned to leave. He was reaching for the handle when the door swung violently open, almost hitting him. Archer dodged instinctively, saw an angry, red-faced Kelsey standing in the doorway, and made his escape, sliding past her with great care not to draw her ire upon himself. Karl just looked at her. He had a feeling he knew what was coming.

"I can't believe you didn't tell me where you were," Kelsey shrieked. She was more overwrought than Karl had ever seen her. "You got shot! You could have died! You could have been stabbed and thrown in the ocean and run over like Fullerton! You could have ended up in a ditch somewhere or been buried in a shallow grave or thrown off a cliff, and I would never have known what happened to you."

Karl just looked up at her, too exhausted to argue that, with a dozen highly trained police officers supervising him at all times, it was unlikely his body could disappear quite so completely as that. He just didn't have the energy for it.

She was actually gasping for breath in her agitation, and Karl reached a hand toward her in an ineffectual attempt to calm her. Kelsey slapped his hand away, burst into violent tears, and sat down hard on the stiff chair beside his bed, her face hidden behind her fingers, her round shoulders heaving. Karl lay, staring up at the ceiling again, waiting for the storm to pass. At last he heard her take a series of deep, shaky breaths and blow her nose with a sound like an air horn. He risked a glance in her direction. She was glaring at him with red eyes, but the tears had stopped.

They looked at each other for a long minute, then her mouth twisted in exasperation and she rose to her feet, pausing long enough to spit out, "Don't you *ever* do something like that without telling me again," and marched out of the room. He watched the door swing shut behind her, but he wasn't sure if it was fully closed before he drifted off to sleep again.

***

Karl signed the hospital's discharge papers the following morning, including the rental contract for a pair of crutches, and used them to hobble to the exit doors. He was wondering if he should call a taxi or try finding his way home by transit. When he finally managed to push through the heavy metal door, he found

Kelsey standing on the sidewalk, leaning against her pumpkin of a car, waiting for him.

"Hey," Karl said. "What are you doing here?"

"I called the hospital this morning, they said they would be releasing you about now. I didn't think you should be driving with that leg, so..." Kelsey pushed off the car, opened the passenger door, and held it, waiting for him to get in. It took a minute for Karl to fold his long frame into the little car, crutches jammed between his knees. Kelsey slammed the door firmly behind him and rounded the car with a bounce in her step. She appeared to have gotten over her previous rage.

"So?" She looked at Karl as she started the car. "Do I drop you off at your place or take you back to the office with me?"

"Is there anything to do at the office?"

"A couple of alimony and child support skippers to track down," she replied.

"I'll do the computer work, you do the legwork?" he asked, his mouth quirking up at the corner.

"Deal." Kelsey popped the clutch, and the little car lurched away from the curb.

44

It took Kelsey's best intercessory efforts, but in the end, Alex forgave Karl for the RCMP's decision to quash her story. She only required a very long and exclusive phone interview detailing every aspect of the smuggling operation and its takedown that he could share. Confidentially, of course. The police weren't concerned about Karl's immediate safety. His involvement in the case would not become public knowledge until the matter went to trial, which, as Kelsey pointed out, could be years. Nevertheless, he was advised to maintain discretion on his participation, and nowhere in Alex's story could he be identified as her source.

Karl had been back at the agency for several days and was getting quite adept at manoeuvring on his crutches, when he finally got around to typing and filing all of his notes and evidence regarding the "case up north," as he had begun to think of it. The euphemism placed the less pleasant details of the case at a distance and let him focus on cataloguing the evidence without thinking about the people or circumstances involved. After a thorough search of the office one evening, he decided that the single remaining Odin's Tear Kelsey had left for him to include in the case file must have disappeared.

He closed the hard file, slotted it into the black cabinet, and shut the drawer with a feeling of relief. He had the satisfaction of including a news item he had come across earlier that day regarding the woman whose house he had broken into. It said that her husband's ashes had been turned in to the RCMP anonymously, with no mention of its connection to the case. Karl even felt grateful to Archer when he saw her tearful relief as she clutched the urn in front of the camera.

Kelsey had been playing taxi driver since his return, with only an occasional mutter of *I told you to be careful* to indicate any displeasure in the task. Karl was about to call her for a ride home when it occurred to him that he hadn't seen Percy in months. Also, that Percy had been John Fullerton's friend, which meant the man had lost two good friends in under a year. He decided a visit to the bookstore was indicated. It wasn't as if Kelsey would be going to bed anytime soon. Carefully manoeuvring his way down the stairs on his crutches, he swung around to the front of the shop and was pleased to see a light still shining in the back room.

Pushing backward through the glass entrance door, Karl smiled at the familiar, half forgotten sound of the bell over his head. He was in the process of rotating on the crutches, careful to avoid tangling his bad leg, when he heard the rattle of the bead curtain and Percy Meiklejohn speaking in the crowded stillness of the dark shop.

"So, young Larsson, you've returned from the dead, I hear."

Karl completed his turn and snorted as he looked down the narrow aisle of books to where the old man stood, straight as ever, framed in the light from the back room.

"Who said anything about dead?" he demanded with mock solemnity, carefully swinging himself along.

"Well, Kelsey certainly seemed to think you came rather close. A veritable brush, in fact." Percy clearly wasn't too concerned now, but Karl wondered what exactly Kelsey had been saying about him.

"I didn't know you knew Kelsey," was all he could think to reply. Percy stood back, holding the bead curtain aside for Karl to pass through then letting it fall behind him and pulling out a chair for Karl to flop into before he replied.

"Oh, yes. She comes down to say hello from time to time. Particularly when you aren't around and she is feeling lonely. Even more particularly when she is worried about you."

Percy smiled his thin smile at Karl as he poured steaming coffee into a mug and held it out. Karl leaned his crutches against the wall, careful to ensure they were properly balanced before accepting the drink and wrapping his hands around its warmth.

"I guess she told you about Fullerton then," he asked awkwardly.

"Oh, yes." Percy's voice was heavy now, all banter gone. "John was a driven man. Especially on the trail of a story."

He didn't seem to have anything more to say about the matter. He certainly did not show Alex's need to discuss the dead man at length. Karl sipped his coffee and stared at the urn sitting on the windowsill. First Mordecai, then John. Percy seemed capable of moving on from loss and grief with an ease that made Karl uncomfortable, but maybe it was the old lingering guilt. John's son hadn't been around to mourn him, but there had been Alex, and Karl himself was sorry the reporter was gone. The paper had purchased a memorial bench in Stanley Park with Fullerton's name on it. Had anyone other than Percy marked Mordecai's passing? Were the agency and this jar the only monuments left to his grandfather's life?

Karl wished he could find the words to ask Percy about Mordecai. He wished he would tell the kind of stories that Alex had told about John, laughing while tears ran down her cheeks in memory of her mentor. But he couldn't find the words. It didn't feel right admitting how little he knew his own flesh and blood. And apparently it had never occurred to Percy that Karl might be curious or want to know. After a silent minute more, he drained the last of his coffee, thanked Percy, and reached for his crutches. Percy seemed to come out of his reverie and rose with creaking formality.

"Don't be such a stranger now that you're back," he told Karl as he again held the curtain aside for him to pass, then crossed the shop ahead of Karl to open the door so that Karl wouldn't have to wrestle with both it and the crutches. Karl returned his smile.

"I won't," he promised. He was reaching for his phone to call Kelsey when he heard the lock click on the door behind him and realized that Percy must have left it open just in case he might stop by.

45

The late fall had turned to early winter before Karl's leg was fully functional again. He thought the slight twinge it gave him from time to time might be there to stay. Coming back to the agency had felt more like coming home than anything Karl had experienced in his life. Even without full mobility, it was a relief not to be playing a part anymore. The last few leaves on the trees along their street were brown and rattled sadly in the chilly wind, but inside the agency was cozy and warm, and the homes in Karl's neighbourhood were starting to put up Halloween decorations. Kelsey was in the kitchen fixing herself a coffee when the agency phone rang one morning in October, and Karl answered.

"Hello, Larsson Investigations," he said.

"Hello, Mr. Larsson?" It was a pleasantly professional woman's voice, and Karl straightened in his seat.

"Yes, speaking."

"I understand that you have been able to provide some assistance to the RCMP in your capacity as a private investigator."

"That's right," Karl confirmed, wondering how she could have found this out when his involvement was always supposed to be confidential. Then again, it didn't sound like she knew what services he had provided.

"My name is Lorraine Sanders," continued the cool voice. "I work for the Ministry of Transportation and Infrastructure. I manage certain contracted services for the provincial government. I was wondering if you would be interested in an agreement to provide background checks and investigations into companies or individuals being considered for infrastructure projects. It would be part of our preapproval vetting process. There would be further checks in place, of course, but it would speed up the early stages of our selection process to have this task contracted out. Your organization was recommended to provide this service on Vancouver Island. Is this something that you might be interested in?"

"Yes, I think that is something we might be very interested in." Karl attempted to keep the excitement in his voice to a minimum. "What would you need from us in order to put something like that together?"

"Well, I've got a contract and a confidentiality agreement that would need to be signed by any staff members, and of course we would need copies of your licensing and criminal record checks on you and your staff."

"Sure, yeah, that won't be a problem," Karl assured her.

"Okay, great." The voice smiled down the line. "I'm going to email you a draft contract and some forms to be filled out, along with a list of the supporting documents we'll need copies of. If you can get these back to me at your earliest convenience, that would be great."

"At your earliest convenience" sounded promising. Karl could envision a backlog of government investigations just waiting for them to get started on. Even if it wasn't exciting work, it should keep them busy, and he didn't mind the idea of steady work without too much excitement for a while. In fact, it was exactly what he needed.

He confirmed his contact information, promising to get back to her as soon as possible, and hung up the phone feeling elated.

"Hey, Kels," he called in the direction of the front office, then bounded out of his chair and around his desk, too impatient to wait for her to join him. Kelsey was frowning over a letter on top of the pile of mail she was opening and appeared not to have heard him.

"Kelsey, you will never guess who just called." Karl's excitement made his voice louder than usual, but he couldn't contain himself. He didn't even wait for her to respond; this news was too good.

"The government. Of the province. Wants to hire us. To run background checks. For them."

He was intentionally speaking in short, goofy sentences, doing a semi-ironic happy dance in front of her desk.

Kelsey was not smiling. "Um, that might be a problem," she said, looking up at him nervously.

Karl paused in the middle of a dance move and frowned. "Why would that be a problem?" he asked, confused. "A major government contract like that is exactly what we need. It'll stabilize the agency's income. I can go off EI, pay myself a wage, and still afford to keep you on board. We'll be twice as busy as we have been. You said yourself, it's boring when there isn't enough to do around here. Well, this should solve that."

When she continued to frown, he said, "Oh, come on, Kels, you can't still be mad at me."

"It's not that. All that stuff sounds great," Kelsey admitted, but she didn't look as if it sounded great. "But we have a problem with our license."

"What problem?" Karl was frowning too now. "What do you mean?"

"Apparently your grandfather would have turned seventy-five this month, which means that he needs to go into the Registrar of Security Services for a physical if he wants to keep his license current." She trailed off, still looking apprehensively at Karl.

"That's impossible," he said blankly. "He's dead."

"I know," she replied. "But they sent this notification after I sent in his license renewal, and it looks like they won't renew him without it."

"You sent in his license renewal?" Karl was stunned by this whole turn of events. He couldn't seem to take it in properly.

"I had to. He's listed as our supervising detective, and we need his license to stay current so that we can complete our licensing."

"Didn't that require his signature, his picture?" Karl didn't know when he had begun moving, but he found himself pacing back and forth in front of her desk, firing his questions at her in clipped sentences.

"It didn't say anything about a picture on the form, and I signed his signature on it when I sent it in."

"You signed his signature?" Karl paused to stare incredulously down at her, and she seemed to shrink in upon herself under his gaze.

"Yeah, I mean, it worked when we applied for our licenses, so I just thought…" She trailed off.

"You shouldn't have done something like that without telling me."

"You were fine with it for getting the business license, what's the difference?"

"I wasn't 'fine' with it. I just didn't know what else to do at the time."

"Well, what else do you think I should have done in this case?" she demanded. "If his license isn't current, then we aren't legal to operate, and if we aren't legal to operate, then we sure as heck better not sign up for any government contracts."

He didn't have an answer for her, but he didn't want to admit it. "When did you do this?"

"When you were away," she replied. "And I would have discussed it with you if I could have gotten hold of you. Since I couldn't, I had to make a decision, and I did!"

Her voice was shaky, but her tone was accusing now too, and Karl's anger bubbled over.

"You don't get it. This," his gesture took in the entirety of the agency, "is just a job to you, but it's all I've got. This is my life we're talking about!"

He turned back to his office, footsteps tramping over thin carpet as he paced its length and back again. Passing the speed bag hanging from the ceiling, he lashed out at it, and it smacked into the plaster, dropping dust onto the carpet as its base rattled. Turning to pace the room again, he caught sight of Kelsey slumped at her desk. Her back was to him, but he thought she might be crying. He turned away. Running both hands through his hair, he walked to the window and stood staring down at the street below while he pulled himself together. After a minute he returned to the front office, where Kelsey still sat, staring down at the forms spread out before her.

"Look," he started lamely. "I'm sorry. I know it's not your fault. I just don't know what to do. Everything was looking so good, and now...I just don't know."

He rubbed his hand across his face, the feeling of a fresh shave still odd after months with a beard.

"I know." Kelsey sounded matter-of-fact. If he'd made her cry, she covered it well, but he didn't look too closely at her face. "It sucks," she continued. "But we'll figure something out."

Suddenly, she brightened. "I know," she exclaimed. "Creepy Uncle Stanley!"

"Who?" Karl asked, confused again.

"Alysa's Uncle Stanley. He's a total skeez. And he'll do pretty much anything for money. He's always trying to bum off Alysa's grandma. He even asked me once. He's her grandma's brother, so technically he's Alysa's great-uncle. But I'm telling you, he would totally take this physical for us if we paid him. I wouldn't even have to talk to Alysa about it. I know the bar where he likes to hang out."

"That's fraud, on top of forgery!" snapped Karl, irritated again. "You can't go around committing felonies just because they're convenient!"

"Signing someone else's signature is only wrong if you do it without the person's permission," she protested. "And since he left you the agency, I think you can read your grandfather's permission as granted. As for the fraud, well, if we don't, we're finished. They'll shut this place down, and we'll both be out of a job."

"I'm pretty sure they'll want to see some ID before they give someone a physical and approve their license," Karl retorted.

"So, we get him a fake ID," she insisted. "If high school kids can do it, I'm pretty sure we can manage. It can't be all that much more difficult than buying a whole heap of drugs in a single weekend."

Karl couldn't believe she was bringing that up now. He forced his anger back down and took a deep breath, then shook his head. "I don't know, Kels. I just don't know. Let... Lemme think about it."

Her shoulders drooped, and suddenly Karl couldn't stand being indoors a minute longer.

"I'll…I'll see you later," he mumbled and turned to the door leading to the stairs and out of the building.

Karl made it to street level, only to find himself standing on the sidewalk, at a loss as to where he was going. Without conscious thought, he turned left then left again, heading down Quadra Street, striding along with his hands thrust into his pockets and his shoulders hunched, as if against wind or rain, despite the fall sun warming his back. He passed trees and shrubs still bearing vestiges of fall colour, their coppers and reds interspersing brown branches, and was again struck by the string of beautiful old church buildings on the street that had surprised him when he'd first started at the agency.

He continued to wander, turning his steps toward the waterfront when he came to Broughton Street, passing more historic buildings, along with the various modern structures that made up the eclectic core of downtown Victoria. He had run this route dozens of times before, but it had never made him feel like this. This was his home. He belonged here. In this city. On this Island. Running his agency. It was the first time in his life that anything had ever been truly his, and he couldn't lose it now.

Unfortunately, acknowledging that fact didn't help him decide what to do. He spun through the possibilities over and over again, bouncing between the chance of successfully fooling the registrar and the more probable outcome of being caught in the attempt and charged with fraud, which would certainly mean he would never be fully licensed. And even if they did pull it off, was he prepared to commit a crime in order to keep his business? Would he really be any better than Gabe Ross in that case? Oh, he could argue that there were no victims in this situation, but he didn't believe his own excuses, even as they ran through his mind.

Considered from a strictly utilitarian angle, he supposed the survival of his little agency didn't matter much. The city was no safer because of him. The Island hadn't really been cleaned up by his endeavours. The sergeant on the Fullerton case had made it clear that they were already working to crack the source of the drugs long before he came along. Surely they would have reached the same conclusions he had, given time. The only difference was that, unlike Fullerton, the police could not act impulsively on guesswork and instinct alone. They had rules they needed to operate within. Rather like the rules a private detective was supposed to follow.

Karl stood on the sidewalk next to the old Customs House, overlooking the Inner Harbour, not sure where else to go. His feet were tired from walking in the wrong shoes, and he leaned against the railing, looking down on the Harbour Centre, idly watching a seaplane fly in and land with a small whoosh on the harbour surface before taxiing up to its mooring. There appeared to be a disturbance of some kind in the parking lot below him, and he transferred his gaze from the seaplane to the cluster of people involved.

A lone officer in Victoria Police Department uniform stood facing two women, his thumbs hooked into his belt except when he was making dampening motions with both hands, clearly trying to maintain calm in the situation. One of the women seemed relatively unconcerned, pushing her fingers back through thick, curly hair, gathering it into a ponytail and snapping an elastic in place. Her friend was another story. She was speaking rapidly, the emotion clear on her face, her sentences punctuated with emphatic hand gestures. The officer looked from one to the other, listened until the emphatic woman had talked herself out, then turned to the small crowd waiting a little way off. With a wide wave of his arm, he invited one of them to join him next to his cruiser, where a new conversation began.

Karl suddenly realized how much he did not envy the man. Listening to so many dramatic, emotional stories. Trying to figure out what really happened in some petty dispute. It all struck him as incredibly tedious, frustrating, and probably disillusioning.

After all, how many people actually made honest statements to the police? Even if they were listening to the truth, the officer could never be sure. That perpetual need to disbelieve must eventually affect the person inside the uniform.

He had his own small part to play in the grand scheme of things, and that part was most definitely on the side of law and order. Whether it was uncovering dangerous drug rings or tracking down deadbeat dads to serve them their summons, they were on the same side. Karl pushed off the railing and turned his steps back the way he had come. He still didn't know what he was going to do, but he was clear on what he couldn't do.

46

It was getting dark by the time Karl hiked all the way back up
Quadra. The lights were out in the agency, and on the floor above,
and Karl wondered where Kelsey was. It was too early for her to
be asleep. The sign on the bookstore said *Closed*, but he could see
a beam of light shining through the plate glass window, probably
from the back room. He realized he should let Percy know what
was going on. After all, it would affect him too if the agency had
to close.

Pushing the shop door open, Karl caught a whiff of cigar
smoke, which surprised him. He wouldn't have guessed Percy was
a smoker. He made his way through the dim of the shop, careful
not to bump into the stacks as he passed between them. Reaching
the bead curtain, he pushed it aside, the familiar rattle making his
heart sink further.

A stranger sat across the table from Percy. He was shorter
and a little wider than Percy, with a thatch of salt-and-pepper hair
and a beak-like nose. He was the one smoking the cigar, and as
Karl stood in the doorway he reached out and tapped the ash off
the end of it into the urn Karl knew so well.

"What. The. Hell," said Karl, staring at the urn.

"Ah," said Percy, his mouth twitching slightly. "I suppose
you recognize your grandson, Mordecai?"

He was looking across at the man opposite him, who was
staring curiously at Karl. A grin broke across his face at Percy's
words.

"I hear I'm supposed to be dead," he said to Karl.

The room spun momentarily, and Karl clenched his jaw, forcing himself to focus on the man in front of him, a man who looked strangely familiar, as if someone had taken his own photograph and digitally aged it.

"You're…what?" Karl looked from the stranger to Percy and back again. Percy began laughing, in his dry, reedy way, harder than Karl had ever seen him, his thin arms wrapped around his stomach as if the extremity of his mirth pained him. The stranger stood up, took a step toward Karl, and held out his hand.

"I'm Mordecai Abrams," he said, still grinning, but with a slightly anxious look in his eye. "And I suppose I'm your grandfather."

Karl didn't know what to say. He shook the man's hand mechanically, but when he turned back to the table to reseat himself, Karl blurted, "Wait a minute!"

Easing into his chair, Abrams looked at him, his face more serious now. "I'm sorry to disappoint you, son, but I never died, just went away for a while." He picked up the mug of coffee sitting on the table in front of him and sipped it, then took the cigar between his fingers again. Karl looked at the urn and then back to the overwrought Percy.

"My grandfather's ashes?" Karl shot the half-question, half-accusation at him.

Percy wiped his eyes with the back of a veined, age-spotted hand. "You know, I never actually lied to you." He practically chortled the words.

"You've let me believe a lie for almost a year!" Karl realized he was shouting and strove to control himself.

"Alright," admitted Percy. "I may have failed to correct your inaccurate assumptions, but that's not the same…"

"Don't split hairs," Karl snapped. "You knew what I thought, and you let me think it."

"Alright, alright." Percy held his hands up in surrender. "It was a bit of a mean trick to play. But it was honestly the best possible mistake you could have made from old Mordecai's point of view, and I knew it."

"Who are you calling old?" Mordecai frowned across the table at him. "Won't you sit down, Karl? Please? Let us explain."

The sound of his name grounded Karl a little, and he pulled up the third chair and sat down, although he did not approach too near the table, and he crossed his arms across his chest.

"Where have you been?" It was the first question he could think of.

"South America, mostly." Mordecai grinned, stained teeth flashing briefly. "I always wanted to get drunk in that bar where Hemingway used to hang out. In Cuba, you know? It's still there," he added. "Practically a national monument."

"But how could I inherit your agency if you weren't dead?" Nothing made sense, and Karl didn't feel particularly interested in Hemingway at the moment.

"Look, I was heading off on the trip of a lifetime, going to celebrate my retirement and visit all the places I always wanted to see before it was too late for me. At my age, you make arrangements for things like inheritance before you go on a trip like that. Seemed natural to leave it with Milly to look after, and she knew that if anything happened to me, I was ready to bet my last throw on you. I planned to get in touch when I came back. It never occurred to either of us that she'd be the one to go first, but there you are, these things happen."

There was regret in his voice, although the loss was not new and he had clearly grown accustomed to the fact of his sister's death.

"I was hiking around Peru, having a grand old time exploring the ruins and camping out under the stars, when it happened. You know it was a brain aneurysm?" Karl nodded.

"By the time I got back to a city and checked my messages, I'd already missed the funeral. And then I called Percy here, and he said you'd turned up and were actually going to try running the place." Mordecai flashed his teeth at Karl in a brief grin again. "It was better than I'd ever expected."

"What do you mean?" Karl asked.

"I spent almost forty years building my agency from the ground up." Mordecai gestured broadly with the cigar. "I wanted someone to pass it on to. Someone who might even enjoy the work as much as I had!"

Noticing that his cigar had gone out, Mordecai paused to relight it, and Percy rose from his seat to fetch the coffee pot and a mug for Karl, who pulled his chair closer to the table and accepted the cup without thinking. Mordecai continued.

"You were my only hope. Your sister may be a lovely person, but she showed no proclivity for this sort of work, and your brothers were too much like your father. I was certain they would sell the second they got their hands on the place, and everything I had built would be gone. You might have done the same; in fact, I thought it was likely that you would, but you had taken that criminology minor in university, and even a business major wouldn't hurt when it came to this place."

"Wait a minute," Karl interjected. "How do you know what I took in university?"

"I'm a detective," replied Mordecai airily, and then, seeing the look Karl gave him added, "My sister Matilda kept in touch with your sister Matilda. They're the pious ones of the family, the ones who set aside past differences for the purpose of family solidarity."

His tone made Karl wince, but he didn't interrupt.

"It turned out to be rather convenient for me that they were, actually. After your grandmother passed, I would never have heard a word about my grandchildren if it hadn't been for Milly's correspondence with her little namesake."

He stopped to puff moodily on his cigar, glowering down at his coffee mug, and Karl was torn between the different questions bouncing around in his brain. Mordecai tapping his ash into the old urn decided matters for him.

"And the ashes?" Karl gestured to the urn, raising his eyebrows at Percy, but his tone was more exasperated than angry now. Percy's laugh was a bit wheezy by this point.

"Kathleen picked that thing up at a flea market years ago. Thought it would make a pretty vase for flowers, or maybe a cookie jar. When I told her it was meant for burying the dead, she got the heebie-jeebies, refused to keep it in the house, but didn't like to throw it out either."

Mordecai snorted. "That woman never could stand to waste anything."

"She had me bring it to the shop, but I didn't think it really suited the decor, so it ended up back here."

"I started putting my cigar ash in it after I broke that old ashtray you used to have, remember?"

Karl couldn't help smiling at his grandfather's reminiscent tone.

"We used to joke that it was the only appropriate use for the thing. Storing ashes, that is. It just sort of stuck."

Percy nodded. "Why bother getting a new ashtray I'd just have to empty when this thing was big enough to use forever without overflowing?"

"I didn't actually mean to deceive you the first time I mentioned your grandfather's ashes." Percy was earnest now, conciliatory despite his twitching lips. "I honestly hadn't realized what you thought. It was only after you left that night, thinking it over, that it clicked. And then I decided to let well enough alone."

He shrugged his thin shoulders. "I thought running the agency might give you a connection to Mordecai, might give you a feel for the man he really is, and maybe, in time, you'd be able to look past what you grew up thinking of him."

"What's that supposed to mean?" Karl's tone was defensive. "I didn't grow up thinking anything about him. I didn't know anything about him at all."

"Figures," Mordecai muttered.

"And it would have been helpful to ask you questions, get tips from you, instead of just guessing based on old files. At least you could have told me I needed a license!"

"Seriously? You went out and started working cases without a license? No training? Nothing?" Mordecai's tone was incredulous, but the glance he gave Karl from under those jutting brows was impressed.

"What else was I supposed to do?" Karl demanded. "I didn't know any better! How did you get into this line of work, anyway?"

"I always wanted to be a cop, ever since I was a kid." Mordecai sipped his coffee, and his eyes had a faraway look now. "I thought of the RCMP initially. But I had a wife, a baby daughter. I didn't want to have to uproot them every half dozen years or so, so I applied to the Vancouver City Police. Got in on my first try, which is rare. Did every job in the book over the years. Finally made it to the Major Crimes Section. I was a Detective Constable. I had been with the department twenty-two years." His voice took on a bitter note.

"And I lost my job because of a complaint that I had misused department resources and abused my position of authority when I ran a background check on my daughter's fiancé."

He set his mug down on the table with a clunk. His jaw muscles were tight, and his eyes were hard. "I wasn't the first guy on the force to do something like that, and I doubt I was the last. But your dad wouldn't let it go. Made a big stink. Threatened to go to the papers, get city council involved. In the end, they decided it'd be easier to make an example of me than to keep me."

He made a visible effort to shrug the tension away. Leaned back in his chair. Looked directly at Karl for the first time in this story. Twitched one corner of his mouth up in a wry smile. "So, I decided to set up shop for myself. Took a payout on my pension instead of saving it for later. They still gave me that, at least." His voice was calmer now.

"I could have stayed in Vancouver. I had more contacts there. Most of the guys in the department knew it was a senseless dismissal. But there were plenty of private investigation firms there already. It was a crowded market. And I wanted to work somewhere that I didn't have to risk running into your father every day of the week. So I came here. It's only two hours away by ferry, less with those fast new boats, but it might as well have been another world. It was a fresh start for me, and I never looked back."

He reached for the coffee pot and poured himself another cup. He seemed relieved to have the story out, but Karl still had questions.

"What about my mom? Why didn't she stand up to Dad, tell him to let it go? Why did she marry him after that?"

His grandfather laughed a short, guttural laugh. Percy blew his nose into his handkerchief with a decisive honk.

"You don't know your mother all that well, do you?" Mordecai asked. "She was mad as a hornet at me when I told her your father was shady. She ran straight to him to tell him what I'd done. She threw in with him one hundred percent."

After a brief pause he added, softly, "Hasn't spoken to me since."

He looked up at Karl's shocked face and hastened to add, "To be fair, I didn't try too hard either. I was pretty mad. Your grandmother kept in touch, though. She refused to take sides, said we'd both been wrong, and she loved us both and she wasn't about to lose either of us."

He smiled as he sipped his coffee. "She was a good woman, your grandmother. She came to the Island with me, no complaints, said she'd always liked Victoria. But she went back a couple times every year, for a weekend or even just a day. She was there when every one of you kids were born, you know. So I got to hear all about you, got to feel like I knew you, even if I never saw you."

Percy got up to make a fresh pot of coffee, and Karl realized that he'd let his cup get cold, listening to his grandfather's story.

"I really thought we'd make it up at your grandmother's funeral," Mordecai continued, watching Percy pour grounds into the machine. "But your father was there, and your mother never took her hand off his arm. I just couldn't bring myself to walk up to them both together, like some schoolboy with his hat in his hand, begging for forgiveness. I hadn't done anything wrong." His fist came down on the table, making Karl jump. The old man was shaking with emotion, but Karl wasn't sure if it was anger or sadness. He cast about for something to say.

"So, what made you decide to get me involved in the agency now?" Karl was genuinely curious. It seemed such an odd decision, under the circumstances. The fit of anger, or sadness, passed as quickly as it had come, and his grandfather leaned back again, surveying Karl through narrowed eyes.

"I wanted to get to know at least one member of my family before I die," he stated bluntly. "Your sister was halfway around the world. And like I said, your brothers are too much like your father. All business and money and no interest in anything that won't make them a buck."

Karl wondered if the fact that his brothers both looked like their father had also worked against them.

"You seemed like my best chance. So, before I went away, I made the agency over to Matilda, asked her to see that it went to you if anything happened to me." He rotated the mug in his hands, staring into the dregs. "I thought there was a better chance that you'd take it on if it didn't come directly from me.

"I didn't know what you'd been told about me," he added after a moment.

"I hadn't been told anything about you," Karl said. "I honestly didn't know your first name, or what you'd done for a living, or even if you were alive. If you were ever mentioned, my dad shut the topic down fast, and we learned not to ask. It was always that way, so we didn't find it weird; it was just one of those unspoken family rules."

He shrugged, not sure if he should feel apologetic about it or not. It wasn't as if the silence had been his decision.

"Well, I'm glad you came when Milly passed. It's not how I'd planned things to go." Mordecai's nod was firm. "But it's good to see someone carrying on the work and doing so well at it, too."

Karl's mouth quirked up at this approbation. "Do you want to come back to work, now that you're in town again?" he asked. It hadn't occurred to him before, but he supposed he couldn't say no if Mordecai wanted part of his business back.

"Oh no, I'm retired." Mordecai held his mug out as Percy returned with the coffee pot and watched the dark liquid stream into the cup before he turned back to Karl.

"You ever have any questions, mind, I'm happy to give you any help that I can. And I still have a few contacts you might find useful."

"My expert consultant?" Karl asked, smiling now.

"Something like that. And I can keep my licence current until you've got your hours in and all that. Not that you seem to need it, but I can continue to supervise you, officially."

"That's right!" Karl exclaimed, straightening abruptly, his head swivelling between Mordecai and Percy. "You can!"

Percy smiled thinly from the counter as he replaced the pot on the coffee machine, "I heard you shouting about it through the floorboards earlier. Mordecai flew back into town when I told him you'd been shot, but we weren't sure how to introduce the two of you. I thought this might be an opportune moment for him to come back from the dead. His year was up anyway, and it was about time he got to know his grandson."

Percy rejoined them at the table, and the three men sipped their coffee in companionable silence for several minutes. An abrupt crash and the sound of muffled cursing from overhead made Mordecai jump, although Percy merely glanced upward then returned to his coffee.

"What was that?" Mordecai demanded.

"Oh," Karl said, with a sudden grin. "You haven't met Kelsey yet, have you?"

About the Author

Arlana Crane is a fourth generation Vancouver Islander, currently living in Calgary, Alberta with her husband James. She loves to read, write, knit, play the ukulele and attend the theatre. Summer vacations will find her back on her beloved Island, enjoying the ocean and spoiling her niece and nephews. For more information please visit arlanawrites.com.

If you have enjoyed this book, please consider writing a review on Amazon, Goodreads, or wherever you shop for books.